"Smart, funny, and unpredictable—*Romantic Friction* is a wild ride that kept me guessing until the end. Readers will love this irreverent, timely novel!"

—Amy Tintera, *New York Times* bestselling author
of *Listen for the Lie*

"Sharply written and impossible to put down. Kept me squirming in my seat with the unrelenting real-ness of it all!"

—Jesse Q. Sutanto, *USA TODAY* bestselling author
of *Vera Wong's Unsolicited Advice for Murderers*

"Witty, heartfelt, and delightful with a side-serve of AI drama and book-world insider gossip—what's not to love about this book? Relatable characters, sharp writing, and emotional turbulence will make you laugh and cry."

—Sally Hepworth, *New York Times* bestselling author
of *Darling Girls*

"With prose that crackles and wit that leaps off the page, *Romantic Friction* opens the curtain to an irreverent, hilarious, and yet decidedly loving behind-the-scenes look at the world of publishing. Lori is a writer readers will be thrilled to discover."

—Chandler Baker, *New York Times* bestselling author
of *Whisper Network*

"A fun romp through the book world, full of humor, hijinks, and envy."

—Catherine Mack, *USA TODAY* bestselling author
of *Every Time I Go on Vacation, Someone Dies*

ROMANTIC FRICTION

LORI GOLD

/II MIRA

/II MIRA

ISBN-13: 978-0-7783-8765-7

Romantic Friction

Recycling programs
for this product may
not exist in your area.

MIRA
22 Adelaide St. West, 41st Floor
Toronto, Ontario M5H 4E3, Canada
MIRABooks.com

Printed in U.S.A.

For my dad, in our hearts, always

ABOUT THE AUTHOR

IT'S A COMMONLY HELD BELIEF THAT IN ORDER TO BE A GOOD author you have to be drunk or tortured. To be a great author? Both. I am a great author. I am occasionally drunk (though not at present). But I am not prone to sprawled-on-the-bathroom-floor bawling. I have not, nor will I ever, utter the phrase: "Please don't make me adult today." And I am not the least bit disturbed by crawling into a king-size bed alone.

All that's to say, I am not, nor have I ever been, tortured.

But there truly is a first time for everything.

The bookstore buzzes like an active hive. Beyond these rolling partitions masquerading as shelves, cushioned folding chairs cradle bums of all shapes and sizes and stages of cellulite. They are here for me. As I am here for them. This is my hometown. And this is the bookstore in my hometown that Jocelyn and Torrence and Callum and little Vance built, word by word, page by page, chapter by chapter, book by book. That I share with no one.

I am not a charity.

My coattails are not for riding.

Tell that to Lacey, my publicist for the last ten years. I already did. Multiple times and with only one expletive. (Which honestly is the definition of *restraint*.) And yet, I am here. Because Blaire, my agent with a heart mushier than a ripe peach, intervened on Lacey's behalf and asked me to be.

Listen, that this industry is harder to navigate than Gen Z slang is not lost on me. I'm not completely averse to the idea of paying it forward, even though when I was starting out no one gave me so much as a linty nickel. But you can be damn sure that if a bestselling author who helped to define my genre had invited me (via said publicist) to a bookstore celebration of their blockbuster series, I'd have been on time.

Not late. By twenty minutes—and counting.

I reach for the partition cordoning off this back room, my rose gold bangles clattering as I wiggle free a chapter book—a tale about monsters hiding in school cubbies that must be the bane of every kindergarten teacher's existence. A ghost of a smile plays on my lips, affection for my kindred spirit of an author who came up with this. I set the book aside and peek through the slim gap.

Heart-shaped helium balloons kiss the ceiling, "library" candles that smell of old books and lavender flicker on the windowsills, and my favorite cushioned armchair beckons from behind my usual signing table, an old desk with legs fashioned out of stacked books. Hanging above the register is a poster of the first nine titles in this series I nearly gave a kidney to make happen (don't ask).

The dozens who have traveled from as close as Boston and as far as Iowa wait with more patience than me alongside half the residents of this small seaside town.

With so many bodies, the room temperature rises. The air

turns electric. And I come alive. I wriggle my head out of my introverted shell and gorge myself on the energy of the crowd. I'm no longer a little girl with debilitating stage fright, convincing my teachers I'd been bitten by a squirrel or had a seven-foot-long tapeworm in my belly to get out of an oral report. Turns out I've always been good at lying.

Lies, fibs, fabrications, tall tales. That's all writing is, really, being good at making things up, convincing others that a little boy with freckled cheeks and a mop of carrot-colored hair can bend universes in one breath and giggle at fart jokes in the next. Ah, little Vance—everyone's favorite character. Which is why he had to die. My socials will be flooded with heartbreak emoji and death threats when fans get their hands on this last book.

My god, do I love my job.

"Sofie, our little Sofie."

I would take these words as a slight, given my five-foot-stature, if they weren't coming from a woman slipping behind the partition with arms outstretched, a half dozen tiny pencils poking out of her salt-and-pepper bun, and a "Roxanne (as in *Bel Canto!*)" name tag on her ample left breast (the right is ample too, but there's just the one name tag).

"Sofie Wilde, the hero of the harbor." Roxanne repeats the same refrain each time I enter this store, be it through the back for an event like today or the spontaneous (read: always-staged) drop-ins through the front to "casually" browse and be photographed with some new release Roxanne's exuberance and penchant for underdogs caused her to overbuy. She posts them on the store's Instagram. Knowing this, some of the younger authors, freed from the decorum handcuffs of my generation, have been bold enough to send extra copies of their books to the store. The feed for Harbor Books is the only place you'll see me posing with a novel that isn't mine.

It's my rule. Roxanne, somehow, over all these years, remains the exception.

"Tell me," Roxanne says, wiggling her phone and pressing the side button to shut it down. "And not even Instagram will hear. Will Vance be able to restore the cosmic balance in time for Jocelyn to choose Torrence? Because she will, naturally. It must be Torrence."

My face remains hard as steel.

"Sofie," Roxanne coaxes. "It's me. We did this together. We built this store as a team. This is ours."

Roxanne also has a penchant for hyperbole.

Still, these days, my fantasy romance series—what this Gen Z, grammaphobic world now calls "romantasy"—is a *New York Times* bestseller, and I have more than half a million followers on social media. But fifteen years ago, I was a thirty-five-year-old woman with mousy brown hair, clear plastic-framed eyeglasses, and self-made bookmarks rolled off my laser printer in need of a yellow cartridge. A self-published author without the financial means to promote myself. That's when I met Roxanne.

When I walked through the door of Harbor Books with my sack of sad-looking bookmarks and shoddily glued-together manuscripts, Roxanne didn't even wait for me to finish my plea to support a local author. She was already slapping price stickers on the back and arranging them in a three-foot-tall window display. Hers was the first store to stock my books. She was the first bookstore owner to host an event with me. In return, I've held every launch party here, and Harbor Books is the only store where readers can preorder signed copies with one-of-a-kind swag. Whenever I have my last launch (a very, very, very long time from now), it'll be here.

Roxanne bats her eyelashes: "I can better serve you and the book if I know how to respond to customer inquiries."

She gives me that syrupy smile we both know is exaggerated. "Truly, there were no advance reader copies printed? Not even for Jenna? Reese?"

"Not a one," I say, firmly, though of course there were. Stripped of the cover with *confidential* and *sharing prohibited upon penalty of death* written across the front (though, as I think about it, no one ever confirmed the use of that perfectly reasonable suggestion).

A small number of advance reader copies are always necessary in this industry that relies on prepublication buzz to anoint its bestsellers, and my publisher plays the game well, distributing copies to high-profile outlets for review. I could have secured one for Roxanne, but Vance's death is *the* surprise of the series and she's terrible at keeping secrets. A photo of her still hangs on the wall of shame at the single-screen movie theater across the street for telling everyone that Bruce Willis's character in *The Sixth Sense* is actually dead. (Ooh, did I just pull a Roxanne? Whoops.)

A ding announces the opening of the front door. Roxanne peers around the partition to confirm it's her.

"Break a spine!" Roxanne says, whooshing out.

Instead of following, I pause to peer through that tiny gap on the bookshelf.

My "invited" guest, the author who will ask me a few questions and then moderate ones from the crowd, hovers at the front of the store, seemingly unsure, eyes scanning the room. Silver hair past her shoulders, flowy cotton skirt, well-worn canvas tote bulging with what can only be useless buttons and cheap pens and glitter tattoos she paid for herself. She has no marketing budget for swag or anything else. She's only here because of me.

No one had heard of Hartley West until a month ago. As

happens (usually thanks to a hefty Venmo transfer), an influencer "discovered" Hartley's self-published debut, *Love and Lawlessness*. That influencer gushed about it and set off a trend among her fellow movers and shakers—leaders of the "next wave" of how books are found, even branded as such by an article in the *New York Times*. Like a snowball, more and more readers "found" and recommended Hartley's book. Said it reminded them of me.

The next Sofie Wilde. That's what they're calling her. Over my dead body.

"Ms. Wilde?"

I turn.

"Are we missing anything?"

The bookstore employee—Amy (as in *Little Women*!) according to her name tag—lifts a large wooden tray as if making an offering to the gods. On it are three black Sharpies with an ultrafine tip, a pad of sticky notes (blue), six peppermint-flavored lozenges, two glasses of water, no ice, and a bottle of hand sanitizer disguised as hand lotion.

I'm not a diva. (Despite how it sounds.) I've simply paid my dues. I've earned the right to be here, to be doing this, and I intend to do it well.

"It's perfect, Amy," I say just as on the other side of this partition, chair legs scratch against the floor.

I return to my peekaboo window. Hartley West has circled the table. She drops her bag on the seat of the armchair. The single armchair. The chair that is mine. She puts her back to the room. Her eyes are closed. Her hand presses against her breastbone, and I wonder if this is her very first event. I'm positive it's her very first event like this. I remember the feeling. And by feeling I mean fear. Maybe that's why she was late. I feel a momentary surge of empathy toward her, understanding what it was like to be just starting out, to be hoping and praying to all the gods and no particular god (to cover all the bases) for the doors of publishing to open even the tiniest crack.

I watch Hartley's chest inflate and deflate, and suddenly I feel like I'm intruding. I lower my gaze, but I can still hear her on the other side, the faint mumbling as she repeats her pitch one final time. Rehearsing the quippy soundbite that we authors spend more time writing than the actual book. We are actors without training. Performers without a safety net. We are thrust into the spotlight despite our desire to avoid it being what led most of our introverted selves to become writers in the first place. When we stand before a crowd, be it one or one thousand, we must be witty and wise.

I am.

Is "the next Sofie Wilde"?

Honestly, what *is* that? Is it supposed to be a compliment? Me being replaced? Isn't that called a coup?

Flump.

Flump, flump, flump, flump.

I resume my spying. Hartley West is plopping stacks of bookmarks on the table beside a two-foot-tall tower of books that she must have pulled from her Mary Poppins tote.

She then reaches into that bag and draws out a single sheet of paper. I watch as she carefully folds it in two. Printed on the front, in big blocky aquamarine letters, is her name and underneath: CO-PANELIST.

I text Lacey: Hartley West, what did you say to her?

Lacey: She's late, I know. Roxanne's been hounding me.

Me: She's here. With a "co-panelist" name card.

Lacey: WTF?

Me: My thoughts exactly.

Lacey: Looping in Blaire.

But Blaire wouldn't overstep. She may have a heart that bleeds so much she needs daily transfusions, but she defers to Lacey on all things publicity related. Lacey started as my in-house publicist, working for a publisher where she had more authors to handle than romance authors have euphemisms for *penis*. Lacey hung out her own shingle after helping me hit the *New York Times* bestseller list with book four, and I became her first client.

Blaire: It must be a misunderstanding.

Lacey: Damn straight, because if you look up the definition of limelight, you will see Sofie right here and now. Not Sofie and Hartley West. She came out of nowhere at the pinnacle of Sofie's career. Sofie cannot validate this flash in the pan at her own event.

Sofie: Isn't that what I said to you? Right before you hit "click" on the posts promoting this entirely predictable debacle?

Lacey: I'll fix it.

Lacey could talk a lobster into a pot of water—then get it to use its own claw to turn up the heat.

And yet . . . in exchange for a blurb, I once offered to donate a kidney to a bestselling author on dialysis (I said not to ask). I had to fight for every reader at the start.

Just like "the next Sofie Wilde."

And if karma exists, I need it on my side. Today marks the beginning of the end for Jocelyn and Torrence and Callum and little Vance. I mourn them. A part of me always will. They've rented space in my head for more than ten years. I know what they eat for breakfast and what they'd wear to a funeral and the fears that paralyze them. Things I barely know about myself. But it's time to let them go, and along with them, shifting universes and alternate dimensions and three-headed beasts. At least for a little while. I'm not leaving romance behind—I may have my flaws, but self-sabotage is not one of them. But the idea of penning a meet-cute that doesn't involve fantastical elements like a talking dolphin or a sidekick with yellow feathers makes me all warm and fuzzy (though honestly, that could also be the hot flashes).

Hartley West places her name card in front of her, testing its ability to stand on its own. I see Roxanne with her phone to her ear, Lacey surely on the other end. Roxanne's lips thin, and she marches forward, a tiny pencil falling to the floor behind her.

I calmly roll the partition aside. I step forward, cutting off Roxanne, secure enough in my books and my fans and the legacy I've built to, just for tonight, share this table in this bookstore in my hometown. I face the crowd here to celebrate with me. And stand behind the table next to Hartley West. Solidarity, women supporting women, one of us rises, all of us rise—yes, yes, yes—all things touted by filtered faces and artsy quotes on Instagram.

Yet if it turns out that this woman *is* trying to make a name for herself by mooching off mine, I'll consider it a declaration of war. And Hartley West won't write so much as a grocery list.

Hartley presses her forearms hard against the table. Wishing she could push through and disappear into a portal that leads to another realm. Or maybe that's just me. Because this is more awkward than I anticipated.

Grooves darkened with time and dust line the top of the wooden table. Amy hurriedly brought in an extra chair, but it's one of the folding ones and the height is a mismatch for the table. I need to scoot to the edge just to land my feet on the ground. I can't see readers beyond the first row, which means they can't see me. But they can see her.

Hartley towers above me, even though we're both seated. She has yet to look at me. Not a word of gratitude. No visible appreciation for how rare this is. No acknowledgment of the shift from announcer to co-panelist. (Though "co" is generous any way you slice it.)

Hartley chews on her bottom lip, unaware that the hem of her blue-flowered skirt is caught beneath the leg of her chair, tugging the waistband down. The top of her underwear is showing. (Red, for the record.) Her brown crocheted cardigan hangs half off one shoulder, the fuzzy pom-poms at the hem dangling like rabbit tails. She's hippie meets prairie with a dash of disheveled that many authors exaggerate to seem more relatable.

I don't think she's exaggerating.

My go-to event outfit is black pants with a hint of sheen and a crisp white blouse. Varied only by a scarf that matches the color of my latest cover. Today it's aquamarine. In honor of the tenth and final book in my series, which officially releases next week.

On the table, a single wireless microphone lies between us. I don't need it. Early on, I was plopped onto hard-core sci-fi and fantasy panels stocked with men and their bassoon voices. A bloodbath for the meek. It was survival of the loudest, so I hired a voice coach. Now, my voice can project to those seated in the cheap seats of auditoriums and ballrooms. It most certainly reaches all who await in this crowd that stretches to the back of the store and halfway down the stairs to the bargain basement where unsold books live out their final days.

I signal to Roxanne with a tilt of my head that I'm ready. She stations Amy at the register and weaves her way through the crowd. A hush swathes the room. Her arms cradle a book-shaped rectangle wrapped in aquamarine paper. It is the magnet that drew everyone here. (And the words you're searching for, Hartley, are *thank* and *you*.)

"Welcome to Harbor Books," Roxanne gushes. "Weeks away from St. Paddy's Day, but the luck of the Irish who founded this town is with us." Roxanne raises the gift-wrapped book, and clapping strikes like thunder. A hoot or two (okay, three) echoes off the shelves.

I can feel the table shift as Hartley drives her forearms into the top. I don't swivel my neck. I don't let my eye slide even a millimeter in her direction. I don't allow the humble half smile I've perfected to slip into resting bitch face. The internet slays you for that.

Roxanne raises her hand to settle the crowd. "Now, she needs no introduction, but—"

I clear my throat, and Roxanne pauses. She forgot Hartley, and let's just put "forgot" in quotes. Roxanne isn't one to eschew potential book sales, but Hartley bringing her own books without discussing the terms first means Roxanne might not get the cut she rightly deserves for providing this customer base (though technically, I'm providing it).

Roxanne nods to Hartley. "But first, a Harbor Books welcome to Hartley West, another local author our great state has birthed!" Roxanne faces me. "And a fan of the woman we are here to celebrate. Now, *she* needs no introduction, but I'm giving her one anyway because she deserves it. She also hates when I make a fuss."

I don't.

"Our very own Sofie Wilde has graciously agreed to let our little store make history. And to let you all be a part of it."

This is my cue, not planned by Roxanne but internalized by me. "To be fair," I begin, and I swear there's an awed gasp from the self-help corner. My adrenaline surges. This feeling, addictive and inimitable, is why I do this. There is no point without it. "Casinos are bigger than this town. And it's February. Tonight, our local events calendar consists of this or an iPad class at the senior center."

Laughter rattles the windows framing the carnival cutout in the shape of a lobster across the street. My fans make much use of it, filling their social media feeds after every event with faces flanked by red claws and topped with pointy antennae. That fish market owes me kickbacks.

Roxanne gives the spiel she has memorized, light on the years spent with dirt under my fingernails clawing my way up the ranks, heavy on the weeks atop list after list.

Hartley listens, a somewhat glazed look on her face as if Roxanne is describing what a landline is to a seven-year-old. But Hartley must be about my age, meaning she's also newly obsessed with the weather and with identifying birds (is that a black-capped chickadee?). She's old enough to understand the difference between how it was and how it is—and that means she should be kissing the ring my finger would be wearing if it weren't for this goiter-like arthritic bump at my knuckle.

I sat in fungus-scented elementary school gyms with a table of my books beside women selling homemade penguin-shaped candles and men hawking neon cephalopod fishing lures. My first series was about a scorpion-loving peasant growing an army of the venomous arachnids to seize the dying realm from an even more poisonous queen. It did not garner me an agent nor a traditional publishing deal.

I self-published in the days when it meant running off copies in Staples. Before it saw the first wave of authors who earned themselves a solid payday and a foothold in the industry. I watched as self-publishing gained a get-rich-quick-on-grammatically-mangled-drivel reputation, experienced the rise of e-books, muddled through the inevitable oversaturation and the back-and-forth of it being "the" place to be or the death of publishing, praised and maligned in equal measure for years. The controversy has largely gone the way of video stores and dial-up internet. Self-publishing is now acceptable for authors big and small. A new breed of hybrid authors extols the virtues of releasing books on their own as well as through traditional publishers.

I am part of that species, thanks to my fans. My scorpion-loving peasant has had a resurgence despite the oft-cringeworthy dialogue and derivative world building. Along with my two standalones and one mediocre series that attempted to invent a brand of superheroes born of constellations.

Roxanne smiles warmly. "Sofie Wilde put our little town on the map."

Well, me and the four miles of unspoiled coastline.

"She built this bookstore."

Not literally. Not with brick or drywall or even the numbers in my bank account.

"She treats us like family."

I'm not even sure I treat my family like family. I just don't understand the word *all* without *in* trailing it. Deadlines and touring rule my life. I wouldn't have it any other way.

Roxanne comes to the end of her introduction and taps the

gift-wrapped book she's still holding. "Now, as you already know, these treasures are under lock and key in our storeroom until next week—"

A bit of grumbling and a "we won't tell" come from the crowd.

Roxanne talks over them. "Even so, Sofie has planned something special as a thank you for being here tonight."

And by that she means Lacey planned it.

Roxanne continues, "Anyone who preorders the final book will receive a one-of-a-kind bookplate designed by the cover illustrator, which Sofie will sign and personalize to you tonight! These won't be available anywhere else and will be included in addition to our exclusive Harbor Books swag." A roar of applause. "And as always, Sofie is happy to sign any of her other books, which are also available for purchase."

Roxanne has a bookshelf dedicated to my past titles that she's planning to roll out right before I begin signing. How convenient.

Because like some decree chiseled in stone and adhered to with more fervor than any religion, publishers only release books on Tuesdays. But this Tuesday, for the first time, I won't be in my hometown.

This year on release day, I'll be in Chicago hanging with the Obamas and hunting down the Bear (the cutie who looks like a young Gene Wilder, not the footballers or the actual carnivores who we've apparently trained to eat from trash cans).

My loyalty to Roxanne, her launch sales, and her Instagram feed is why we're here tonight for what we're calling (or rather what Lacey is calling) a "Celebration of Sofie Wilde."

And, apparently, Hartley West.

Roxanne spreads her arms and gestures to the room. "We here at Harbor Books are honored to welcome Sofie back, in celebration of *Light As*, the final book in her *Weight of Feathers and Stone* series. Tonight, our every question will finally be answered—unless it spoils the book, of course," she adds, winking. She directs that saccharine smile at the prize nuzzled by her bosom. "My heart has never beat faster. Inside are the words that will either set it soaring or shatter it to pieces. But I, like all of you, will love it and her either way. She's the reason we are here."

Roxanne turns toward me, this a planned cue, but just as I begin to rise to my feet, a soft bubble of words releases from the chapped lips of the woman beside me.

"Quite literally," Hartley West says. "She saved me. Sofie Wilde saved my life."

RESTING BITCH FACE

THIS. IS. BULLSHIT.

Sorry. Bull. (If I want to maintain my crossover readers, I can only have twelve curse words per book. And yes, they count them.)

Hartley West has been talking for—I subtly check my watch—eight and a half minutes. Eight and a half. Without a single opening to step in.

I can't make one of my spontaneous (painstakingly concocted) quips.

I can't launch into my inspiration for Jocelyn (which is, well, me).

I can't explain to doe-eyed young writers (with full truth despite my proclivity for lying) how writing my first book was the equivalent of a personal MFA that ultimately led me here. (*"You have to write it wrong to learn how to write it right."* Trademark pending.)

I can't subtly gloat over being given headliner status (*for the first time*) at the annual Romance US convention in Chicago, where I'll hold my first-ever ticketed launch party. Followed by a fifteen-city tour, my biggest one yet.

I can't because Hartley West hit rock bottom. And then she found my books.

"Tucana made me smile," Hartley says, returning to when she first read my constellation-superhero series. "So sweet, with that beak that she always thought was too big." Hartley briefly rubs her pointy nose with the back of her hand. "But then she used it to slice a car in half and free a troop of Girl Scouts trapped under the ice by the evil Hydrus, and well, Tucana knew she was special. She knew she was needed. No one could do what she did. And then, when Tucana and Delphinus began to fall in love, despite one being a bird and the other a dolphin . . ."

(I know what you're thinking, and it reads much better on the page. Besides, I was in an experimental stage.)

"Let's just say," Hartley continues, her voice stronger than it was when she first began, "it changed me. If they could find purpose, if they could find each other, then I thought, maybe I could too. Maybe I was worthy."

Someone in the back says, "You are, dear, we all are."

The folding chairs birth murmurs of assent and affirmation and I nod. My smile could be drawn on by a caricature artist because that's how very much I need to force back my resting bitch face right now.

It's not that I don't empathize with Hartley. And if not empathize, sympathize, then, or at the very least, conceptualize how hard life can be. But putting this all on me here, now, at an event for *my* book, an event for which she was supposed to be little more than Vanna White, is inappropriate.

Social media did this. BookTok, Bookstagram, BookTwitter, and Book-Things I'm too close to living in a crypt to even

know about. They started a hashtag: #TheNextSofieWilde.
That hashtag "went viral," which I honestly don't understand
because five people can't even agree on the toppings for pizza
let alone pick a movie while scrolling through Netflix, so how
do thousands, tens of thousands, more, agree on anything?
#TheNextSofieWilde. Seriously?

Once the clamoring bubbled up on Lacey's radar, she took
off with it like a getaway car.

(And no, Swifties, she didn't invent that phrase.)

I'm only active online because of Lacey. I don't directly
engage, don't have open DMs, don't click that little heart
icon on photos of my books with my followers' fluffy dogs
(look who else loves this read!) or pumpkin spice lattes (first
of the season!) or flickering penis candles (you can't make
this stuff up).

Don't get me wrong—readers voluntarily giving up their free
time to spread book love are my definition of saints. I wouldn't
be here without them. It's just that I've always preferred to meet
my fans in person. Lacey claimed that responding to my online
fans would make me seem relatable. As if a forty-nine-year-old
woman living alone (no plants, no pets) in a four-thousand-
square-foot house with a view of the ocean that she bought by
torturing imaginary people could ever be relatable.

Lacey pushed to invite Hartley, saying we should meet (and
document it for Insta) since we only live an hour apart. An hour
and another world, if I had to bet.

So now I'm here, begging my resting bitch face to stand
down, trying to come up with some polite encouragement for
Hartley West when all I want to do is scream, "Vance dies!"

A stillness shrouds the room, and I almost wonder if I did
just that. All eyes are on me. I was lost in my own head, an
essential skill for authoring but less so for promoting. I don't

know if someone has asked me a question or Hartley has said something profound or if we're having a moment of silence out of respect for little Vance.

I lower my head, staring into my lap, in case it's that last one. A couple of throat clearings and the shuffling of sneakers against the wide pine floors let me know it's not. I should have done what Lacey demanded and let her listen in on my phone. At least then she could be sending me a text right now, telling me what the hell to do.

My palms begin to sweat. This used to happen all the time in the early days, but I haven't been nervous in front of a crowd in years. It's a feeling I despise. And so, by extension, I despise this woman next to me for putting me in this position.

"Is that truly the correct question, though?" a deep voice says.

With the force of an unforeseen squall, the energy in the room shifts. A man in the standard preppy coastal uniform of jeans, checkered button-down, and puffer vest awkwardly stuffs his hands into his pockets.

The tush of the occasional male has been known to occupy a seat before me, lavishly lauded for accompanying his female partner or daughter. That male tush belonging to an actual reader (or one willing to admit as such) is as rare as a snowy owl sighting on our local beach in January. (A fact I now happen to know. Thank you, middle age.)

I'm wondering which category this man fits into when he begins to sway. Could it be? An actual reader? I feel guilty for hoping he is, and that he might pass out from nerves. At least the ensuing chaos would take the focus off me.

Hartley eases her forearms off the table. She slides deeper into her chair, but the end of her skirt is still caught beneath the leg. The tugging reveals more of her red underwear. Instinctually, my arm darts out. I set my hand on her shoulder to stop her from shifting farther before subtly yanking the hem free. A collective "aww" circles the room.

My heart sputters, but I go with it, pressing my hand more deeply into Hartley's shoulder, causing the bangles I favor to clank together. A middle-aged woman in a "Team Torrence" tee pulls a tissue from her purse. She dabs at the corners of her eyes. An older woman beside her places a hand on "Team Torrence's" forearm and pats twice.

"An inspiration for us all," the older woman says, and a rolling wave of applause builds to a crescendo.

Hartley still hasn't looked at me. My fingers continue to sink into the fabric. (Corduroy? Seriously?) Whatever question I was asked before Puffer Vest interrupted, this gesture was resoundingly the correct response and one I damn well never would have consciously chosen.

Hartley's pale blue eyes, shades lighter than Jocelyn's but with the same undertone of gray, finally seize mine. She says, "Thank you, Sofie."

I nod to Hartley, not letting go of the confidence I learned to exude no matter what when in front of a crowd, partly thanks to those bassoon-voiced men. "Of course." I begin to lift my palm, but she swings around and clamps her hand on top of mine. Cell phones lift, capturing this moment.

She removes her hand, and I carefully and casually retract my own. In unison, we resume our original positioning and face the sea of folding chairs. The energy in the room has shifted. Something has changed. And I have no idea what it is.

The remainder of the event plays out like they all do. Author inspiration, check. Fancasting, check. Hardest to write: first or last page, check. And everyone's favorite: call out a number, and read from that page of the book, me knowing well enough to leave out spoilers—something Hartley had to learn the hard way tonight after revealing that her main character had to shoot her beloved pet pig when it attacked her newborn baby girl after turning rabid (do pigs turn rabid?).

I'd smiled along, assuring karma that, post-event, I'd offer Hartley a tip or two on how to more deftly handle an event reading. It's only now, as my signing line forms, that I realize how eerily reminiscent that scene was of the one in my third book, the one that inspired the stuffed version of Goldie given out as swag exclusively by Harbor Books. I'm told that coveted launch party plush bird now sells for hundreds on eBay.

Jocelyn had nurtured its likeness, a yellow wingless passerfly (like an American sparrow, that same long thin tail and dark smudge in the center of its chest, and honestly why do I know this?). She'd cared for it ever since she found its cracked shell on the sill outside her bedroom window. She had just learned Callum was dead (though he was simply kidnapped and remained very much alive that first time, and the second). She'd thought he'd sent it to her, a way to remain together even in death. She fed it, carried it with her in a sling, taught it to hop across great distances, watched it learn to hunt for itself. It was her child until Vance came along. But then poor Goldie ate poisoned berries that ravaged its mind. It went after Vance. Jocelyn had to break its neck. It was the first time she understood the sacrifices of being a mother.

Same as the character in Hartley's book. Addie, was that her name? A coincidence, purely a coincidence. Motherhood is universal. Even when you are only a daughter. I steal a glance at Hartley, wondering if she has children. I didn't read her bio. I didn't look her up online. I most certainly didn't read her book. Why would I read "the next Sofie Wilde" when I *am* Sofie Wilde?

Hartley fiddles with a pom-pom at the end of her sweater. Her line has yet to form. Readers are given sticky notes to write their names on, so we don't have to try to carry on brilliantly entertaining small talk and absorb how to spell their names at the same time. Which is *a skill* with all these "Cindees" with two *e*s and "Izobelles" with a *z* and a double *l*.

Those hoping for my Sharpie swirl of an "SW" will have blue sticky notes. Those awaiting Hartley will have yellow. The room is awash in an ocean of blue.

It could be worse. Like arriving at a signing to have the throng of people turn out to be waiting not for you but for the fifty-five-year-old dude in a banana costume making balloon fruits. Or sitting with a mile-high stack of your books beside the bookstore entrance, desperate to deliver your pitch, buoyed when someone finally makes eye contact, humiliated when they ask directions to the toilet. Or the ultimate mortification: the single reader. No one showing up to an event cancels it outright. But a single person? No one—not the reader, the author, or the embarrassed-for-you bookstore employees—have any idea what to do. Fortunately, I learned a trick early on from my one-sided nemesis Rosie Gardens—a bestselling author in my genre. When we first met a lifetime ago, she offered what turned out to be sage advice: when only one or two people show up to an event, ditch the store and take everyone for drinks at the closest bar. Me and my maxed-out credit cards gave many of my early fans such a night.

As my signing line coils through the store, Roxanne sets my special Harbor Books swag on a stand beside me: a replica of the scarf I'm wearing. Lacey's pissed she didn't do scarves for every tour stop. Next time. Though next time will be without Jocelyn and Callum and Torrence.

It's taken months of convincing, but I've finally succeeded

in enlisting Lacey's help. We have to make a good case that switching genres won't tank my career. My readers will follow me. My fans want "Sofie Wilde," whether it's "romantasy" or "romance" or maybe even, one day, historical fiction or (cue hot flash!) a murder mystery. Tonight's celebration, the reader convention, the fifteen cities—it's a goodbye *and* a hello tour. I intend to subtly plant the seed with my fans. With Lacey's help, all those book prefixes on social media will build and spread buzz, proving fan interest in an expansion of the Sofie Wilde brand. Maybe we'll even start our own hashtag.

While I've floated the notion to Blaire, she doesn't yet know how serious I am. She wanted to come tonight, but I asked her to hold off, to wait to celebrate all together at my final tour stop in New York City. If Lacey and I do what we're planning, and it works, we'll have much to discuss. Blaire will support me; she always supports me. But she's going to need all the help she can get in making the case to my editor and publisher. Me staying on brand is currently what's making us all money.

As children, we find comfort in the familiar. We read the same book or watch the same movie ad nauseam, relishing what we know, the lack of surprises, the safety inherent in it. Adults may not read the same particular book multiple times, but they too gravitate toward the familiar. They "auto-buy" books by authors they love, craving and expecting an echo of the story they remember with slight deviations in characters and premise and cover but underneath, an ever-flowing river of the same. But I think readers are underestimated. And publishers need to take the risk.

I'd rather not change editors and publishers in order to do something new, but I will. I'll even take a smaller advance, with a bonus on the back end. I've earned the right to bet on my fans—and myself.

Jocelyn and Torrence and Callum gave me that right. They helped me land Blaire twelve years ago. She negotiated a meager deal for the first two books that wouldn't buy me a new love seat. And yet to me, it was like a leprechaun had delivered a bucket of gold. Still, there were no two-martini lunches with the publisher, no campaign-strategy meetings with the marketing team, no publicist to ensure I had three ultra-fine-tip Sharpies and a place to use them. But I had my scorpion-loving peasant and my constellation superheroes behind me.

I am a hustler. I am perhaps a better hustler than I am a writer. Even before the ink on my first publishing contract was dry (oh, how I curse you, DocuSign, stealer of that fabled signing mystique), I was already working. I compiled spreadsheets of bookstores and libraries and sent handwritten, professionally printed book-release postcards to every single one. I put together my own media kit. I sought blurbs from my favorite (and less favorite) authors. I applied to every festival from Ellsworth, Maine, to Dundee, Oregon, and paid my own way to the handful who took a chance on me. I was deferentially humble. I networked and pleaded and tweeted my way to a second book deal.

Then came little Vance and a write-up in *People* magazine that I sold my soul and my flat-screen to get. Quickly followed by a photo of that fetus from that CW show holding my books that I sold my grandmother's engagement ring to pay for. And that second book deal became a third and a fourth, and I bought my grandmother's engagement ring back and a house and a car and another house and here I am.

In this bookstore filled with fans eager to experience the end of my best era (to date), I pick up my ultra-fine-tip Sharpie. My heart thrums with excitement. I'm about to signal to Roxanne to unleash the fans when that same guy in the puffer vest approaches our table. A yellow sticky dangles from his left index finger.

It reads: Brad.

I would have pegged him for an Oliver or a Noah. Maybe it's the tattoo. The small compass rose on his wrist doesn't scream "Brad."

An actual "Brad" is a little nondescript. Plain Jane. A "Brad's" defining feature would be a tuft of dark chest hair poking out the top of a tucked-in golf shirt with some tech company's logo across the pocket. A true "Brad" doesn't have Puffer Vest's chiseled cheekbones and those thick brown curls that would make McDreamy jealous. (RIP, another plot point spoiled courtesy of Roxanne—that woman needs a three-second delay.) This guy is more of a Noah. Maybe even Hunter. Either way, a missed opportunity by his parents some forty-odd years ago. He steps forward without Roxanne giving the go-ahead, and Hartley immediately snags a copy of her book from the pile beside her.

She digs into the open canvas bag at her feet. The cheaply made bookmarks are starting to bend at the corners, crammed as they are among tattoos (glitter *and* reflective), a book on marketing and publicity, a bag of potato chips, three protein bars, and a large yellow box that reads EpiPen. She finds a blue Sharpie with such a blunt tip that it makes everyone's writing look like a two-year-old's scribble. "Should I make it out to you?" she asks, a tremble in her voice. "Brad? And hi. I'm Hartley."

"Brad" gives a small amused smile and presses the sticky with his name on the table before Hartley. "I know. I'm a fan."

"You are?" she says.

"There's not a Sofie Wilde fan alive who wouldn't also be. You truly are uncanny."

A prickle up my spine.

"Oh, well, I don't know about that," Hartley says. "I mean, it's *Sofie Wilde*." She whispers the second half of that sentence.

Brad nods toward me. "An honor." Like me, he lacks that throaty, drop-the-*r* South Shore accent—a sign he's a rare non-native too. People are born here, people live here, and people die here. Everyone knows everyone. It takes three generations to no longer be an interloper. It's the perfect spot for a transplant who prizes her alone time. He adds, "I'm not quite Kathy Bates–level fan, but close."

Readers think this is cute. Comparing themselves to the actress famous for playing the deranged Stephen King character who held her favorite author hostage. She demanded he right the wrong of killing off a beloved character, hobbling him for incentive. With Vance's impending demise, the reference is even more unnerving. And so I thank Brad but can't help adding, "The *close* is the key there though, isn't it?"

He's taken aback, though recovers quickly, adding, "Touché." He turns to Hartley, who's frantically penning a diatribe of appreciation in his book. "Addelyn is beguiling," he says to her.

Addelyn? Addie is an Addelyn?

Like Jocelyn? Another coincidence?

Roxanne begins to wave my first fan forward, but I hold up a hand to stop her. I perch myself on the edge of my chair and reach across the table for one of Hartley's books. Flipping to the first page, I skim.

"Eyes like the ocean on a cloudy day."

"Hair the color of wheat."

"Curves of hip and lip and an invitation to stare."

"That's not . . ."

My description of Jocelyn from the first book:

"Eyes like the sea when a storm rages."

"Hair the color of fallen leaves."

"A swell of breasts, a rounding of lips, a body of perpetual curve that causes one to linger longer than they should."

"What the actual fuck?" slips out.

Roxanne sucks in a breath, but Brad offers that same jaunty smile. "Uncanny, like I said."

I murmur assent, heat rising in my cheeks, actual steam spewing from my nostrils not out of the question. Closing the front cover, I slide the book back toward Hartley without a word.

"How did you do it?" Brad asks, accepting his signed copy from a flustered Hartley.

She manages a slight shrug. "I worked hard, sat in the chair every day. Butt in seat and all that."

Brad nods along as if this is heart-stopping news. "Sure, sure. But how'd you do *it*? Sound so much like Sofie? Was it just a lot of reading and rereading or did you write fan fiction or—"

"Excuse me," Roxanne says, coming to the table. "We have a large group to accommodate and I'm afraid we must impose time limits per guest."

Brad offers a simple, "Course, course" but stays his ground.

Roxanne's brows knit together, not wanting to make a scene with so many eyes of the world in people's pockets.

With a hang of his head and resulting undulation of those chestnut-colored waves, Brad retreats. An exhale worthy of the maligned author trope of "releasing a breath she didn't know she was holding" comes from the "author" beside me.

What I read isn't plagiarism, not exactly, but it's something. I endure the rolling boil beneath my skin and plaster on a smile for my first reader.

"Maddisyn" hands over her blue sticky and trills a request for a photo just as Brad's voice resounds through the bookstore.

"It's just, it's so similar," he says. "Even the cadence. Especially the cadence. Wait . . . is this for real?" He wags a finger back and forth between the two of us. "This isn't a collaboration? Some stunt to help promote book ten?"

I'm at a loss for words, quite unusually.

"Sir," Roxanne says. "Let's get you on your way. Amy's waiting at the register right over there."

That same "Course, course." That same standing his ground. "Sorry, I just can't help . . . I mean, I've been reading Sofie Wilde from before she was *Sofie Wilde*. Tucana? Sure, I was all in even then. The arachnids? I've got the original Staples copies on my shelf." He holds up his phone. "Look, I can show you."

This has veered into creepy territory, and my line of readers is starting to get anxious. I rise to my feet. "Brad, as always, I appreciate my long-term fans, and I'd be happy to speak with you after the event, but right now . . ." I scribble in the air with my Sharpie.

He nods. "Much appreciated, Ms. Wilde, but I'm still waiting for an answer from Ms. West."

"An answer to what, exactly?" I say, veering not just into resting bitch face but active bitch face.

"How Ms. West was able to write with so much resemblance to you. Don't you want to know?"

I don't actually. And wouldn't ever have had to wonder if Lacey hadn't insisted on this ridiculous pairing. This is ruining my night and making my carpal tunnel flare. "Craft for all of us begins by studying authors we admire. It's perfectly natural that a resemblance can be seen in our first works—"

"It's more than a resemblance."

"An echo, then."

"More than an echo."

"A likeness." I pause as Hartley's head drops into her hands. With a stern look at Brad, I continue, "A similarity. A common sentimentality. Fine, yes, that can happen. I'm sure if the books have a homogeneous quality, that it's simply a coincidence." I widen my lips into a smile. "Imitation is the sincerest form of flattery, isn't that right?"

"Is it, Ms. West?" Brad presses, and I can't believe this night is going to end in a call to the police. "Ms. West?"

I move closer to Hartley because it feels like this guy is starting to bully her. "You don't have to answer him. He's probably from some hater blog or trolling Goodreads account or—"

"Your biggest fan," Brad says. "Which is how I know she's a fraud."

Hartley's head lifts, her cheeks are wet, her eyes already tinged with red.

Remembering the audience's earlier reaction, I gently lower my hand to her shoulder. This time, she winces.

"No." She pulls back, shaking me off. "No, no, no, no. I can't do this. I can't . . ." She peers up at me, a pleading in those blue-gray eyes.

She's flustered. She's nervous. She's scared. I remember feeling the same. I hated feeling the same. So I ensured I wouldn't. At the start of my career, I forced myself to stand before a mirror, reciting my pitch, rehearsing the answers to questions, memorizing "off-the-cuff" amusing stories. Preparation was my key. And the door it unlocked was the door to all of this.

I pass her one of my glasses of water and stand beside her, side-eyeing Brad as she gulps the entire thing and covers a burp.

Lacey is in for an earful.

"Listen, why don't we take a break." I nod toward the back of the store. "Roxanne? Maybe in the meantime, do the giveaway?"

I start to pull Hartley's chair back, but she's bigger than me and I have no leverage. I lean in and whisper, "Hartley, it's okay. There will be other events." I purposely don't say *with me.*

"That's not—" she shakes her head "—important. Or what's most important. You don't know, you can't know, but—" Her chest rises and falls and sweat dots her upper lip. "I admire you, so much. I can barely breathe with you beside me. Sofie, you saved me. *Saved.* I was so lonely, and I'd lost Artie—"

"Artie?" I ask.

"My cat, this molten brown stray who loved bananas of all things."

"Awws" from the room. Then, everyone goes quiet, intrigued by the start of Hartley's response to Brad's question.

"I was at my lowest . . ." Her head bobs. "Then I found your books. I devoured them, and yes, I read and reread and reread again. So many books, but I needed more of them. They weren't enough. I needed something more than just reading your words. I needed your words to be mine."

A foreboding radiates like a spider web. "I'm not sure I'm following."

"She copied you," Brad says in his bassoon voice. "Can't you see it?"

I swivel, fixing a stern gaze on Brad. It's so silent you can hear seaweed growing in the harbor across the street. I lean against the edge of the table facing Hartley, my back to what I don't need to see to know are phones filming this moment. I breathe deeply, ensuring my tone is calm and soothing, my muscles loose, my body language welcoming. "If there's something you need to tell me, you can. I'll understand. I've been exactly where you are, Hartley."

"You haven't. I'm sure you haven't."

"Try me." I angle myself toward her but also so my profile is more fully in view to the crowd. (Seizing every opportunity for self-promotion is ingrained.) "See this?" I point to the short white crease under my left brow. "Fan-fiction hazard, though they didn't call it that when I was in high school. Word to the wise: creative rush and light saber pencils don't mix. For me, it was *Back to the Future*. I sent Marty to rescue his newly married parents from a virulent moss from outer space. With every mow of the lawn, Marty's dad got greener." I sigh. "I learned a lot. We all do. Writing in the style of an artist we admire is how we all begin. I'm honored." (I'm not.)

Hartley stares at my scar, unable to look me in the eye. "You are so kind." (And a very good liar.)

She presses her hands into the table. "But you don't know what I've done. He's right—Brad. I didn't write in your style. The computer did."

I give a light chuckle. "See, you're a writer! Careful about word choice. Sure, we use a machine, but—"

"No *but*." She grabs one of the paperbacks with her name in tiny letters beneath a stock photo of a woman in a whispery white gown stroking a chocolate-colored horse. "This was written by AI."

ENTER: THE ANTAGONIST

INNOVATION IS THE NEW INSPIRATION: HARTLEY WEST, A WRITING Prompt Puppeteer.

Art Is in the AI: Love and Lawlessness, *a Delightful Debut.*

Who Will Be the Next "Next Sofie Wilde"?

Doomscrolling, that's what this is, apparently. Roxanne says I need to stop. But Lacey keeps sending links to me. My text chain with her is going to max out the storage capacity on my phone.

"Sofie," Roxanne says, sliding me a cup of chamomile tea that I slide right back to her.

This is not what I asked for. She shakes her head, and one of those tiny golf pencils tumbles out of her bun, landing safely in her bounteous cleavage. She leaves me in the pink tufted chair in the window of her living room above the bookstore and returns to the kitchen.

I pick up my phone, feeling the strain in my eyes that I nicknamed Not Today, Reading Glasses as I return to my texts.

Lacey: It's been two days! The trolls are asleep at the wheel! I've never seen a publishing scandal so, well, unscandalous.

Me: How can that be? What about integrity?

Lacey: Did you seriously just ask about the integrity of trolls?

Me: No, in general. General integrity.

Lacey: We all can't be Torrence.

Me: I'm serious!

Lacey: So am I. You've been living in your own book world too long. The truth has Jell-O for legs.

Me: But my fans... why don't they care?

Lacey: They do. They're psyched to have more Sofie Wilde books to read.

Me: They're not my books!

Lacey: Semantics.

Me: And my publisher? When will they have a response?

Lacey: You didn't just ask that of an industry that moves slower than a tortoise on a molasses sled. Which is why we need to get in the game. Better: define the game.

Me: Blaire wants to lay low, let it unfold before we say anything.

Lacey: So very Blaire. Sometimes she's an agent without agency. We're going to miss out. We could proclaim it a dialogue opener, at the very least. Other authors are, you know.

Me: Let me guess... Grace Chang.

Lacey: For one.

Me: She's always hated me.

Lacey: You've always hated her.

Me: Fiona Finley. Loose morals, that one.

Lacey: Manipulating bookstore reporting to hit the list remains a rumor.

Me: Uh-huh.

Lacey: Moving on... There's also—

Me: No.

Lacey: Yes.

Me: Rosie Gardens is okay with this? She's actually good.

(Better than me.)

Me: And we talk. Sometimes. About things.

Lacey: The definition of BFFs. Told you being a lone wolf would get you eviscerated.

And yet, one can also be eviscerated by a BFF.

Me: Rosie really supports this?

Lacey: No. She's sidestepped. But she wants to talk to you. United front, Sofie.

Roxanne reappears, a bottle of bourbon in hand. She pours a splash into my tea. "I don't condone this." She then does the same to her own.

"Right, I can see just how much."

"You have a flight in the morning and a convention to headline. Me? I'm just here. Watching my bookstore sink into the sea."

"Melodrama doesn't suit you."

"Nor jealousy you."

I grit my teeth as texts from Lacey fly in.

Lacey: You need to come to grips with this.

It's happening.

We have to strategize.

Approach it the right way.

Could bolster sales.

If you don't screw it up.

I'm sending you a statement. Sound bites. For Romance US. Memorize them. Don't deviate.

Me: Sound bites? Shit.

(Shoot. I mean, shoot.)

Roxanne dumps her tea into the jade plant coiling over the arm of her chair and pours in straight bourbon. "Still, I agreed not to stock *Love and Lawlessness*. And you don't even consider me a friend."

My head snaps up. "That's not true. I never said that."

"Nor the opposite." Roxanne swirls her cup and tilts it toward me. "You come here for this. Industry talk. Occasionally you'll look at my grandkids photos and we commiserate over creaking knees and our inability to start a movie past seven. But I've never even been to your house. Your work comes first, I know that. I support you. This whole town does. Your fans love you. But I do wonder if it's asking too much to expect them to love *only* you."

"That's not what this is. Hartley is a fake. She's making a mockery of me. Of you. Of all of us."

My phone buzzes.

Lacey: Be nice when you see her.

Hartley's going to be at the convention? I didn't get invited to the convention until book four.

Me: This is bullshit.

Bullshit, bullshit, bullshit.
Fuck the crossover readers (no offense).

I gulp down my bourbon-chamomile tea, burning my tongue and throat, and tears spring forth and I refill it with more bourbon that I swallow in a single sip.

"Sofie, hun, slow down," Roxanne says.

I close my eyes, but all I can see is Hartley West. That ugly flowered skirt. That tragic crocheted cardigan. Fingers with unpainted nails and ragged cuticles tapping my book. She unwrapped Roxanne's prop after her confession, and the internet was flooded with images of her holding my final book.

I pour more bourbon.

Lacey: Advance copy of the BuzzFeed article is in.

Me: Tell me or don't. I don't care.

(Liar.)

Lacey: Direct quote: "My novel is an homage to the incomparable, iconic Sofie Wilde. Creating it made me whole again. And I guess, well, I started to feel like it was a gift I could give to others. I could share this with those in need and they could experience the same. I wanted them to have this joy and love it as much as we all love her."

Me: Let me comment.

Lacey: No. You're too close to this.

I *am* this!

I slug back the bourbon in my teacup and pop to my feet. I need air. I race through Roxanne's nautical-themed living room, past bowls in the shape of fish and a giant wooden crab on the wall, and bound down the stairs.

I am the top-selling fantasy romance author in the country. We're fielding offers from television studios right now. My books will become three-dimensional. My words will exit the mouths of famous actors with smoldering eyes and high cheekbones. They will snap selfies with me and praise my work, even though we all know that in the early days, they would have let me and my scorpion-loving peasant die of thirst or dysentery or zombie disembowelment without a whisper of regret. I did all of this. *Me.* Not some goddamn machine.

In the middle of the bookstore, all the air leaves my lungs. It was here where Hartley admitted to my "loyal" readers that she used artificial intelligence to "write" a book that would feel like mine. I expected them to wage a war on my behalf and renounce Hartley West as a charlatan. Brad and Roxanne (as in *Bel Canto*!) and Amy (as in *Little Women*!) and the woman in the Team Torrence T-shirt—I expected them to defend me, my art, my life, which are all one and the same. Instead, by the time we regrouped, every single person in my signing line held not just a blue sticky but a yellow one too.

Traitors.

The bottle of bourbon is still in my hand. I upend it and guzzle.

Roxanne startles me. "Easy there," she says, appearing in front of me.

I hear a ringing in between my ears, and there's no "easy" here, there, or anywhere.

I'm circling the store. Pulling books off the rolling partitions. Muttering to myself because Hartley West is a complete and utter imposter and no one cares. In fact, everyone loves her. In just a couple of days, she dismantled everything I spent years building. She's made a farce of my life's work—and Grace's and Fiona's and Rosie's and that of every other author who actually uses their minds and hearts and souls despite overdrawn bank accounts and advances that wouldn't even buy a Dyson.

But it's fitting, isn't it? Laughter bubbles up my throat. "Why should this be any different from everything else about this industry? It's all an illusion. At least this time the readers are in

on it. At least Hartley West admitted the truth. That's something. Can you imagine any of these authors actually telling
the truth about their success? Like this one?"

I hold up a book and point to the fleur-de-lis stamp on the
front: A Riley Read. Some actress turned literary expert by
way of Instagram. She's rivaling Reese and Jenna and all the
rest for dominance in the book recommendation space. She's
never featured one of my books. Ever. But this one? This drivel
about a woman trekking across the country to forage for mushrooms with her dachshund, Wiggles? "A Riley Read. For her
debut. And do you know why?"

Roxanne's eyes leave mine, float to the other side of the store,
as if she's contemplating making a run for it.

"Her husband's a producer," I say. "Rights were sold, Riley
Moore attached to star, before the publisher even signed on.
This Bill Bryson rip-off will be trending on every poor
sucker's Netflix, and they'll have no idea it was all rigged." I
drop the book on the floor. Snatch another. "And this one?"
On the cover, two people lock lips on the bow of a cruise
ship. With my hand to my forehead, I mimic one of the influencer blurbs on the back. "'So dreamy.' Christ. I was on
a panel with the author and she went on and on about how
word of mouth led to her book becoming a hit out of nowhere.
An organic reader-fueled sensation." I toss the book on the
floor. "Horseshit. Her publisher paid those influencers. Each
and every one. She bragged about it after." I reach for another
with a forlorn-looking woman stroking a piano on the cover.
"And this? Every interview, the author waxes on about her
inspiration—a musician mother with paralyzing stage fright.
Lie. Outright. Packager all the way from story idea to story
beats to character arcs. They hired her to write it. And no
one knows."

Roxanne stands. "Sofie, these are interesting insights, but I think—"

"Interesting? It's fucking criminal!" My hands dart out, grabbing book after book. "At least political ads have to tell you who paid for them." I fling a book to the ground. "TikTokers paid for by Big Five, or is it four now? Three?" And there goes another. "Instagrammers, paid." One more. "Celebs, paid, paid, paid."

I seize another book and pause. It's a title I've never heard of. "Oh, Roxanne, you truly are 'salt of the earth,' aren't you?"

She does this, stocks the books that have less support than a bra from the dollar store. The books that aren't projected on billboards in Times Square. The ones that aren't "coincidentally" reviewed everywhere from the *New York Times* to the *Washington Post* to *Cosmo* in the same week. The ones whose advance reader copies aren't printed in the thousands and sent to influencers and celebrities in special boxes that spew glitter and nestle the book amid eye serums and cashmere throws and bubble baths in the character's favorite scent. The ones that aren't granted all of these marketing efforts upon acquisition, preordained as bestsellers before the book even hits the shelves. Roxanne does what she can to support the books that get dropped in the publisher's next season catalog with as much fanfare as an advertisement for hemorrhoid cream. Just waiting for someone to believe in them.

I clutch the book. "From the land of misfit toys. An unsupported book. A single copy ordered by a bookstore owner with a soft spot. It will linger here, gathering dust, until it finally makes its way to the seventy-five-percent-off bin where some old lady will find it and use its pages to line her parakeet's cage. The author to be shit upon once again." I balance this sad sap of a book on the shelf, face out. "Here's your chance, little one. Godspeed."

"Yes, well," Roxanne says, her voice tight. "Lessons for us all. But I need to close up shop. It's after hours, and you need some coffee, maybe some Advil."

She starts walking toward me, and I bolt to the bestsellers' table at the front of the store where the first nine of my *Weight of Feathers and Stone* books are artfully displayed among a handful of others.

"Paid," I say, tapping the nearest and then each one in succession, including my own. "Paid, paid, paid, paid, paid, and, oh . . . right, paid. The same goddamn books at the front of every single store because the publisher paid for them to be. And yes, my books are here too, so am I as guilty as the rest of them? No!" Roxanne winces, but I can't lower my voice any more than I can stop. "I *worked* for this. I have a bathroom closet full of craft-fair penguin candles that make me nauseous every time I grab a roll of toilet paper. Writing a book using AI? A coward's move. A brainless coward's move. And yet readers are too stupid to see it. They have murdered us one and all." I bring my hand to my chest and bow my head. "Here lies the remains of a breed of human we once called Author. They are no more. Extinct. Rest in peace. Rest. In. Peace."

In one fluid motion, I sweep my arm across the table and send bestsellers flying.

Roxanne gasps in front of me. And someone else does from behind.

I turn. A cell phone looms high in the air, filming my every word.

The middle-aged woman who wore the "Team Torrence" T-shirt at my event stares at me, jaw open. "M-my mother-in-law," she stutters. "She hasn't started the series yet, and in all the fuss, I forgot to get her a copy of the first book, so I thought I would just come back and . . ."

I swipe the first book in my series off the floor and hand it over. "Here."

"Would you mind signing it?"

"Yes, I would."

A CRIME OF PASSION

"YES, I WOULD."

I tug the brim of my floppy hat farther down my forehead and slink into my first-class seat. My voice floats down the aisle, exiting the speaker of at least a couple of phones as boarding passengers in puffy coats jostle my elbow with their carry-ons. I'm a meme. I'm not even sure what a meme is, but I am one. And not a good one, according to Lacey.

Team Torrence posted the video. My rant is all over the internet. My social media is locked down. I can't post (well, Lacey can't post for me). No one can comment or message me. A day before my book drops—a series conclusion a decade in the making—I have no online presence. But Lacey assures me that's better than the alternative.

The announcement comes that this Boston-to-Chicago flight is pushing back. We're asked to place our phones in airplane mode. I dash off a quick: Taking off to Lacey and On my way to Blaire, who assures me that this will all blow over in a couple of days. I'm not the first public figure to have stepped into this particular storm of shit, and I won't be the last.

But it is my first time, one I regret in myriad ways. I regret trying to heal my wounded ego with bourbon. I regret my hypocritical tossing of the work of other hardworking (and not-so-hardworking) authors on the floor. I regret not recognizing the ringing between my ears was actually the ding of the opening door.

And yet, this business isn't a meritocracy. The blatant manipulation is what people should be in an uproar over. Some are, or so Lacey patronizes me by saying. But what they're truly in an uproar over is what I said about Hartley West. It was the *brainless coward* bit that did it.

After Hartley saying I saved her.

Admittedly, when taken in concert, it's not a good look, as they say. (As Lacey tells me they're actively saying, quite loudly.)

I also called readers *stupid* and basically accused them of murder. My biggest regret of all. And not because of a fear of what that will do to my sales numbers (well, not *only* because of that fear). Because readers aren't stupid. They've simply been lied to.

I shut my phone off entirely, slip from the aisle seat to the empty one beside me. I angle my body toward the window and let my mind wander, to a new world with new problems and new characters whom I will torture for thousands of pages. I am at peace.

Three hours and one time change later, I've abandoned *Pick Me*—my animal shelter meet-cute where a fun-loving man-boy stand-up comedian and a disciplined Boston ballet dancer clash over the Labrador/poodle/German shepherd mutt they both want to adopt—and returned to my safe space. I'm deep in the underground world of Palladium, the last habitable zone for the human race. Brianna/Sylvia/Laurel (names are so important) is either a spy or pawn and is in love with either the head of a criminal gang or the leader of a coterie determined to replenish the climate change–ravaged Earth. In turn, she's, naturally, the opposite of whomever she's in love with.

My mind asks what-if questions, spins from idea to idea, gnaws on twists, visualizes the color and fabric of Brianna/Sylvia/Laurel's surroundings. I am a plantser—a cross between a plotter, a writer who painstakingly plans the details of their story in advance, and a pantser, an anarchist who fires their brain and their fingers at the same time, creating story on the fly or "by the seat of their pants." Plotting takes too much time up front and can feel like writing in a straitjacket. Pantsing mires one in revision for what feels like decades and too often results in a scrapped manuscript with no way to knit together a hundred thousand words of loosely related tangents. The mix gives me a solid map: a starting place *and* a destination. But the roads are fuzzy, some only dotted lines, some nonexistent. I pave them into existence as I go. The more my brain lives in a fictional world, the more that fictional world is revealed. Cows spend nearly eight hours a day chewing, and when I'm working out a story, my mind does the same, both consciously and subconsciously. The constant rumination leads to what could be construed as epiphanies—disparate story ideas suddenly fitting together. But it's actually the result of my mind tirelessly working, of a full immersion in the story world.

It is maddening.

It is glorious.

It is easier with Palladium than with *Pick Me*.

But that doesn't mean that *Pick Me* is wrong. Palladium benefits from mental muscle memory. *Pick Me* is new. Different. That means it might be a heavier lift at the start. I must remind myself that this is the process; this is how it always begins.

I love and hate this part in equal measure. The freedom to

create something new is as thrilling as it is daunting. I try not to imagine the comparisons to Jocelyn that will come. Those blurred-vision, heart-thumping panic attacks are future Sofie's problem. As is the fallout from my viral rant. And so as we land, I relish the quiet, keeping my phone turned off. For just a little while longer, I will allow myself to remain oblivious.

I let myself explore this story world I'm building out of nothing as I deplane, as I find the driver holding a sign reading "Wilde," as I check into the hotel, wash my face, apply a heavier layer of makeup than I normally wear, and gather myself in front of the floor-to-ceiling windows of this suite that overlooks the Chicago Bean and the waters of Lake Michigan beyond.

I could live here. I have the same thought every time. A city whose architecture is actually art, built around a wide snaking river they will dye green for St. Patrick's Day. The world's fair was here in 1893, and it's easy to imagine it. Chicago feels both set in the future and the past at the same time.

I slip on three thin gold bangles and loop a purple scarf around my neck, echoing the coloring of the first book in my series—the one I tossed at the woman in the Team Torrence tee. My phone is still off; I need just a bit more respite from reality, especially since no events are scheduled for today, only the evening VIP meet and greet for attendees who paid extra to have dinner with the authors. "With" meaning sitting at separate tables, eating differ-ent food, and taking photos from afar. Though we do "mingle" post-dinner. The authors behind a velvet rope strung across the stage in the largest ballroom of the convention center, the one where I will join the ranks of the romance literati who have come before me and give my keynote speech that will bring this three-day event to a close and launch my expansion of the Sofie Wilde brand. By then, Hartley West will surely be on her way to becoming nothing more than an obscure answer on *Jeopardy*.

My mind is sharp, my body light as I stride through the lobby to the attached convention center. Only then, in full event mode, do I finally turn my phone back on, confident that Lacey and Blaire will confirm the strong winds have whipped through and this has all blown over.

I face the entrance to the grand ballroom. I would be lying, and not convincingly, if I said my throat didn't swell at the sight before me. My name in swirly letters three feet high—aquamarine, a nice touch—the cover of my final book on one side, my author photo (with my face five years younger and Photoshopped) on the other. I've been here six times, half of those as a VIP author, but I've never been the headliner. (WTF is right.)

Tall ladders flank both sides of the entrance. At the top of the one on the right, a man in a yellow safety vest tugs on the cord holding up the banner. They must have just finished putting it up. Impeccable timing.

I lift my phone to take a photo, and it buzzes as if set to Taser mode.

The man on the left, also in a yellow safety vest, shouts something I can't make out. I lower my phone. Flip it around. And the banner with my name snaps like thunder and plummets to the ground.

Lacey: There have been developments.

Lacey: You need to call me.

Lacey: It's not blowing over.

Lacey: Call.

Lacey: Me.

Blaire: Good flight? Get in a catnap?

Blaire: Just a heads-up. Things are percolating.

Blaire: But I'm on it! Don't panic. We'll fix it.

I message Blaire back first: Fix what?

Blaire: The keynote is being… reimagined.

My chest tightens as I lift my phone and take a photo of the banner strewn across the floor. I send it to Lacey and Blaire on the same text chain.

Lacey: Such disrespect. To not even tell me!

Blaire: This is a misunderstanding, I'm positive. We have a contract. They can't… Oh, my word.

Lacey: Just seeing it too. Oh, no, oh, oh, oh. Oh.

Lacey is the person you want taking the controls when the pilot has a heart attack. Lacey is not an "oh, no" person. Certainly not an "oh, oh, oh" person.

Me: Whatever it is, you can make this right, can't you, B?

Blaire gives a thumbs-up. Nothing else.

Lacey: Get yourself a drink. On second thought, no. No drinking for you.

Me: It's that bad. Spill.

Blaire: She's going to find out anyway. So…

Lacey: She's getting a review.

A vice grips my heart, and small little dots float in front of my eyes.

Blaire: We haven't heard about yours yet, but it's coming. I just know it.

Hartley West is getting a *New York Times* book review. The thing that will surely lead to her hitting the list.

"Spectacular work, Sofie." I look up from my phone and straight into the judging dark eyes of Grace Chang. "Just spectacular."

"Grace," I say curtly. "I'm in the middle of something."

"I'll say," she says. "A steaming pile of shit. And I woke up this morning smelling it because you're dragging us all in behind you."

I glue my lips together. Lacey would scold me if I said what I actually want to say, which is that Grace and every other author younger than me is only at this convention, in this world, because my books created a readership for them.

"Funny," I say, watching as a group of early attendees or maybe volunteers try to sidestep the banner. "It's only my name currently being used as a doormat."

What turns out to be a volunteer in a red Romance US shirt bends his dark curly-haired head to free his foot from the heavy plastic.

"For now," Grace says. She's in the middle of her five-book Sapphic paranormal romance series about shipwrecked ghosts. Her writing is compelling and vibrant and she really brings the characters to life. (Oh, come on, how could I not go there? In truth, she's quite talented, and hello, have you met me? Those are not words I dispense lightly.)

Grace exaggerates the arch in her back. "But when Hartley West takes the stage, what then? She appears beside us as an author without ever having written a word. She becomes more and we become less. Like that." She snaps her fingers and her neon rubber bracelets slide down her arm. She modeled in the late eighties, the last time she updated her wardrobe. Her hair helmet is news-anchor lacquered and she has a slight British affect despite her Nashville roots.

Grace crosses her arms in front of her chest. "She can't do the keynote."

My pulse thrashes. "She's not. The keynote is mine."

"Is it?" Grace raises an eyebrow at my banner, being stuffed into a gigantic orange crate. "That's not what my agent says."

"And mine." Fiona Finley strides toward us, nodding to Grace as if this were planned. Her red curls skim the bottom of her shoulder blades. It's a wig. Part of her signature. She dresses as though she stepped out of one of her books—true bodice rippers. Today, her gown is light blue with a lace collar and a train. It's not even three o'clock, and she's already in full costume. Some might call that commitment; I call it excessive.

Fiona bunches up the fabric at the front of her dress and smooths it back down as she stands before me. "You're out, Sofie. Normally, I'd be giddy. But this affects—"

"All of us." I spin around to face Rosie Gardens, whose presence confirms this is an ambush.

"But mostly me," I say, embarrassment over (potentially) losing my keynote soaring.

Rosie's lips thin. "No, Sofie, it is all of us, truly. We know you think you've worked harder than the rest of us to get here, and maybe you did, maybe you didn't. But we all worked hard. We're all here, just like you."

I do think I worked harder than most everyone here, except, perhaps, for Rosie. She's like me. She has just as many bestsellers as I do, has been a Riley Read twice, and has been writing as long—longer. But she's also not like me. She is a Black author in a white-dominated industry—romance, even more so. She's never been given the keynote either. If she were replacing me, I'd be fine with it. Well, not fine, but okay. Actually, I'd still be fuming, yet I'd not only understand the choice but applaud it.

Rosie's books tend toward the literary, with most of her novels being historical romances about marginalized women who have so rarely been featured as protagonists, in books and in life. Her literary style is the embodiment of what I grew up thinking a writer was, though my reading tastes ran the gamut from *Sweet Valley High* to Stephen King to Margaret Atwood. In my first writing workshop, surrounded by writers who eschewed all but the authors whose names were accompanied by Pulitzer or Booker or Caldecott, I realized my style fit in the commercial or (dreaded) genre bucket. I nearly collapsed under the weight of the chip on my shoulder. Until I wrote my first sex scene. And that was it. Romance gave me a place I could call home.

It is a home we all share, though that doesn't mean there isn't dysfunction. Rosie walks a tightrope, literary on one side, romance on the other, and she does it better than anyone I've ever read. And she does it by never making anyone feel that they are less, that there even *is* a less.

Before me, Rosie's stacked bob shines, the dark strands framing her petite face, the tips at the front dyed a subtle shimmery gold, her book accent, the same as my scarf. We get asked about it on panels—if we came up with the idea together. We tell a story about how we did, how we came up with the idea of matching the hues of our book covers one late night after a book event where no one showed up so we took ourselves to the bar across the street. Only half the story is true. No one showed up. But we didn't go to the bar. She invited me, and I said no.

I've never been good at engaging with my peers. I was a shy kid, small for my age, with crappy coordination and fragile bones that gifted me with sprains and broken limbs and a learned aversion to soccer balls and monkey bars. My parents must have wondered if there'd been a mix-up at the hospital, because I was nothing like them. For a couple who prided themselves on costume parties at Halloween and Christmas in July cookouts complete with fake snow, I must have been a disappointment. By the time I was in the fourth grade, I had established myself as the girl who helped the teacher clean the classroom during recess. Except, that year, I gave them a reprieve. I still remember the way my mother's eyes danced when I came home and told her about Sandy.

The über-popular Sandy had one day appeared inside the classroom at recess. She'd broken her leg in a nasty fall off the balance beam. Of course, Sandy was in gymnastics. She was the prettiest girl in class. Dirty-blonde hair and actual heart-shaped lips that were naturally shiny and bubblegum pink. Except they weren't. I caught her sneaking an application of lip gloss. For some reason, she offered it to me. And that was it.

For the next seven weeks while her leg healed, I read my favorite books aloud to her, and then we began to make up stories together. She soon realized that I was the better writer and she was the better artist. We collaborated on eleven illustrated books while her leg was in a cast. Nine of them about squirrels—Sandy loved squirrels.

They sawed off the cast, but nothing could cut through our friendship. She introduced me to chopped apples in pancakes and I ushered her into the world of V.C. Andrews. We were both small with glasses and each had a giggly laugh we saved for the other. And for the next three years, we were the definition of BFFs with those split-heart necklaces to ensure everyone knew it.

Then came a transition from elementary school to middle school and the arrival of a new girl. Another Sandy, but this one with an *i*.

If my Sandy was pretty, Sandi with an *i* was Cindy Crawford in the *Sports Illustrated* swimsuit edition. Puberty had come in hard and fast. She had luscious dark hair, eyelashes like feathers, and a rasp to her voice that felt far too sexy for a thirteen-year-old.

Unlike me, my Sandy shot up in height. Her dirty-blonde hair turned white-blonde. And she mastered the art of jabbing hard contacts into her eyes, something she tried to teach me. But after three scratched corneas from my own fingernails, my mom took my contacts away. As my face lost its baby fat, my nose appeared longer and narrower. The boys dubbed me "George Washington" while Sandy became "Christie Brinkley."

The class's running bit of calling out "Sandy with a *y*" or "Sandi with an *i*" bonded the two of them. I hated sharing Sandy. For her birthday, I thought I could win her back by returning to what had brought us together. I wrote a book about friendship with squirrels as the main characters and brought it as my gift to the birthday party at her house. My stapled-together booklet had blank spaces for her to draw in the pictures. As she tore off the squirrel gift wrap, she accidentally ripped the book in half. I'd warned her to be careful.

Later, I heard the giggly laugh I knew in my sleep from the kitchen. Sandy and Sandi shushed each other as they exited and strolled past me. I found my book in the trash beneath melted pools of strawberry ice cream. I told Sandy that no one likes strawberry, but Sandi with an *i* said the opposite. Sandi was wrong. I was right.

That day I learned I didn't need an illustrator. Or half of a heart necklace. Years later, it would be a different heart, given and taken and taken back, that would teach me how to navigate this world and eventually find my place in it, which I did amid the people I wave to on the beach, the barflies I chat with in town, the books I create, the fictional people I invent, and Blaire and Lacey and Roxanne and my parents' pickleball videos. And my fans. Whom I very recently called stupid.

I filmed an apology, heartfelt, almost embarrassingly so. I just hope my fans can see that. Especially since, as I stand here in the trap set by Grace and Fiona and Rosie, I know that my fellow authors aren't going to jump in to help. I can't really blame them—though I'm trying, really, really hard.

I'm an anomaly in this industry. Writers, published and unpublished, live in a miasma of codependency. They squee over one another's cover reveals (*"dying, I am dying, dead, I am dead over this!"*). They high-five one another's agent signings, and when book contracts are announced, they send balloons emoji on "nice" deals (read: three grand). Add confetti cannons for "very nice" (okay, now maybe you can buy a car—a used one, after agent commission and taxes). A cancan dancer with "good" (new car territory). A few champagne bottles at "significant" (now we're talking down payment on a house). And countless mind-blown ones on "major" (all the zeros). They celebrate what arguably deserves to be (typing "the end") and what categorically does not ("deleted more than I added today but PROGRESS").

All to mask the vinegary bitter taste of jealousy. A lie said enough times becomes a truth.

Grace, Fiona, Rosie, and I aren't friends. We're barely even colleagues. I don't owe them anything. And they don't owe me. Clearly, a sentiment they share.

I can't stand here looking at the empty space where my banner used to be. I need to extract myself from this group that would burn me at the stake, except as authors we're all too fond of witches to disparage the genre by using that metaphor. "Blaire says she's going to fix it. If there's anything to even fix. Maybe they just decided to move the banner to a more prominent spot."

Two young women roll a cart toward the ballroom. Books fill all three shelves, the spine reading one thing and one thing only: "*Love and Lawlessness* Hartley West."

Rosie leans closer. "She can't have this. Hartley West taking that stage doesn't just end your career. You were right about that. She used AI to write a book that is more than likely on track to become a bestseller. She's being lauded as a pioneer. As the heralding of a future where *writing* no longer exists. Where *entertainment*, not creators reign. She lived in obscurity before your tirade brought her front and center. This may not have started as your fault, but you made it your responsibility. Blaire or no Blaire, this has to be fixed. Here. And now. She can't hit the list."

"She won't," I say, suddenly realizing just how hard that would be. To be in range of hitting the bestseller list, there have to be enough actual books in print, able to be bought in the current week. Most authors, even those traditionally published, have small print runs—another thing that separates a top-selling author from everyone else from day one. The chance isn't even there. Dreams of breaking out and the power of word of mouth are at odds with this basic mathematical fact. Everyone from Oprah to Reese to Taylor Swift could endorse the same new release on the same day and still the book wouldn't be in contention if there simply weren't enough copies in cir-culation. "She can't have enough."

Rosie eyes the bookshelf with skepticism. "And what if she does?"

A huff of frustration erupts out. "What would you have me do?"

Rosie shrugs, her shoulder nudging the bottom tier of her chandelier earrings. "You're creative. You've plotted your way out of deeper holes, haven't you?"

"This? It's barely worthy of the flap copy."

"Make sure it stays that way."

THE MEET AND GREET

A SERVER WEARING A TALK WORDY TO ME TEE SETS AN EDIBLE rainbow in the center of our table. Small macarons in bright pink and yellow and green and blue call to me. It's an *Alice in Wonderland* moment. I didn't eat dinner. Nerves from expecting Hartley to walk in at any moment (she hasn't yet). But also, my crisp white blouse does not mix with wilted salad drenched in balsamic glaze any more than the deep-dish Chicago-style pizza aligns with my gluten-free diet. Lacey had ordered a special meal for me, but she apparently doesn't have the pull she once did.

Macarons, though, they're gluten-free. I reach for a yellow one, the lemon zest wafting toward me, when the entire platter disappears. Yanked to the far side of the table by Grace, a move that receives a conspiratorial nod from Fiona. If they think starvation will help me invent a way to stop Hartley, they've never heard of Uber Eats.

Another server, this one in a When I Think About Books, I Touch My Shelf shirt, rounds the table offering final splashes of red or white wine. I've had neither, per Lacey's instruction (read:

command). But I haven't eaten anything since the two hard-boiled eggs I brought on the plane, and I need calories if I'm going to make it through the rest of the night. I order a dirty martini with extra olives and shoot Grace a victorious smile.

No one has talked to me since we sat down an hour and a half ago. I may not be a social butterfly, but I'm also not a mute. I can commiserate over bad reviews and chide my publicist (sorry, Lacey) with the best of them. Tonight, it's like they all signed a pact to ensure I'm extra chilly.

Honestly, what do they expect me to do? Bribe the *New York Times*? Isn't that Fiona's area of expertise?

With a casual swivel of my neck, I check out what a server in a Reading a Good Book Is Like a Kidnapping of the Mind T-shirt is dropping off at the author table next to us. Sad fruit cups, no macarons. If this were high school (and by the way, publishing is totally high school), we're the cool kids and they're, well, not. We get the best panel time slots, our books are featured on the event posters, and our rooms aren't simply rooms but suites facing the lake.

I was one of the uncool just six years ago when I attended my first Romance US convention as an invited author. Not only did I not get macarons, I didn't even get the gooey fruit cup. I wasn't included in the VIP dinner—I didn't even know there was a VIP dinner.

Back then, I was over the moon that they'd paid for my hotel room. (I had to shell out for the flight.) But I was here. Not just at *a* convention but *the* convention. Every single one of my books would be sold by an actual bookseller without me having to ask (read: beg). No checking two suitcases of my own books and having to make change myself. Fans had reached out ahead of time to tell me how excited they were to meet me. I'd thought I'd arrived.

I would soon learn that I'd barely made it through the door. And that it was the first door of many. Some authors pay their own way, some get their hotel rooms comped, some receive an "honorarium" that involves no honor since one author may get a hundred bucks and another author three and another five. One author may be on a single panel, another on multiple panels, and others on multiple panels at the best times in the best venues. Author events are like chubby nesting dolls with hidden layers of ever-more exclusive perks and parties.

Well-known authors with larger fan bases get and can demand more. Inherently, that makes perfect sense. And yet, a lesser-known author cannot become more well-known without exposure to more fans. A catch-22 that pervades every facet of publishing.

I slide forward in my chair, about to make a grab for some slimy pineapple, when Rosie lowers herself into the seat beside me. She holds a plate of macarons. My fingers stretch out, and she draws the dish back.

"This is absurd," I say. "You think withholding food will somehow motivate me when I can't fix this anymore than any of you can. I notice none of you has stepped onto the pulpit."

She ignores me. "Did you hear? The post-dinner mingle is now a panel, followed by a signing."

"But . . . it's never a panel or a signing. This is a casual meet and greet." I dig my phone out of my pocket. The din of the room must have masked a call from Lacey, but the transcript of her voicemail confirms the change. It ends with a reminder to "be nice," that she surely knows will set off alarms in my head. "Did your publicist say why? Lacey didn't."

Rosie leans in, her chandelier earrings swaying. "Lacey must believe in that shooting-the-messenger thing."

Oh, no. No, no, no. No. "Her? Why?"

"It seems Hartley West couldn't get here in time for tonight's dinner."

Late again, like at Harbor Books. (This is what happens when there aren't consequences for bad behavior.) I scoff. "And so that translates into needing a full panel?"

"A bunch of people standing around mingling isn't exactly the most exciting content. They're going to film the panel and break it down for reels or something."

"Film it?" I've been doing this long enough that instead of nerves, I get a surge of adrenaline. But that's not the case for everyone. Like the two first-time attending authors at the table beside ours who cowrite as "Tara Kara." The editor who let them get away with that name mashup is totally phoning it in. I gesture to them. "They'll be eaten alive."

"I'm not so sure. They're super popular online. They started as bookstagrammers before they signed with that snake from LA. Perfected this Adam Levine–as books Instagram account, matching book covers with photos of him, mostly bare chested. Stellar following, obviously. Not to mention their writing-tip videos do tremendously well. They're definitely comfortable in front of a camera. Still, they weren't invited to be on the panel."

See? High school.

"Then who was?" I ask.

Rosie sweeps her hand across our table like a game show model. "Told you this affects all of us. She can't be normalized, Sofie. This is the start of something that will change everything. Who are we . . ." She trains her eyes on me. Her hard confidence slides away to a look of sadness. "Who are we without all of this? And I don't mean this." She places the macarons in front of me and gestures to the room. "The conventions and the cosplay and the book trailers where some muscled general from the future disguised as a potato farmer rescues Fiona from a leviathan-filled swamp. I mean *this*." Rosie taps a closed fist against the middle of her chest. "We write because we breathe. Take one away, and we cease to exist. I would cease to exist. And I know the same is true for you."

A cold rush of goose bumps tingles my skin. If this were a movie, I would clutch both of her hands, swear allegiance, promise we will fight the good fight, we will prevail, we will band together to conquer the enemy heading our way. Exactly the effect Rosie is trying so very hard to achieve. As I said, she's better than me.

"How many revisions on that?" I ask, reaching for a lemon macaron.

Rosie shrugs. "Only one. Truly, it writes itself." She holds up her hand, and I notice how goiter-free her skin is. "I take that back."

I bite into the pastry. The tangy curd filling wakes up my taste buds and the sugar sharpens my mind. "I do understand the danger. It is me she's writing as. Maybe it will come for all of you, but right now, I'm the meme. I'm the one whose banner is in a dumpster. I'm the one whose final book in a series that makes menopausal women feel seen is being overshadowed by a hack. If there's a fight here, it's mine."

"Then pick up a goddamn sword." Rosie points to the macarons. "And try an orange one. The marmalade inside is orgasmic."

Laughter buoys the entire ballroom. Fiona is a better storyteller in person than she is in her books, and that's what's required on a panel such as this one. This audience is not made up of fans but experts, steeped in our books and us.

From this elevated stage, the hundred and fifty readers still seated at their round dinner tables wait in anticipation for us to share a secret, tell them something they can't read online or haven't already heard at the half dozen other conventions they've attended. If we rehashed our inspiration, our writing process, our favorite scenes, our most beloved characters to write, they'd know, and there'd be a mutiny.

And so we remove our author hats, grab a whip and a chair, and become lion tamers.

To be democratic, we're seated in alphabetical order, which means, I'm on the far end, Hartley beside me. She appeared right before the panel began, giving her no chance to interact with any of us. She's upped her game. A cardigan still drapes over her shoulders, though no longer crocheted and with nary a dangling pom-pom. Her skirt is now a dress, still flowered, but at least this time no underwear is showing, the colors match, the quality of the fabric is less thrift store and more Macy's, possibly even Neiman Marcus—especially the shoes. Black boots of leather so supple I want to pet them. Someone's celebrating their uptick in sales.

Tara of "Tara Kara" clinks the microphone against her teeth. The sound reverberates through the room. "Super sorry!" she cries. "Wee bit excited to be here. I mean, *come on.*" She points at the five of us on stage, and her mouth drops open. Apparently after a call from their agent, she and Kara, were asked to moderate tonight's Q&A. I'm not sure if they're good at acting dumb or if there's no acting involved.

The audience wrote questions on index cards during dinner and dropped them in a heart-shaped box. Tara Kara has been posing things to us for the past forty-five minutes. This question needs to be the final one if we're going to get to bed at a decent hour. I'm mildly nauseous, having eaten a dozen macarons for dinner, and a little post-climactic hazy (Rosie was right about that marmalade).

Tara digs into the box, making a show of feeling around, as if willing the perfect one to manifest into existence, though from my angle I can see the cards with the actual questions, chosen in advance, in her lap. Before we started, I caught the tall guy in the red volunteer shirt from earlier handing over the cards. Tara conceals the true questions with a copy of her book. Maybe not so dumb then, recognizing the opportunity for self-promotion.

"Aha, here we go!" Tara sweeps her arm in the air and flutters the planted card. "Ooh, a saucy one! Is this the best audience ever or is this the best audience *EVA*!"

The crowd erupts.

Okay, so Tara has definitely been coached. Granted, by someone who apparently also casted *The Mickey Mouse Club*, but still.

Kara leans in to read the card and then tilts her head toward the mic. "She's not kidding, y'all."

Y'all. She's from Vermont.

Tara drapes her arm around Kara, and one of the sequins on her shirt gets caught in Kara's hair. They're young enough to wear sequins—metallics too, maybe even together—and get away with it.

Tara frees her sparkly sequin and nestles the microphone between her and Kara. Together, they read the card: "What's the most cringey thing anyone's ever said to you at an event?"

It's as if a stiff wind has blown through. This is a minefield of a question and one that should never be asked—especially without warning. Especially of me right now. My fans need a reason to forgive me and to be behind a shift in my brand, not to worry that I'll use their excited utterings against them as an amusing panel anecdote.

But it's not just me who's unnerved. I swear I can hear the wheels spinning in each of our heads as we wrack our brains for a semi-truthful response that won't offend, for one that won't take this PG-13 event straight into triple X. I need time, more time to invent an answer that ticks all the safe buckets but still entertains, still delights, and I beg Tara Kara to see the fear gripping my face and start at the far end with Grace, because it's her turn, isn't it?

"Sofie, since you're about to go on tour, would you like to kick us off?" Tara or Kara says this, and I don't know which because I'm so pissed I can't see straight.

I scooch to the edge of the chair, sending the pillow I'd requested for height off the edge. I clench my thighs together to keep it in place. "'I'm your biggest fan'?" I say, miming the swing of an axe.

Tara guffaws. "We've all gotten that one! Come on, Sofie, dig a little!"

Kara grins smugly. Apparently, this is what happens when you don't make author friends.

Always qualified. "Author" friend. "Writer" friend. Because this is a business of rivals. Like overhead space on a plane, success is limited. Agents max out on the number of clients they can service. For bookstores to carry a new title on their shelves, they have to roll off an old one. Publishers do not have endless stacks of "major" deals to hand out like lollipops at the gas station. If your "author friend" gets a million dollars from a particular publisher, odds are, you won't. You'll get that "nice deal" of three grand for literally years of work. You can't be "friend friends" with someone whose gain increases your chance of loss. Still, not having author friends means they delight in watching you squirm. I have renewed respect for Tara Kara.

My brain continues to whirl through my rolodex of inappropriate comments made at events over the years. Can I sign my own boobs for a photo, how do I enjoy the kiddie rides at

Disney World, have I masturbated while writing Torrence or Callum or—my god, Vance?

I stop the grinding of my teeth and smile. "Let's just be honest, here, there's no way I'm telling you the most cringe-worthy thing, because I signed a morality clause as part of my contract!"

I mean this as a joke (even though it's true), but the audience doesn't quite follow, until, from the middle of the table, Rosie slaps her hand against her thigh and offers a hearty chuckle. I see her nudge Grace, and she joins in, followed by Fiona and Tara Kara. The fans all laugh and beside me, Hartley offers a polite smile that for some reason makes my hands sweat.

Biting my bottom lip, I glance down the table at my fellow authors, as if I'm trying hard to remember the details, though I haven't forgotten a thing despite it being several years ago. "I don't believe any of you were there. It was a good size festival, but not huge, something I was grateful for because I was still getting my feet under me." I gesture beneath the table where only my toes reach the floor, inciting a few giggles. "Anyway, after my panel, I was browsing the books for sale. The local store had stocked our titles, including most of our backlist, though they wouldn't allow any of my self-published ones."

Awws and even a "snob!" comes from the crowd.

Whoosh goes my whip. I've got them.

"No, it's okay. Inventory costs money, I understood that, even then. In fact, I was thanking the bookseller for bringing in so many great books. As I flipped through a young adult fantasy about a modern-day genie, the bookstore employee—the owner, for full clarity—asked what I wrote. I pointed to my book, the second Jocelyn at the time, and the woman picked it up. She said, and I quote, 'Yeah, I read romance sometimes. Well, not read, listen to the audio, you know, while unpacking the dishwasher or running on the treadmill or watching TV, when I don't have to pay attention because the writing's, well, you know. It's not like it's *War and Peace*."

Silence, complete and total silence. And then someone cries, "My word!"

The bookstore owner actually said "James Patterson." I love Mr. Patterson's books. I grew up reading them. And today? He celebrates authors whose voices haven't been traditionally heard and lifts up bookstores. Every year, James Patterson gifts half a million dollars to help indie bookstores stay in business. This isn't a slight against James Patterson. But if I use his name, that's all anyone will think. (See, Lacey, an old dog can learn new tricks.)

"Let's be clear, this story is not about *War and Peace*. It's not even about me." (Or Mr. Patterson.) "But it is about respect. For art. For an author's hard work. But also for the reader. Books are books are books. Subjectively—wonderfully subjectively—loved. Without subjectivity, we wouldn't have so many books in the world, and more books is the best thing." I glance at Tara Kara. *"Eva."*

Applause to the rafters, and I toss my self-satisfied smile to Tara Kara. I've just taught them a little something about experience and respecting one's elders.

And then Hartley West clears her throat. "I couldn't agree more," she says with a hint of a tremble beneath her words that takes me back to when I was surrounded by those bassoon-voiced men, trying to not be overlooked. Up until now, she's only answered the questions posed directly to her, keeping her answers to a minimum. This is the first time she's engaged in conversation. "I don't have the breadth of experience these authors do. I can count the number of book events I've been lucky to do on one hand. I can only imagine what may come and hope I can handle it with the deference and skill that I'm sure these authors have."

"You will," Rosie says. "Shall we—

"I'm not done," Hartley says curtly.

As well-trained as we are, a couple of eyebrows rise at the author table. I feel the downturn of my lips and fight against it.

"My apologies," Hartley says, more to the audience than to Rosie. "This is all so surreal. To be here in front of all of you. With these authors. I never imagined it. I also never imagined what being here would cost me." She turns to me. "I said I hoped that I would handle difficult reader situations with skill, but I never expected that it would be a difficult situation with a fellow author that would serve as my training ground."

Oh, no, she's not . . . she's not doing this. Not here.

Her hand slips into her pocket and she extracts her phone.

Holy. Shit.

She taps the screen. *"A coward's move. A brainless coward's move."*

From Hartley's other side, Rosie slants forward the tiniest bit and her hair falls forward, shielding her face from the audience but letting me see her eyes. And the urgency in them.

In addition to that reel for my fans, a formal statement of apology for my behavior was extended via my social media and website to all those whom I disparaged. The honorable thing to do, I suppose, was to seek Hartley out and offer a direct apology—even though I've yet to receive one from her for stealing my work.

Still, "brainless coward" . . . something doesn't have to be untrue to be unkind.

"Hartley," I say, "my regret over that moment, of those words, is profound."

She shoves herself back from the table, her long torso and legs and heels of those gorgeous boots pushing her into another stratosphere. "Wait, Sofie. I'm not sure all of these readers recognized what you did right there. I very much believe they're smart enough, but they haven't studied you and your words the way I have. The way you can say something and mean another. Or not mean anything at all."

"Oh, come on, let's call what you did what it is: stealing!" a heckler shouts and I want to kiss them—sorry, that's inappropriate. Tip? Can I tip them?

Hartley draws in a breath and places her hand on her chest. Her fingernails are freshly gelled in a dark brown that matches the horse on her cover. I want to bring Rosie's attention to this copycat move, but she's staring straight ahead.

"That's what some think," Hartley says. "Thief, imposter, fraud, I've been called it all. Fortunately, my self-worth does not depend on strangers. I approach every negative article and comment as a chance to glean something I can apply to make my work and myself better."

A smattering of applause, but someone cuts through with a "But it's not your work!"

Do I have any hundreds in my wallet?

Hartley shakes her head, her silver hair trailing across her face, but she rights herself, brushes her locks behind her ears and doesn't back down. "You know, I've been thinking. And I realized something that no one's brought up. Which I'd know. I told you, I've read it all." She laughs softly, letting it fade like a wisp of steam above a hot teacup. "*Stupid* is not a nice word. We all know that. But what about *untrained*? Is there anything wrong with that? Not inherently, I'd say. I'm untrained in lots and lots and lots of things. Plumbing, changing a car battery, downhill skiing. And what do we do nowadays when we need to become trained?"

"YouTube!" someone cries.

"TikTok!" from another.

Hartley nods vigorously. "Apps I use, same as all of you." Hartley pauses as if to show the audience how alike they are, and my hackles begin to rise. "And now, there's something else, isn't there? AI? Just the latest in a string of new technology for us to learn from. Something I used because I was in a very dark place. I found the light because of Sofie Wilde. I *loved* Sofie Wilde."

Emphasis on *loved*, past tense, in case you missed it.

"I'm embarrassed to say that I became a tad obsessed. The books weren't enough. Reading and rereading . . . Sofie had become a constant in my life, and I didn't want that to end. She doesn't reply to comments online, she doesn't DM with her fans."

Because I'm writing. You know, *doing my job*. I force myself to keep smiling.

"At first," Hartley says, "using the AI was almost like a way to talk with Sofie. This may sound strange, but reading her books felt like getting advice from someone I trusted and admired."

Nods in the audience. A "Same" and a "Ooh, yes," which seem to encourage Hartley.

She continues, "Life gets hard . . . My life was getting hard, and I felt like Sofie just might be able to help. I craved Sofie's advice, the things her books would teach me if only there were more of them. So I used AI to get more of Sofie's words. But then her words started to mingle with mine. You all know this, you've heard it already. Except what you've heard is that I used AI to write like Sofie Wilde. That's only one piece of the narrative. Another piece, what I, myself, didn't fully understand until all of this attention found me is this: I may have been untrained in writing, but I wasn't untrained in story. I *know* story. Which is why I loved Sofie Wilde! But Sofie didn't become

Sofie Wilde all by herself. She has an agent and a publicist and an editor. Critique partners and beta readers."

No, I don't.

"You've seen author acknowledgments, haven't you? Oscar speeches name less people. Authors like Sofie have a whole team who know story and what can make her stories better. Talk about stacking the deck against those of us who can't get a foot in the door." She dips her chin. "Fortunately, my understanding of story is strong. And AI allowed me to be more efficient than most authors because I cut out the middlemen."

Middlemen? Did she just call me and the rest of publishing "middlemen"? Good luck getting an agent or editor now, Hartley.

She continues, "I used AI to write *Love and Lawlessness*, yes, I did. And then I took what I coaxed that AI to write and I edited the living heck out of it."

Heck. Even Hartley West is attuned to crossover readers.

"I made it what it is today. *Me*. This is a collaboration no different from what all these talented women have been doing with their teams of experts for years. Except maybe being faster than the average two-year lead time." She smiles with a confidence she has not yet shown. She's being intentional now. She's clearly learned the art of embellishing stories to appeal to the crowd since Harbor Books. "But I'm not just a member of the team." My god, she orchestrated this. Every piece of the puzzle. "I am the team—it's me, and only me, in the finished work. And I, for one, think readers are smart enough to see that."

A cacophony of sound—chairs sliding and forks tines clinking glass and a few "Yeah, we are," and even an "I love you!" followed by applause as loud as the roar of a jet.

Hartley West has become a performer. And she's just gotten a standing ovation.

She takes two steps back from our table and—no, she wouldn't. She does. She bows.

While Hartley's head hangs down, the hot stare of every set of eyes on this stage—including Tara Kara's—lasers in on me. Heat blooms in my own eyes, and together we could light the stage on fire. We are not friends. But we don't have to be friends to be of one mind. With a gentle tuck of my chin, I nod at Rosie, Grace, and Fiona. We all then arrange our faces into supportive smiles, Grace even getting to her feet and aiming a few claps in Hartley's direction.

Not a resting bitch face in sight. You don't have to look like a bitch to take one down. Which is exactly what I'm going to do.

LOVE AT FIRST WRITE

THIS IS WHERE I LIVE NOW. THIS BARSTOOL. THIS BARSTOOL IN this mod-glam lounge with ebony wood and brass fixtures and vintage etched glasses. I signal for another martini and pick up my medium-rare burger without a bun. Yolk drips down my fingers, and I think adding the sunny-side egg on top might have been a mistake until the salty creaminess coats my tongue, and this is bliss. Maybe I should forget about Hartley West and become a food critic.

AI can't take over that too, can it?

My second martini arrives loaded with olives. I wipe my hands on the black napkin given without me even having to ask. No white fuzz on my black pants. I make a mental note to tip well.

I have a sudden urge to text Roxanne a picture of my drink. My house has a fully stocked wine fridge but little hard alcohol. Roxanne fancies herself an amateur mixologist and I'm her very willing focus group. I begin digging into my tote, which is hanging from a hook beneath the bar top, when I remember that I don't have my phone. Rosie insisted on taking it from me when I said I was going to the bar.

Hartley must have checked a dozen Mary Poppins suitcases full of her books. At the signing after the impromptu panel, she certainly wasn't lacking for copies. Good thing (for her), considering her line of eager fans outnumbered everyone else's. You could say it's because we've all been here before, same as the majority of these readers who paid extra to attend the meet and greet. I recognized at least half. Books signed by us must wallpaper their homes. You *could* say that. Or you could say something else. Hartley West is on the precipice. A novelty that cannot turn into a sensation.

The last text I received before Rosie took my phone was from Blaire. No news is no news! Hang tight!

Tell that to my banner crammed inside an orange crate somewhere.

The flump of a bag onto the bar to my right sloshes olive juice over the rim of my martini.

"That looks disgusting," Fiona says, pointing at my crumbled soggy mess of a burger. "Can I have a bite?"

The growling of my stomach begs to be echoed by the same from my lips, but I push the plate toward her. My hips will thank me. Past the age of forty, you gain weight simply by smell.

"I didn't eat dinner. Keto," Fiona adds by way of explanation, grabbing a fork and knife I didn't think to use. She carefully crafts a morsel perfectly layered with burger, egg, tomato, and lettuce. "S'just okay." She creates another little amuse-bouche for herself, and I want to yank back my plate, but Lacey's words about being a lone wolf repeat in my head.

Lacey is as sociable as my parents. She doesn't understand that I can be as animated as I am in front of a crowd and still call myself an introvert. But introverts are like reusable batteries. We need time to recharge. Another reason why I didn't socialize much at events early on. I'm only realizing now that the other authors might have taken my early lack of engagement as a snub.

"Did you hear?" Fiona says, pushing the long strands of her red wig over her shoulder. "The featured panel, the one they didn't ask me to be on, Beautiful on the Inside? Riley Moore's moderating it. I loved her in that gender-swapped Robin Hood. She does period *so well*. You or Rosie, slip in my name, would you?"

I give a noncommittal nod and look past Fiona to where Hartley leans against the wall beside the entrance to the lounge. I almost don't recognize her. She seems taller despite wearing the same boots. She's changed into jeans and a bomber jacket, her hair piled atop her head in one of those stylishly haphazard top knots. She's talking to a man nearly equal her height.

With dreamy dark waves.

Wearing a puffer vest.

He turns slightly as he digs into his pocket.

What the—

The "volunteer" handing Tara Kara the index cards.

The "early attendee" who nearly tripped over my banner.

One and the same: Brad.

A perfectly seeded plot twist I didn't see coming. I scrunch down behind Fiona and watch as Brad places something in Hartley's open palm. Drugs? Is it drugs? *Let it be drugs*. Drugs have to trump the "brainless coward" remark. Though it'd be better if the transaction were going the other way.

I reach for my phone. Which is in Rosie's purse.

Fiona slides the plate across the bar. She's left me a perfectly layered bite. I gulp it down followed by half my martini.

"Our editors are pissed," she says. "Mine's been blowing up my phone all night."

"Give it to me," I snap.

"What?"

"Your phone, give it to—"

Hartley is the definition of smug as she pats Brad's puffer vest and saunters off.

Dammit.

"They're all talking," Fiona says.

"What?" Did Fiona see Hartley talking to someone other than Brad?

"Sofie, are you even listening?" Fiona says. "How many of those have you had?" She gestures for the bartender, slices her finger in front of her throat, and jerks her head in my direction. "They've been talking amongst themselves."

"Who?"

"Our *ed-i-tors*," she enunciates. "Mine, yours, Rosie's, Grace's. They were concerned before, but with Hartley and her AI buddy now directly threatening their livelihoods, to say nothing of ours, they're livid. The names my editor is calling my house's legal department and CEO and board and everyone else can't be said in public. She's been trying to insert contract clauses against our work being allowed to be used to train AI for years. Ahead of the curve."

Brad inhales a deep breath, rakes his hand through his hair. He turns. Looks directly at me. And runs.

I snatch my tote and the last olive-laden toothpick from my drink and take off after him.

"Can I finish that then?" Fiona yells after me.

Frostbite, this is how I'm going to die. Lacey would call it fitting, perhaps Roxanne too, if my untimely death were to mirror my somewhat frosty persona. We're outside the hotel. In February. Neither of us has a coat. Despite my short legs working overtime to catch up to Brad, I'm freezing. He's nearly at the Bean. At the edge of Millennium Park, a cart sells hats and scarfs and sweatshirts. I grab my wallet out of my tote as I pass. I shove several twenties into the cashier's hand, jarring her from her phone, and seize an orange Bears sweatshirt, a red beanie, and a Burberry knockoff blanket scarf from the shelves. I'm pulling the sweatshirt over my head as I land two feet in front of the gigantic silver sculpture in the plaza. There's no sign of Brad.

I pull the beanie low over my ears and drape the scarf around my shoulders. Adrenaline and the extra layers warm me as I search, eating my olives and pacing around the iconic kidney-shaped installation that still fills me with awe.

I look up. I see him reflected in the Bean. He crosses in front of one of the lights projecting up from the ground. It kills his night vision, and I beeline for him.

My fistful of his puffer vest surprises him and he lurches back, his heavy winter boot crushing my ballet flat. I squeal, and a couple strolling the edge of the park glance our way. Not needing any more viral in my life, I tamp down the anguish in my voice and shout, "Foot cramp."

Brad holds up a hand to them and rests his other around my waist. "Such a man, I am. Twenty-two years, you'd think I'd be better at picking up the warning signs. I've got her. Come on, darling, back to the hotel."

My blood boils, but I allow myself to lean into him. I ease the weight off my screaming toes, and the couple waves and continues on their way. Satisfied, apparently, that self-deprecation is not a would-be assailant's trait.

"So," I say, removing Brad's hand from my waist and turning to face him. "Would you like to tell me what the hell you're doing here?"

"Admiring the Bean. It's actually called Cloud Gate."

"Really? How fascinating," I say, feigning interest, as if this man isn't trying to destroy my life.

"The Bean is just a nickname. The artist hated it at first, but he came around."

"Well, aren't you cultured," I say with sarcasm, immediately followed by a snipe of, "A necessity in your line of work, is it?"

"I'm a farmhand, so not really."

"A farmhand? You work on a farm? Like, slaughtering lambs and chickens?"

"Now that's dark. What about squash? Potatoes? Haricot verts?"

"You grow squash and potatoes and haricot verts?"

"No, but I'm just saying, when you mention a farm, most people don't immediately think murder."

I narrow my eyes. "And when you attend a romance novel convention, most people don't think drug deals."

"Ooh, is this a game I don't know about?" He lets go, and I wince as my full weight hits my foot. "So, when you attend a rodeo, most people don't think—"

"Enough," I bark. "I'm serious. I saw you. After the day I've had—because of you—I deserve the truth."

"Everyone deserves the truth. Some people are just better off without it."

"You're infuriating."

"Thank you?"

I breathe. Roxanne always tells me to breathe. But it's usually followed by her handing me a paloma. "How did you even get here?"

"Route 3A to 93, on at Braintree, straight shot to the airport tunnel, direct from Logan, I got in about noon. You?"

I'm so flustered that I mumble a "Same."

He slaps his chest. "Were we on the same flight? We could have carpooled."

I really, really wish Roxanne and her palomas were here. "This is absurd."

Brad leans against the polished silver of the Bean, not a single seam visible, and I realize I have no idea how they constructed it. Brad probably knows.

"You know what's absurd?" he says. "And a missed opportunity? When they commissioned this, they narrowed it down to two options. The other was a slide. Ninety feet in the air. Some artist from New York proposed it, but the committee thought it was ostentatious. To think, a slide, pretentious, but a giant silver kidney's totally natural."

I find myself saying, "A slide sounds like a liability nightmare."

"True. But isn't a little danger what makes things fun?"

"A philosophy expected of a drug dealer."

Brad's eyebrows scrunch together. "Oh, sorry, not that kind of farmer." He whispers, "Mar-i-ju-ana. I can barely keep a succulent alive."

"I saw you. You dropped something into Hartley West's palm. You're here, same as you were at Harbor Books."

He laughs. "So what, you think I'm her drug caddie?"

"Aren't you?" Disappointment makes my foot hurt even worse. "And if you're not, then what did you give her and why are you here and goddammit I need some ice for my foot."

Brad looks at me. Even though he's wearing his puffer vest, it's only over that volunteer long-sleeved red tee, and his cheeks are flushed from the cold. "Come here."

"What?"

He takes a step toward me. "Do your books have any declarative statements or are they all questions?"

"Shouldn't you know, as my biggest fan?"

"Sofie, just give me your foot."

"Wh—" I stop myself and kick my leg in the air. He catches my ankle and slips off my ballet flat, part of my standard event uniform because they're elegant and easy to walk in. (One hundred percent *not* because bending to put on a sock risks pulling a muscle in my groin.) He presses my foot against the Bean. It's freezing. It feels both awful and glorious at the same time. We stay like this, Brad holding my foot, until both sets of our teeth begin to chatter. I draw my foot back. He lowers it to the ground, gently sliding my shoe back on like Prince Charming. Which he is. Tall, dark, and handsome, right out of one of Fiona's books and—

Christ, I'm so naive.

"A room key," I say. "That's what you were giving her. You two are a thing. You met after the event at Harbor Books, and she forgave you for outing her. Of course, she did. Without you she'd have never gotten so much attention and—"

Oh—oh, goddammit.

"Outing her at Harbor Books wasn't by chance."

Brad pats the top my foot and stands. "Let's get you some real ice."

Every muscle in my body tenses. "The truth. Now."

"It won't help. It won't change anything. It won't make anything better."

"And yet . . ."

He sighs deeply. "No, it wasn't by chance. None of it was. I was a plant."

FAKE RELATIONSHIP

"WE MET AT A CRAFT FAIR OUTSIDE OF STURBRIDGE A COUPLE of months ago. It was pilgrim-themed—neither of us knew."

I grip my hot chocolate spiked with brandy. We're in the lounge of a restaurant two doors down from the hotel. My foot is elevated, soothed by a bag of ice wrapped in a white napkin, lint already clinging to the hem of my black pants, confirming my need to leave a substantial tip for the bartender in my hotel.

I urge Brad to continue.

"Have you ever seen a chair built out of dried corn cobs? Here, wait, I think I have a picture." He pulls his phone from his pocket, and my nostrils flare. He sets it back down beside him. "Right, so pilgrims. Fantasy romance and apocalyptic worms devouring the earth are not their bag, it turns out."

"Hartley writes about apocalyptic worms?"

"She better not! That's my claim to fame."

What is going on here? I should leave. Now. Confront Hartley and . . . and do what, exactly? This isn't illegal, it's not even frowned upon by everyone. It's just a game, one that will quite possibly play out in her favor. I try not to clench my jaw as I press on. "You're a writer, then?"

"Or do I just play one on TV?"

"Are you for real?"

"Are you? Is any of this? *The Matrix* meets *The Truman Show*—a premise I'm spinning and—"

"You're . . . strange," I say.

"Thank you."

"You're welcome."

Brad has a round velvet pillow on his thighs and clutches another against his chest for warmth. He ordered a double espresso, which would keep me awake for a week straight at this hour, though I'm not exactly sure what hour this is.

I check my watch, but it's a black box, out of charge. "Let's speed this up. Whatever time it is, I know it's late. I have the Jam Session breakfast and my book launch, and—"

A lump swells in my throat. My final *Feathers and Stone* book launch is today, and it's about to be ruined by Hartley and Brad.

"Of course," Brad says, either not recognizing or choosing not to acknowledge the pained look on my face. "Where were we?"

"You were a plant." I raise my palm. "And no going on about what kind of plant you would be if you were an actual plant or how much to fertilize this here ficus or whatever this is." I gesture to the green-leafed plant on the coffee table between us.

"Money plant."

I'm not surprised, but whatever she paid him, I can pay more if it comes to that. "How much?"

"No, not me, that." He points to the round leaves. "That's a money plant. The shape of the leaves was thought to resemble coins and so—"

The thinning of my lips is enough to curtail his tangent.

He sips his espresso, his large hands grasping the tiny mug like he's raided the kitchen of a dollhouse. "Sorry, I'm a nervous talker."

"I make you nervous?"

"This whole thing makes me nervous."

"Which brings us back to what this whole thing is."

"Sure, sure." Brad picks up his espresso and the story. "The craft fair. We had side-by-side tables, and some of the pilgrims would occasionally pause to listen to our pitches. I even made a sale. But I'm pretty sure the woman thought she was buying a gardening book. She pointed to the worms on the cover and asked if I'd included specific pH levels of the soil."

His lips turn up in apology and his cheekbones rise even higher. I could use them for Brianna/Sylvia/Laurel's love interest. Except I've just decided that Brianna/Sylvia/Laurel is going to be the Boston ballet dancer who wants to adopt a dog because I am a great author and I am up for the challenge that comes with plotting *Pick Me*. I'll need a name for her love interest—the comedian. With it being a contemporary novel, his name needs to be unique enough for readers to see him as dreamy but familiar enough that he could be *their* dream. Not a Brad. But Bradford? Fordham? Ford? If I'd kept Brianna/Sylvia/Laurel in Palladium, her love interest's name would have to be something less recognizable. Bragger? Hammel? Hammel. Rhyme it? Laurel and Hammel?

"You're in it, aren't you?" Brad says, jarring me back from the place I'd rather be.

"I'm sorry?"

"Woolgathering, my grandmother used to call it. When your body is in this world but your mind is off in another. I used to think everyone did it. I was in college when I took my first creative writing class and realized not everyone goes through their day cataloging gaits and speech affectations and eyelash lengths to employ later. I'd spend the first half of every frat party hugging the walls, inventing backstories for everyone there. Still do."

"At frat parties?"

"Less so. But . . ." Brad gestures to the table behind us. "See that server with the shaved patch behind his left ear? I've been coming up with the reason why since we walked in the door."

I inspect the man in a white shirt and tan apron holding a flip notepad. Average build, a brown bowl of a haircut. He turns, and I see it, the bare patch of skin reflecting the light.

"Go for it," I say, challenging him. "And it better not be a biopsy. Or to give a lock to his sweetheart before he goes off to war."

"Please, amateur hour." Brad sets his espresso down. "The spot makes you think brain."

"Naturally."

"Communication."

"Possibly."

"Or a portal."

"Go on." I lean forward, and the ice falls from my foot. Brad reaches for the dripping bag. He wraps it in his own napkin and gently sets it back over my toes. I once again notice the compass rose tattoo on his wrist.

"I'm partial to aliens, always, but he just doesn't look the type. To be one or to have been abducted by one. Something about the way he moves, with confidence but clocking everything around him—and everyone."

"Time travel," we say at the same time.

"He's here to find someone," Brad says.

"Kill someone," I say.

"Or stop the killing of someone."

"To save the world."

"And his lover."

"Child!" Again, that's both of us, loudly.

My heart pumps pure adrenaline. I've never written with anyone else. After that first disastrous workshop and a handful more like it, I stopped using critique partners. I don't even bounce around ideas with Blaire. I could never understand writing the way Tara Kara do. But now, my brain feels alive, craving more, to keep going.

"Okay, so you *are* a writer." I hope Brad doesn't pick up on the energy in my voice, though what we've just done together and the smirk on his face says he already has. "Then you must understand the implications of what Hartley is doing. At the very least, how it makes me feel—how it would make *you* feel. Yet, you're still here?"

Brad tosses the pillows to the side and bends over his thighs. He presses his forearms into them, outlining the muscles beneath his long-sleeved tee. He breathes in deeply, his chest broadening with his exhale, as if he's struggling with what to say. Extending the moment. Increasing the tension. Attempting to make me less inclined to want to smother him with one of those pillows. It's textbook—and I should know, I write romance for a living. But there's nothing cute about this meeting.

"I'm here because she's going to help me," he says finally. "I've been at this for fifteen years, Sofie. Is it all right if I call you Sofie?"

I nod, surprised at his admission.

"Well, to understand fully, you need to know that recently I've been mired in my very own existential crisis, one might say."

"One who is melodramatic might."

He rubs the back of his neck, his eyes lowering to the floor, and I almost feel bad—then remember he was a *plant* for Hartley.

"Melodrama," he says. "From the Greek, the combination of music and drama, neither of which sound as bad alone. But together . . . tanks a story. One of the many things we writers agonize over. To set a story in New York or in Chicago or on Mars? Present day, near past, future? Is the character an introvert or an extrovert? Rich or poor? A sweetheart or a curmudgeon?"

"No." I shake my head. "We're not doing this."

He ignores me and continues. "Do they kiss on a first date? Reclaim their stolen sword? Swallow poisonous nuts? Choices and choices. Writing is not for the indecisive, is it? People don't get it. The weight of making all those decisions on top of choosing to write in the first place instead of doing a thousand other things. Time is not simply a construct for most of us. The older I get, the more I find myself thinking of all the time I've spent writing and asking why? Have I wasted all those hours? Will anything come of this? Is any of it worth it?"

"Writing is a job for which your salary is delayed," I say automatically, one of my standard answers on panels when young writers ask about combatting self-doubt. When pressed, I add what I say to Brad now, "And, yes, the hard truth is that sometimes you write something that never earns you a monetary return. Or less than the cost of a new set of pots."

"Sometimes?" He cocks his head. "Most of the time for us mere mortals. Which is who we all are. How arrogant am I to think I have anything to say? Anything worth not just my time to write but someone's time to read? My words won't cure cancer or stop school shootings. So why?" He shakes his head. "See? Existential crisis." He sits back and hugs the pillow. "And along comes Hartley West. I haven't read your books, I admit that. But I do know your story. Hartley told it to the pilgrims. It was the only thing that got them to pause braiding wheat long enough to give her book a once-over. I know you got yourself here by putting in the time. Butt in seat, like Hartley said at Harbor Books."

"No, not like Hartley. Because it was *my* butt. One that is human not robotic."

"Same here." He pinches the skin on the back of his hand. "Though I guess that's not entirely convincing."

"Cylons," I say.

"Nice pull. And that right there convinces me to read your books."

"You should. Read them. They're a phenomenon for a reason. In no small part because they were written by *an actual person*."

"And we're back to Hartley West." He tucks his chin and glances at me from beneath stubby lashes, perfectly embodying the subplot of sexual tension that every story needs. Is it possible he doesn't realize how poorly this will work on someone who does this for a living? (A very good living, at that.)

I laugh to let him know I'm fully aware that he's playing me—me, a heterosexual middle-aged woman with pancake breasts and gray pubic hairs who hasn't had a relationship in nearly five years. But still has sex—I have sex regularly. Despite being a middle-aged woman with pancake breasts and gray pubic hairs, that's easy to do. Men are men, after all.

"Hartley?" I prod him to continue. "She's helping you how?"

"She's going to give my book to her agent."

"Oh, Brad. She doesn't have an agent."

"She does now."

"Who? Wait, don't say it."

"Max Donner."

"I told you not to say it." A groan escapes my lips. Max Donner is Blaire's biggest rival. He represents Tara Kara. He tried to lure me to him a year ago, saying I was a "talent this world has never seen before" and I deserve "an agent of equal ability" who has an affection for "beauty of all forms." He offered to lower his commission and get me attached as screenwriter to whatever film deal we'd make. He made the same offer to Rosie. And Grace. Verbatim. Copy and paste is a dangerous thing. Authors talk. Even me. (Though to be honest, I might have been loopy on cold medicine at the time.) That year, I gave Blaire a bonus.

I pick up my hot chocolate. "So she's going to give your book to her agent."

"Not just give. She's going to make sure he signs me."

Sure she is. "Uh-huh."

"Listen, I'm not stupid. It's a long shot, I know, but it's sadly my best shot. Maybe my only shot. Fifteen years of manuscripts living only on my computer, plus an existential crisis, Sofie."

When he puts it like that, is it any worse than offering up a kidney or selling your grandmother's engagement ring? Yes. Yes, it is.

"Fine," I say, "so she says she'll give your career a boost and in exchange you do what, exactly?"

"Help her become the next Sofie Wilde. Though I'm pretty sure you ended up helping more than me."

I take a sip of my drink, the only heat left the burn of the brandy. "She couldn't have predicted my—"

"Self-sabotaging tirade."

"Unfortunately captured industry critique."

"Wordsmith, you are, indeed."

I can't tell if he's purposely trying to distract me from learning the full truth or this is just who he is. Either way, I push on. "But before whatever *help* I gave her, Hartley must have had a plan. And that plan included everyone finding out she used AI to become 'the next Sofie Wilde.' She arranged for you to prod that, to force her to tell the truth. She took advantage of the opportunity at Harbor Books—"

Brad's eyes dart.

"What?" I say.

"Nothing. Go on. You're doing great. Real understanding of human nature."

"No. There's something else . . ." All this ruminating allows my plotting brain to slot in the puzzle pieces. "#TheNextSofieWilde—she started it? Along with the online fervor for us to meet in person? She did both of those things, didn't she? Maybe not directly but through intermediaries? Encouraging bookstagrammers and influencers and maybe even through her own fake accounts?"

Brad shrugs but mouths, "Yes."

I'm disappointed in myself. I'm not even that calculating. (Yet.) "So she angled to get herself a platform grand enough that word would spread fast. Hence the meetup at the Celebration of Sofie Wilde. Stories about writing using AI are commonplace now. It wouldn't get enough attention without her 'confession' spilling while she sat beside me. I understand that." (*Admire it, even?*) "But what made her think that attention would be positive? It could have gone either way."

"Perhaps, but when she talked about you to those pilgrims, they listened. Talking about you makes her come alive. You've seen her, twice now. She has a way with words."

I roll my eyes so hard it strains a muscle in my eyelid.

"You were there, Sofie, you saw that audience at Harbor

Books. And earlier tonight. You heard the audience here. Hartley spun the answer to that question about cringeworthy comments better than anyone. Better than you."

"Because she planned it. You gave the questions to Tara Kara. Which means Hartley gave them to you. She wrote that question and she had AI write the response."

"Even if she did, you're missing the point. Whether they were her words or AI's, they had exactly the effect on the audience that she was going for." Brad gestures to my foot before lifting off the ice. "She took a risk, perhaps, but one that's paying off."

I swing my foot to the ground and test putting weight on it. "So she's at Romance US. They added tonight's panel and included her because she's trendy for a *hot sec*, as her precious AI would surely write. Maybe they'll put her on a couple more panels, but her reach will only extend so far. What does she think will happen when the convention ends and she's out of the spotlight?"

Brad's phone buzzes beside him. He looks at it, his face stoic, but then he signals for the server with the time-travel portal patch. "This is on me."

He signs the bill and trains his eyes on the floor as I pull on my beanie and loop my scarf around my neck. "What is it? What aren't you telling me?"

"Nothing. It's not my place."

"Which is it? Nothing or not your place? Because it can't be both."

He clutches his phone. "You're going to find out in the morning anyway. I'm surprised your agent hasn't already called."

I tap my pockets before remembering. "Rosie took my phone when I went to the bar."

"Smart. Maybe keep it that way? Get a good night's sleep? And then tomorrow—"

"Just tell me."

He reluctantly unlocks his phone, opens his text messages, and rotates the screen. Unlike me, he hasn't made his font size big enough to see from space, and I have to squint.

Hartley: I'm in.

Hartley: We're in.

Hartley: They're pulling her. The keynote is mine. Happy Thanksgiving, Coop!

My lungs squeeze like Jocelyn's did when Callum appeared at Vance's bedside, the boy he didn't yet know was his exhaling shallow foreboding breaths. The engagement ring from Torrence was still unfamiliar on her finger. She was convinced Callum was a ghost. Ashamed how much, even in that ethereal form, she wanted him still.

This can't be happening. If I lose that keynote, all my publisher is going to see is me on a downward trend. And downward trends do not bode well for taking risks. They don't even bode well for the status quo. Rosie told me to pick up a goddamn sword. But swords are heavy.

"Phone," I say, my voice cracking. Then again, louder, stronger. "Phone, now."

I dial my own number. No answer. I could stop right here. Give Brad his phone. Go back to my room. Not bother with a heavy sword that requires more hands, maybe find a small knife or really sharp tweezers? But all I can hear in my head is *Would you mind signing it?*

Yes, I would.

I'm still a meme. I can't become another one. I begrudgingly dial again. And again and again and again until, finally, on the fourth call, she answers.

"What the hell? Who is this? Do you have any idea what time it is?"

"Time to form an army," I say, somewhat dramatically, though meaning every word.

"Sofie?" Rosie says. "Where are you? Wait—are you safe? If you need me to call the police, say *banana*."

"Banana? How exactly would I work in the word *banana* if I were being held hostage?"

"I'm hungry for a banana. I hope my mom feeds my pet monkey a banana. My ankle still hurts from tripping on that banana peel. Come on, Sofie, you write for a living." Rosie pauses. "Oh, was that it? Was that you using *banana*? Stay on the line, I'm calling the police with the hotel room phone."

"No, Rosie, no. I'm fine. I'm not being held hostage."

"Sure, of course not," she screams loud enough for her voice to be heard through the phone to my would-be kidnappers.

If only someone would whisk me away until the next Twitter scandal of author or agent or editor behaving badly relegates me to quaint old news.

Or whisk Hartley away. She's been here for a blink of an eye. If she disappears, scandal-seeking brains would easily forget, I'm sure of that.

She *needs* to be whisked away. Now.

"Get the others." The bitter taste of resentment rises up my throat, but I swallow it down. "Grace and Fiona. In your room. Five minutes." I ask for her room number and she gives it without hesitation.

"What is this about, Sofie?" Rosie says.

In a stream-of-consciousness burst, I tell her everything, including the apparent loss of my keynote.

"What. The. Actual. Living. Breathing. Fudge." Despite the last part (crossover is ingrained), the venom in her tone chills even my iced toes. "I told you to fix it."

"And I told you I couldn't. I need—" oh, how I can hear Roxanne having a good laugh over this "—your help. All of you. We have to do this together."

"Do what?"

"Stop Hartley West."

THE PLOT THICKENS

"You. Come." I hike my tote higher onto my shoulder and jab a finger at Brad.

Except . . .

Happy Thanksgiving, Coop!

Her text. "Coop? Did she call you Coop?"

He gives a half bow, half curtsy. "Cooper Armstrong."

Knew it. Noah, Oliver, Hunter, Cooper, little difference.

We leave the restaurant lounge and exit into the frigid air of late-night Chicago in February. Cooper Armstrong.

"Let me guess," I say, limping slightly as I lead the way back to our hotel. "Your ancestors were on the Mayflower."

"And founded Plymouth's first suburb, living right in Duxbury Harbor, very close to where my farm is now."

"Your farm. In Duxbury Harbor. What are you? An oyster farmer?"

He tips his chin.

"You're joking," I say.

"I never joke . . ."

I roll my eyes.

"About farming *or* seafood," he finishes.

"So you and your worms know nothing about the pH of soil."

"No, but I can tell you the pH of isochrysis galbana algae must be kept at a constant eight."

"I'm starting to think you either know everything or nothing."

"One of those is entirely accurate."

We enter the convention hotel and pass through the lobby on our way to the elevators. Inside, I hit the button for the third floor where the ballrooms are located. He presses the button for the tenth floor.

"Oh, no," I say. "You're sticking with me." Because Cooper Armstrong, Mr. Wonder Bread himself, just heard me vocalize my intention to end the career of his craft-fair friend.

To his credit, "Coop" simply nods, and when the elevator opens to the third floor, he follows me out and to the grand ballroom.

Hartley knows me. Perhaps not personally, but she's read my books and "written" like me. That means she knows how my brain works. All fiction writers put themselves into their work, no matter if they're writing about medieval Europe or aliens on Mars or apocalyptic worms. Our struggles with our mothers, our partners, our fear of failure or small spaces, our love of mint chocolate chip ice cream—some of "us" seeps into our stories, both on purpose and not. Hartley has the upper hand. I need the same. I need to read *Love and Lawlessness*. I don't care that an AI spit it out. If she truly "edited" it as she says, there have to be pieces of herself in it. I'm sure there must be a copy leftover from our impromptu signing.

We round the corner, and my legs morph into cement.

"Now that's gotta hurt," he says.

"Shut. Up."

A gaggle of volunteers in red Romance US shirts stands outside the entrance where my banner once hung. They're constructing a shape out of books. Letters, specifically. The first is already completed. An *H* the size of Brad. Vertically stacked using copies of *Love and Lawlessness*.

The *W* is about to get under way as a young woman in a I Have a Sleep Disorder: It's Called "Reading" shirt drags over a ladder. She collects three books, my name on the spine of two of them. Feeling returns to my legs and I step closer, Brad—I mean, Cooper—on my heels.

"They're using mine," I whisper.

Hartley having only one title means there aren't enough of her books to build two letters the size of human man. So the books serving as bricks are hers *and* mine.

"Don't." It slips out, raspy, like it's been dragged over sandpaper.

Before it fully registers, Brad—Cooper, *Cooper*—is taking off his puffer vest, pressing it into my chest, and marching toward the cluster of volunteers.

His red Romance US shirt marks him as one of them. He uses what he has—height, deep voice, male genitals—to command authority. I slink back toward the elevators as he informs the volunteers that there has been a change of plan. I don't hear what that change is. I don't particularly care.

The next Sofie Wilde and Sofie Wilde. Together. For how long? My series has ended. The timing fits for that baton to be passed. Or, more accurately, violently ripped from my death grip.

A wave of nausea sends my hand to the wall. Short rapid breaths make me dizzy, and I bend at the waist.

This is a world of business masquerading as art. Profits drive all. And profits come and go as quickly as a wrongly worded quip online. And what I did was much more than that. Is this how it ends, then? At my own hands? With me unable to do anything except sit back and watch as that velvet rope is drawn, secured, with me on the wrong side, metaphorically the same way it was literally years ago when I first learned of its existence?

Purple it was, a deep royal color, strung across the entrance to a world I thought I had finally become a part of. Back then, only Rosie was behind it. Grace and Fiona were still fetuses. It was my very first book festival, this one in Texas, a state I would come to learn regularly sees a tsunami of amazing and dedicated readers pouring into convention centers and bookstores to meet authors like children gleefully storming a Disney World character breakfast.

My publisher had sent me, or so I thought. I found out years later that Blaire had used her own money to foot the bill and her powers of persuasion to convince the publisher to include me.

Inside I was a ball of nerves, but outwardly, I projected that same confidence that sold a book about superheroes born from constellations to shoppers who had come to the holiday fair for penguin candles. Still, I flubbed my author pitch at my first panel—my only panel. But I was determined to learn. I sat in on every other author talk and panel, prioritizing the writers from my same publisher, taking notes, memorizing their names and genres and story premises. That night, the publisher was hosting a dinner for all of its authors attending the festival.

When I arrived at the party, clutching my first traditionally published book, in a navy suit I couldn't afford, tears pricked the backs of my eyes. A sign with my publisher's name and all the divisions in it, including my own romance imprint, hung on the wall beside an entrance guarded with a purple velvet rope.

"To protect us from going in or them from getting out," I joked to the woman holding a tablet.

"In," she said brusquely.

I gave her my name, and she scanned the list, shaking her head. A mistake, it had to be a mistake, because I was so new. I opened the front cover of my book, pointing to my imprint and publishing house, the same names staring down on us from the sign behind the velvet rope. I unearthed my wallet, then my ID, from the black leather clutch I'd borrowed from my mother to prove that I was who I said I was. This book, this publisher, this life, was mine.

The rope remained in place. As if it were protecting a secret algorithm for guaranteed placement on the NYT bestseller list (which, in retrospect, it essentially was). I thought I belonged there, that I was one of them. Surely, someone on their end had messed up, and yet I was the one with clammy hands and burning cheeks.

I made a call to Blaire. She made a call, several, I'd learn after the fact. But in that moment, she took the blame, saying she had neglected to RSVP for me. The hotel had strict room-capacity limits. There was nothing anyone could do.

I was every version of myself in that moment. I was a seven-year-old girl paralyzed by the fear of embarrassing myself in front of my peers and I was a twenty-year-old college student pretending my heart hadn't been clawed from my chest and I was a twenty-five-year-old woman apologizing for not writing "real literature" and slumming it by writing "cheesy romance." Never good enough, smart enough, funny enough, likeable enough, talented enough, *enough, enough, enough.*

Enough.

The pedestal I'd put publishing on was cracked. That was the first step in realizing that this world was no different from the one I left, from any world, really. I wouldn't be given any-thing. By the time those cracks revealed themselves to be fault lines, I was well on my way to not expecting anything and simply taking.

"Sofie?" The voice is far away, at the end of a long tunnel. "Is everything okay? Are you in pain?"

He stands before me. Cooper. Brad. Names are so important. They breathe life into a character. You can't write a hundred pages and not be emotionally tied to your character's name. Changing a name that late in the game is like killing a friend. Cooper. Brad. Cooper-Brad. Cooper-Brad has one arm out-stretched as if to steady me. Tucked under his other arm are two books. I'd recognize the purple spine in my sleep.

"They're taking it down," he says. "And if it makes you feel better, it wasn't sanctioned."

"They did it on their own?"

"After a variety pack of hard seltzers in Clarice's room."

"Clarice?"

"Which begs the question: did the parents know? And what's worse? Knowing they'd chosen to let their daughter share a name with a character viciously tormented by the most odious serial killer in all of literature or not knowing?"

"They knew."

"You're guessing?"

I shake my head. "Clarice has been the lead volunteer ever since I started coming. She may truly be my biggest fan. At least she used to be."

Cooper-Brad's head hangs down. He shifts the books from the crook of his arm to his hands. One mine, the other Hartley's.

I grab *Love and Lawlessness*, drop it in my tote, and point to the first book in my series. "I appreciate it, but I have reached the stage of my career where I actually get more than ten author copies. In fact, I have that in twenty languages, large print, and Braille."

He lifts his head, blinks those stubby eyelashes. "This one's for me."

I introduce Cooper-Brad simply as someone who wants to help and stash him in the corner of Rosie's suite before marching into the center of the room to command their attention.

"It's not being announced until the evening of," I say, holding up my phone, which is heavy with missed texts from Blaire. Including a heart-stoppingly cryptic one about my upcoming fifteen-city tour. "So we have two days."

"You have two days," Grace says. She angles herself in a leather slingback chair in Rosie's suite like she's in a perfume ad. As a former second-tier model, she can't let go of posing no matter where she is or how many people stand before her. It's like she's perpetually shilling coconut-scented deodorant and absorbent tampons. Her wide-legged pants are pleather. Her bra strap's pink, peeking out of a rainbow-colored tube top at four in the morning. In Chicago. In February.

Fiona, on the other hand, is curled into the sofa in her *Outlander* pajamas. None of us has yet to reach pajama-level success. Diana Gabaldon is the standard by which we all measure ourselves—and by all I mean us, our editors, publicists, agents, and everyone else who only makes money when we do. Whether this line of work is symbiotic or parasitic depends on one's perspective.

Rosie, the gold tips of her hair askew from sleep, hovers near the coffee maker in yoga pants and a long-sleeved athletic tee. "Cut it out, Grace. Or should we have all had that attitude when you told that copy editor that she could stick a semicolon up her skinny tight rump?"

Fiona giggles. Her blonde hair, her actual hair, is clipped tight to her head, making it easier to don her various wigs. I've rarely seen her like this—not playing a character from one of her books. "Priceless," she says, still with a pearl of laughter clinging to her throat.

Rosie opens a creamer and pours a drop into her freshly brewed coffee. "Exactly, Fiona, like the time you called librarians *prudes*, and we hit social media to spin it as *prunes* for culling expert TBR lists?"

Grace stands. "Whose side are you on, Rosie?"

"Ours. All of ours." She wraps her hand around her mug and leans against the kitchenette counter. "Sofie hasn't exactly been one of us."

Pointed looks in my direction.

Rosie says, "Not in the way we would have liked." Surprise makes my brow begin to lift until she adds, "Once upon a time. Still, she's here now. She's asking for our help, something I doubt any of us would be inclined to give it if it were only for her benefit." She shrugs at me. "Sorry."

"Don't be," I lie.

Christ, eating raw pigeon would be preferable to this. I despise asking for help. I hate being in the position to *have* to ask for help. Especially from a group of women who now think I'm responsible for the apocalypse.

"What's going on here is criminal," Rosie says, "perhaps not in the legal sense but in that it is an affront to her, her name, her brand, her person. Copyright issues have been a part of the conversation surrounding AI from the beginning, and everyone at every level, from the government to our publishers have been too slow to integrate protections. But common sense says if Hartley used Sofie's work to create that book, Sofie at the very least deserves credit. Maybe even financial compensation."

"My agent is pursuing all of that," I say, my phone tight in my hand.

Blaire: Legal's on it.

Blaire: If her books infringe on or plagiarize you in any way, we'll find it. It may take time, but we won't let it drop.

Blaire: And the keynote? I've heard nothing concrete. Just your anxious inner author speaking. Same as Lacey's fears of the tour being tweaked. I'm sure it's A-OK! Positive thinking, lady!

This is even worse than I thought. Blaire knows me well enough to not push *positive thinking* on me. Or *lady*. I feel myself starting to sweat.

Rosie, however, remains calm and focused. "I would expect nothing less from Blaire. But two days won't be enough for her or legal to make any traction. We could put a spotlight on it, here, together. Especially since my agent says every publisher is waiting for the other to step up first. They don't know if they should condemn this or maybe—"

"Maybe what?" Grace says. "Support it? Be okay with it? With machines writing our books?"

"No one is saying that," Rosie says.

"Yet," I say. "Think about it. This is an evolution the publishers couldn't be accused of creating but that would benefit them the most. Hartley cut out the middlemen, but what if the publishers could eventually cut out Hartley? AI doesn't require an advance or royalties. At least not yet."

The ball on the couch that is Fiona says, "They can't. We'd rebel."

"But it wouldn't matter," I say. "They wouldn't need us."

Fiona shakes her head. "The fans. Readers. They wouldn't stand for it. Not when it's more than just Sofie." She shrugs. "Sorry. That's not what I meant."

Though it probably is.

Rosie sips her coffee. "Fiona isn't entirely wrong. Even now, many readers haven't embraced this. Some care the way we care, and they always will, no matter who the author being copied is."

I address Rosie. "I'm betting the key word there is *some*."

"Unfortunately," Rosie says, ramping up in a way that is truly impressive. "The industry won't change overnight to embrace AI, but what's happening with Sofie and Hartley has shown that a good segment of readers won't have that same slow reaction time. Right now, we see readers who appear to be fully accepting of the use of AI. What we don't yet know is if that acceptance is unconditional or only because this is a curiosity, which is understandable, to an extent."

Rosie sets down her mug and gathers her thoughts, and I swear her body shifts into a slight superhero power pose. "What comes next, how we behave, how our publishers behave, how this convention behaves, can tip the scales. We must control the direction. Everything that happens now is under scrutiny to see if this is a footnote to history or becomes actual history. If the keynote is taken from Sofie, Hartley will be on that stage, and we won't be. The optics alone will send a message that Hartley West is the future of publishing. It will sanction her actions to writers and readers. Using AI won't be seen as just acceptable but laudable. That is a door that will open and never close. Because it's been blown right off its hinges. Which is why we have to help."

Grace tries to cross her legs, but the unforgiving pleather won't allow it. Instead, she places her hands in her lap. "So we go to the convention directors. We make our case. We have all the leverage. They can't have a convention without us."

"I wouldn't be so sure," I say. "How many first-time authors would strike with us? I wouldn't have given up my shot then. With the big names gone, I'd see it as a chance to stand out."

"Of course, *you* would." Grace waves her hand, her fingers long and slender, and I wonder if they help her type faster. "Considering this is a carnival attraction, turned into a spectacle by you."

I fight the urge to argue. It's like they all think I asked for Hartley to target me. When the reality is that I was dragged, full-on kicking and screaming, into this mess.

Grace again tries to adjust her skirt, finally giving up and standing. "This won't become a thing. The convention coming on the heels of Hartley's confession and Sofie's rant has fueled the buzz. But once the convention is over, the buzz will die down, and Hartley will be forgotten within a week. Hartley will realize her stunt doesn't have legs, and she'll be gone."

A deep throat clearing from behind me, and Cooper-Brad steps forward. "I'm not so sure about that."

Grace's eyes challenge him. "The lurker finally speaks. And you are?"

"Cooper Armstrong," he says.

"Apocalyptic worms are his specialty," I say, wryly.

"Don't forget time-traveling waiters."

Is this banter? Did we actually just banter? But this is a manchild who is helping to ruin my career. I don my resting bitch face to ensure he knows his place.

Grace wiggles one of those long fingers at us. "What is this? Is this all some practical joke?"

Cooper-Brad shakes his head. "Not at all. If there's one thing I know about Hartley West, it's that she takes this one hundred percent seriously. She's in it. Full on. She's not going anywhere."

The temperature in the room drops a few degrees, the chilling effect of his words silencing us all. I let Rosie make me a coffee as Cooper-Brad summarizes his role, all the way through to the aborted "H W" tower the volunteers were erecting. He's a good storyteller. Starts with an inciting incident, identifies his quest, shows his strengths and weaknesses, builds to the moment where he had to make a choice. His sentences have clarity and precision, efficient but not without voice. Blaire might even be impressed. I'm not. I know he's up to something. He has an ulterior motive for delivering this so eloquently. Older and wiser is a cliché for a reason.

Fiona swings her feet onto the floor. "You've known Hartley West a while then?"

Cooper-Brad says, "Not too long."

"But you're friends?"

He shrugs. "More like craft-fair friends."

"I don't know what that means."

Of course, she doesn't. Fiona is a publishing unicorn. One of the rare authors who wrote her first book in three months, got an agent with it in a week, an editor in two, and the support of the entire imprint who invested in advance reader copies swaddled in cashmere scarves and appearances across the country and advertisements in Times Square that all shot her to the top of the list. Or so her story goes. She conveniently leaves out the dozens of speaking engagements that preordered thousands of copies of her book just in time to report to the list thanks to her oil tycoon of a father. She's not undeserving—no one stays at the top without talent—but she underplays how well she understood and played the game to get there. And how that's too often an unfortunate but necessary component of success in this industry.

Cooper-Brad shuffles his feet, and I remember what this

was like: being this close to people who have the thing you've always dreamed of.

"Fiona," I say, "what are you getting at? This isn't one of your books. We don't have time for flowery prose that meanders for a hundred pages just to get to the potato farmer glimpsing the fair maiden seductively washing herself in the river."

"Once—I did that one time." Fiona's voice is curt. "And you won't let me live it down. Shall we decipher all your tropes? I mean, what's more hackneyed than a love triangle?"

"Careful now," from Rosie.

"Watch it," from Grace.

Cooper-Brad pulls his hands out of his pockets. "She wants to know if she can trust me."

"Well, the answer is obvious," I say. "Of course not."

The only sound is the drip of the brewing coffee into the waiting mug.

"I don't trust anyone," I say, to which Rosie sighs but Grace nods in agreement. "What I do trust is that we all want something."

Rosie holds up a packet of sugar, and I gesture for two. She rips them open and lets the grains trickle into the hot coffee before handing it to me. "Relationships as purely transactional? That's a sad way to go through life, Sofie."

"My bank account hasn't noticed," I say with a completely straight face. I blow on the coffee before taking a tentative sip. It's dark as mud and tastes both over-brewed and under-brewed at the same time. I take another sip. "What Cooper-Brad—"

He cocks his head at me in a way Rosie would describe as *ambrosial*, and Fiona as *luscious*, and I refuse to acknowledge the unscripted tingle in my traitorous nether regions.

"Right. Cooper. What Cooper wants is a seat at the table. A publishing deal for his apocalyptic worms."

"Actually, I've moved on to killer manatees released by melting Arctic glaciers. The worms were a series back."

"Manatees in the Arctic?"

"From the woman who wrote about superheroes birthed by constellations?"

"I love Tucana," Fiona cries.

This unnerves me. That Fiona read my books—and not the more popular *Feathers and Stone* series but the early ones.

"Access," I say quickly to keep us focused. "Cooper wants access. Hartley promised it to him. But she has an agent, maybe, certainly no editor or book deal, and she's been in this business for, what, five minutes?" I set down my coffee and stick out my finger, making a show of counting. "Four. There are four of us, each in this business for a decade, if not longer. Four times ten? Fifteen years? I know authors aren't good at math, but I'm sure even Cooper can do that calculation."

Grace sighs. "Fine. He helps us, we help him. And you . . ." Grace scans everyone in the room, and a smugness that makes me wary takes over her face. "You help us." She perches herself on the arm of the sloped chair. "I'll go first. I want your cover designer."

Maddie Li has designed my last eight covers, building on the stock images used on the jackets of books one and two, before I became Sofie Wilde and could ask for an artist of my choosing. Maddie went to the Rhode Island School of Design and is immensely talented. She's also a total badass who, along with two other young women, took down some sleazy tech founder when she was only a teen. She's under exclusive contract with me and is paid well for it—part of my advance goes directly to her, ensuring no other author has a book cover with even the barest echo of mine, a fail-safe I now realize can be dismantled by AI.

I feel my crow's feet deepening. "One cover."

"Two," Grace says.

Unbelievable. "Not in the same year."

"Acceptable."

"More than," I mutter as I sip my coffee, bracing for what's next.

Fiona's feathery voice floats through the room. "At least two posts on my next book release. Plus a giveaway. A big one."

Grace clucks her tongue. "Not enough."

"We aren't negotiating," I say.

"Aren't we?" Rosie says. "You started this."

Actually, Cooper-Brad started this, but now doesn't seem the time for technicalities.

"And a blurb," Fiona says. "I also want a blurb from *the* Sofie Wilde."

I don't do blurbs. Since keeping my kidney, I've learned that readers don't care. Blurbs don't equal sales. They're simply a way for all of us authors and publishers to try to out-peacock one another. They're also not to be trusted. A lot of authors who are asked to blurb don't even read the books. You can see those a mile away. Every generic "gripping page-turner!" and "edge of my seat!" equals "my agent/editor/blackmailing frenemy forced me to blurb this."

I face Fiona. "You do realize I just went viral and not in a good way."

Fiona kicks her feet out on the couch. "Exactly why I'm asking. Your follower numbers are blowing up."

"They are?"

Fiona looks at me quizzically. "You aren't checking? That's willpower."

"Lacey won't let me."

A snicker from Grace.

Fiona leans in. "Lacey does your socials? Not an assistant? But you do have the login, don't you?"

"No," I say, cutting off whatever she's planning. "No manipulating likes or comments or whatever else you're scheming."

She widens her eyes, places her hand to her chest in a "who me?" trope, and I can't help releasing a little snort. (And the tiniest dribble of urine because . . . middle age.)

Cooper-Brad, Grace, Fiona—they've all said what they want in return for helping me deal with this mess. Just one blackmail to go. I slowly turn toward Rosie, meeting her gaze. "I'm over the proverbial barrel, so you might as well take full advantage."

"I can ask for anything?"

"Within reason. I can't double your advance or manipulate the list unlike others."

Fiona clears her throat.

Rosie says, "That's not what I want."

A foreboding builds, and whatever it is that Rosie wants, it's going to cost me. I know it. "Then what do you want?"

"I'll tell you after."

"After what?"

"After we stop Hartley."

"Speaking of, how are we doing that?"

Rosie rests her back against the counter of the kitchenette. "Are you saying you brought us all here without any notion of how to put an end to this?"

And this is what's wrong with fully pantsing. Full steam ahead only to crash into a wall.

"I sure hope not," Fiona says, hugging her knees to her chest and wrapping her arms around the pattern of Jamie Fraser on her pajama bottoms. Beside her, her phone dings and she taps the screen. "Especially since it looks like that keynote isn't going to be just a keynote."

Grace unearths her own phone. "Share it."

Fiona nods, and we all hear the ding of a notification on Grace's phone.

"Well, drown me in a bucket with Fiona's potato farmer," Grace says.

Rosie's lips thin. "What is it?"

Part of me doesn't want to know. I can't take much more.

Fiona and Grace have a silent debate. It's Fiona who unfurls herself and says, "It's from one of the convention organizers, someone who is seemingly in that camp of never accepting the use of AI. She heard a rumor . . ."

Grace's impatience takes over. "Hartley is planning to use her keynote as a call to action. The organizer snuck a peek at notes Hartley was making in the bar. She wants to level the playing field by encouraging others to use AI to write like their favorite author, to get more stories out in the world. She's going to even offer to help."

Rosie swallows. "You mean Sofie? So there can be a *next* next Sofie Wilde?"

"No, I mean their favorite," Grace says. "She's going to encourage them to write like their favorite author. It could be any one of us."

Fiona reaches for the short ends of her blonde hair. "I'm not done being Fiona Finley. I don't want a next me."

I set my coffee down too hard, and hot liquid spills over the back of my hand. I bring my thumb to my lips, trying to cool the burnt skin, but I'm too incensed to even exhale a breath. She can't do this. If she does, every single author at this convention—and outside of it—is going to blame me. They're going to hate me, will say I gave Hartley the spotlight she needed for this to take off. Their editors—the ones I need if I'm going to establish myself in a new genre—will never want to work with me. Publishers will blacklist me. Book clubs will ban me. This cannot happen. The only "next Sofie Wilde" is the one I become.

Hartley West cannot step onto that stage. No matter what.

I clasp my hands in front of my stomach. "We need to stall. We need to give Blaire time to find a solution legally. We need to give Lacey time to pull every string and call in every favor she's owed on my behalf. And if all that fails, we need the convention directors to have no choice but to proceed with the original plan. We make sure Hartley does not walk onto that stage."

"How do we do that?" Fiona asks, still tugging on her hair.

"By kidnapping Hartley West."

TROPES AND WHY WE USE THEM

"THAT'S RIDICULOUS," FIONA SAYS, CHOMPING ON FIFTEEN-dollar potato chips from the minibar that the convention will pay for without even asking because we're in Rosie's room. "One, we'd need a goat, and two, *we'd need a goat*. Next."

"A goat is easier to get than a box of hand grenades," Grace says.

"Really?" Fiona snorts. "Have you watched the news? We Americans love our firearms. Walmart, here we come."

"Grenades aren't firearms."

"A fact gleaned from your extensive military training, no doubt."

Grace paces the room, the hem of the yoga pants she borrowed from Rosie skimming her calves. "Then we're back to hiring a professional. It's Chicago, isn't this the birthplace of the mafia?"

Fiona smacks her leg, which echoes in my thighs. "Of course, why, they must advertise in the Yellow Pages. 1-800-Mobsters-R-Us! Quick, give me a phone book!" She frowns. "Wait, sorry, we're not in a Scorsese movie or the Prohibition era."

Apparently, Fiona shifts into sarcasm when she doesn't get enough sleep. She shakes her head. "Almost had it though!" She hits her leg again, and I try not to wince. At some point, her feet went from butting up against my leg to full on in my lap. Rosie has been eyeing me, testing me, but I've left Fiona's feet right where they are. (Fortunately, she has lovely feet.)

"Although," Fiona says, as if getting an idea, "we are in the right place. This hotel has a hidden speakeasy. We all went on a tour last convention, remember?"

The others nod, and I stare at my cuticles. I didn't go. Or maybe I wasn't invited.

Fiona glosses over it. "Under renovations, they said when I checked in. The work's done, but they're waiting for the city to inspect it, so it's not reopened yet. They're hoping to make it *the* place to be, same as it was during Prohibition. We all know Sofie would have lived there."

I ignore her and say again, "Food. I still think this centers on food, somehow."

"Like ET?" Grace says. "Set out some Reese's and she'll follow? Are we really this uncreative? Isn't this what we do?"

I yawn, setting off a chain reaction of mouths opening. "I haven't slept in twenty-four hours. What's your excuse?"

"Being woken at three in the morning?"

"Four," I say. "It was four."

"Ten to four, to be precise."

We've been at it for three hours, and we're no closer to a successful kidnapping plot than we were when we started. And half of us are due at the Jam Session breakfast in less than an hour.

We didn't just jump in. Debate did follow my declaration. Outrage and disbelief (Fiona). Ethics and morals (Rosie). Desperation and foolishness (Grace). Silence and admiration (at least I think that's what it was) (Cooper-Brad). And yet, no other solution came.

So here we are. Kidnapping. Stellar storytelling, really. It solves one thing but creates a host of new obstacles. But those obstacles are future Sofie's problem. Full immersion will lead to epiphanies that will lead to the way out, same as it does with writing.

"This isn't going to work, is it?" Fiona says. "We're authors, not criminals."

We couldn't even play them on TV, as Cooper-Brad would say. *Cooper-Brad.* He's been dozing on and off in the chair beside Rosie's bed as we've been hashing ill-conceived plans in the living room of the suite. *Cooper-Brad.*

And . . . this is why I'm a plantser. Only when the quick-sand reaches your waist do you think to use your bra as a lasso.

Cooper-Brad and Hartley are friends—maybe only craft-fair friends but friends nevertheless. They're also coconspirators. They had a deal. We're the ones buttering his bread now, and not just a little. If Hartley were a dab, we're an entire stick. Of the good stuff, artisan, maybe Irish, not store brand. He promised not to rat us out. But he owes us—*me*—more than that. And I just figured out how he can start living up to his end of the bargain.

I shove Fiona's bare feet off my lap. Little white flowers swirl on her red toenails. She does them herself, and I understand why her books meander. If she only spent more time revising than painting her toenails, maybe she wouldn't have to manipulate the list to land herself on it.

"Cooper," I say loudly. I forget about my bruised foot and put full weight on it, wincing. I ease off as I walk toward the open pocket door separating the two rooms.

His left eye cracks open.

"Cooper," I repeat. "You, in here, now."

Both of his eyes flutter open. He reaches for something on the floor, and I realize it's my book. He folds down the top corner of the page (sacrilege!). He's nearly halfway through, which means he hasn't dozed as much as I thought. He's been reading.

A flush starts at my neck, and I spin away from him. Rosie stares straight at me. She's been mostly silent, weighing in only to curtail our most ludicrous ideas. I honestly didn't realize how creative Fiona could be. I only read her first book. And by read, I mean skimmed. And by skimmed, I mean flipped through it on my phone while on the toilet. (Oh, please, you all do it.)

"Esteemed authors," Cooper-Brad says as he nods to the room. "Any coffee pods left?"

Rosie points to a box of fifty that housekeeping delivered an hour ago. She's made a dent in it all by herself and I'm not sure how she's not using these walls like a bouncy house right now. "Help yourself. Anything but the hazelnut."

"Gotcha. I've got plenty in my room. Hartley's allergic. Didn't even want them in her suite."

"She has a suite?" Grace says. "What? Did this woman train under Elizabeth Holmes?"

I watch as Cooper-Brad tears back the covering on two pods. He presses down the grounds in the first to make room and dumps in as many grounds from the second as he can fit. Rosie watches me watching him and I want to tell her to knock it off, but I don't know what she's going to ask for in exchange for helping me and I don't want to give her more ammunition to make the request even grander.

Once Cooper-Brad settles himself in the corner of the sofa, likely still warm from my tush, I begin. "My editor's always telling me to simplify. Even with an epic tale over ten books, threads don't have to be complicated to have complexity.

The answer has been right here." I tilt my head. "Cooper and Hartley are friends of a sort. Business partners, and in her mind, still are. She doesn't know he's here with us. She'd have no reason to suspect he's not her puppet still."

Cooper-Brad raises a finger. "I prefer yes-man."

I stifle my laugh. Cooper-Brad is still the enemy (and I'm not wearing a Depends).

Fiona sits up straighter, her green eyes darting between us. "I like where this is going."

"All we need to do is have Cooper ask Hartley to meet him. Say he has some new information about me. A way to upstage me. There's no way she doesn't come running, that silver hair of hers flowing behind her, same as her tacky flowered dress."

Fiona nods. "She shows up to his room. He lets her in—and we've got her."

Grace says, "Lacks originality, but it'll work. So what, we need rope, a hood, and duct tape?"

"A hood is stifling," Fiona says. "I wore one for two days to understand how my potato farmer would feel when Princess Ciara crammed him into her travel trunk on the way to the Isle of Forbidden Teeth." Fiona taps her lip. "Muzzle? Less constricting. Maybe there's a pet store close by." She pulls out her phone.

Cooper-Brad places his coffee on the table. "A lesson in craft right here. As much as I appreciate learning from masters, you'll have to find another way. I'm not committing a felony."

Fiona laughs. "Of course not. We're not asking you to kill her. Are we?"

Grace's brow crinkles before easing into a patronizing look. "Fiona, there are other felonies besides murder."

"I know that." She bites her bottom lip in a way that proves she didn't know that at all. "Like what, for example?"

"Like this. Kidnapping," Cooper-Brad says. "I can't be a part of it."

"But we're not committing a crime," Fiona says. "We're just stopping Hartley from doing the keynote. We'll let her go after."

Grace opens her mouth but no words come out. She's rethinking this. I should be too. Because when you put it like that, we are planning a crime. An actual crime.

I turn to Rosie. She gets up and walks to the window of the suite. I join her, and together we look down on the entrance plaza to the convention center. It is a sea of aquamarine. Scarves hang about the necks of dozens of women. In honor of me and the final Jocelyn. A lump forms in my throat.

And then the crowd waiting for the doors to open parts. Hartley strolls to the center of the group, and just before they surround her, she lifts my aquamarine book into the air, magnanimous, perhaps to show that she holds no ill will. She then swivels her neck and kisses my book like it's a trophy at Wimbledon. Cell phones rise, capturing her as she raises her book to be equal to mine.

If Hartley takes the stage in my place, her feet where mine should be, her voice reaching pitches mine does not resounding through the ballroom, it will be a literal and metaphorical passing of that baton. She will become me, my brand hers to consume. But my brand doesn't just belong to me—it is me. The same way it is for Rosie.

"We have to," I whisper.

Rosie's finger hooks around mine. She lets go and faces the room in one swift motion. "We're all a part of it now. Being privy to the planning of a crime of this magnitude is a felony all by itself. So either you help ensure it works and we don't get caught, or you go to the police right now and stop us."

The only sound is my growling stomach.

"All right," Grace says. "But emphasis on *not getting caught*."

Fiona bobs her head to agree. They might be doing this for the future of books, globally, but on the micro-level they're doing this because Rosie asked.

Cooper-Brad has yet to respond. If I were writing this, this is where his storyline would evolve. He may be in because he's one of us, an author, who understands how important this is and what it means for this industry we love and hate in equal measure. He may be in because of Jocelyn, the book nestled beside him that he's been reading with the speed of a true fan. He may be in because of the ocean air that is part of his DNA, like me, or because of the time-traveling waiter, or the feel of his hand against the skin of my bare foot.

He tucks his chin. "I'm in. Deal's a deal," he says.

But I'm not writing this, and this is his true why. He's in for the access to the agents and the editors. He's in for himself. And yet, he's not exactly looking at me with expectation or demand or entitlement. He pulls my book into his lap, glances at the cover, then back at me. He smiles. And I feel the same way all those menopausal women who read my book do. I feel seen.

"So," Rosie says. "Let's start storyboarding this thing."

I hurry down the hall post a breakfast of scrambled eggs and my continuous plastered-on smile in response to:

"Don't you love Hartley's aquamarine cardigan?"

"She crocheted it herself. On the plane here. What a talent!"

"Jocelyn is such an inspiration for Addie. You must be so flattered."

It wasn't all a Hartley West lovefest, but it was enough of one that I could use a heating pad to ease the tension between my shoulder blades. And yet, a side benefit of all the enthusiasm for Hartley is it reinforced our need to do this. Fortunately, Rosie was there to witness it. Unfortunately, our countermove of making ourselves fully available to our fans meant the breakfast ran late. I've had no time to shower or change, something I lament as sweat breaks out from my every pore (making me deeply regret those raw onions in my eggs).

A standing sign with my face and name on it perched outside the function room at the end of the hall comes into view, and I slow my breathing. Just as I reach the side door, my phone dings with a text. It's from Roxanne. A video— even I hope not from this morning—of a cocktail. It's blue, made from something called a butterfly pea flower. When she adds lemon juice, the liquid turns purple. She's upping her game. Every release, she invents a cocktail that somehow matches the cover of the newest book. The whole Hartley West coup meant we didn't get to enjoy our usual release day ritual. She says she's planning to perfect this one for when I get back from my tour. She hints (fine, says outright) that it would taste better with a view of the ocean. Then she wishes me luck, knowing this is a first for me.

I slip through the side door and heat builds in my eyes. I blink and blink, but it's no use. My eyes blur with tears. The function room is *Feathers and Stone* come to life. Posters of every book cover on the walls. Fairy lights strewn across the ceiling like glittering stars. A swirling black hole made of papier-mâché in the middle of the room. More than ten years of my life, a life that I'm preparing to say goodbye to, is on display. I'm awed and humbled at the same time.

This is the official launch party for the release of *Light As*, the final book in the series, my last-ever *Feathers and Stone* book. It's a ticketed event—a convention fee add-on. For the first time, readers have paid to be at one of my launches. The ticket comes with this private talk with me, a copy of the book, exquisitely bound, series-long bonus content in the form of deleted scenes, and, not just one like at other signings, but all four of the new exclusive tour-only bookmarks.

Four different styles, each one a silhouette of a main character, including the pint-sized one of Vance. I oversaw the design myself. Maybe out of a habit formed during the days when I bled my printer dry of yellow toner, when I was not yet tortured but possibly drunk (definitely—apparently our livers do not believe in that ten-thousand-hours thing, and hangovers really do worsen with age). But being involved in the creation of my swag goes beyond habit.

Swag is an extension of the book, an extension of me. It needs to be true to us both. I don't want my face on an earring dangling from some woman's lobe (or any other part of their anatomy). *Total miss there, Lacey.* Unlike the scarves. I flatten my hand against my chest, instinctually feeling for my own.

I tuck my tote beside one of the two blue velvet armchairs at the front of the room. It looks like I'll be signing books here, one-on-one.

Though my last few launches at Harbor Books have certainly had more of a celebratory feel than when I first started out, I've always acknowledged my "book birthdays," even when it was just me and a glass of cheap prosecco that I smuggled onto the beach. As much as it seems like you can't throw a rock and not hit someone trying to be a writer, the truth is, most of the billion people on this planet won't publish a book. So I celebrated, because who needs the validation of readers?

(Well, we all do, but you get my point.)

Those days when it was just me, I didn't dream of this—I strategized for it. I brainstormed high-concept story ideas. I took a highlighter to the bestsellers. I wrote hundreds and hundreds of pages because I believed in that ten-thousand-hours thing.

And now I am not just good, I'm great. Without being drunk (most of the time) or tortured (until now).

As my final launch party for a book in the *Feathers and Stone* series begins, my chest swells with pride and my heart with a nostalgia I didn't expect. I plant my feet on a box behind the single podium with the microphone perfectly tilted for my height.

Fans greet me with colorful feathers twined through their hair, infinity bracelets like Jocelyn wears circling their wrists, and plush Goldies clutched to their breast. My true fans. The ones who've been with Jocelyn since the beginning, when she was a scared soul who only wanted to find a sense of calm amid the continuous skipping through time and space. She found a best friend in the adventurous, daredevil Triana, for whom she would give her life, though the opposite came to pass. These readers rooted for Jocelyn, then Jocelyn and Torrence, then Jocelyn and Callum, and back and forth, again and again, thanks to my manipulation. They always rooted for little Vance. (Ah, poor readers, such devastation awaits them.) Hartley West will never have what I've spent the past ten years building. And she will not stop me from what I will create in the next ten. As I clutch the sides of the podium and read the first chapter, half from memory, riveted eyes meet mine. I am home.

My signing lane winds around the perimeter of the room. As readers approach me, versions of *"There's no 'AI' in author"* and *"She will never be you"* and *"I'm so sorry, Sofie"* buoy me. On the heels of this oversold room for my book's release, they make me feel like I can do anything, be anything, overcome everything.

They also help settle the twitching in my right eye over what we're about to do. These fans prove that we do have a window of time before readers are swayed, before writing with a machine is normalized. Before my fans will have so many "Sofie Wilde" books not actually written by me that they may not care about the ones I do write. In this genre or a new one. I have been confident that my fans would follow my writing wherever I take it. But I never imagined that would extend to where *other writers* would take it.

The carnival sideshow that is Hartley West is having her sword-swallowing moment, but she will not become a headliner. She will not carry the show. So long as she never gets on stage for that keynote.

My speech must be its own call to action, one that shuts down Hartley and all that she represents. One that ensures any directive she'd give for writers to follow in her footsteps falls flat. One that puts the emphasis not on Hartley's imitation of me but my own reinvention to come. It may be the hardest thing I've ever had to write.

In the back corner of the room, Cooper-Brad continues to read my book. He's nearing the end. Grace and Fiona, who went shopping for kidnapping supplies since they don't have convention commitments until this afternoon, took his phone away and dropped him off here for me to keep an eye on. We don't trust each other much less someone we just met. Someone who flexed that square jaw and outed Hartley in Harbor Books because she bribed him. That's a felony, isn't it? At the very least it counteracts our bribing of him. I don't actually think he'd go to the police, but we can't risk it.

My long launch party signing line is impressive, even for me. I snap a photo of the bodies clutching my aquamarine book, wearing Team Torrence and Team Callum and Little Vance tees, boasting scarves in the colors of my books around their necks, and send it to Lacey. If any bookstores are having niggling feelings about hosting me, this is proof of my popularity (and their impending profits). This morning has reassured me that there is a way back from my viral mess.

Before I reach for my Sharpie, I grab my hand sanitizer disguised as lotion off the table beside me. I squeeze the bottle, and a white glob that smells like almonds oozes out. I rub it in between my hands. It's actual hand lotion. And this is how the mighty fall. One botched event rider at a time.

My phone buzzes with a text just as I'm about to signal for Clarice to send forth the next person in line.

Evil Spawn: Buggered up this one, haven't you, Wilde?

I should ignore it. And yet . . .

Me: Cut it, Donner, you're not British.

I've never been good with "should."

Evil Spawn: And you're not the keynote speaker.

I suck in a breath. If he knows, that means they really did ask Hartley. And that he really is her agent. But this is Max. He could be phishing. All I have is Cooper-Brad's word that he's Hartley's agent.

Me: Where'd you hear that?

Evil Spawn: I'm like a doctor. Can't reveal my sources.

Me: That's journalists, you knobhead.

Evil Spawn: Are you mocking me?

Me: Always and forever, love.

Evil Spawn: And here I was, going to get your keynote back.

Me: There's no back.

Evil Spawn: Wilde, I *know*. Same way I know I can get it back for you.

He's bluffing. But maybe he knows something that can help Blaire.

Me: Blaire's working on it. Has it nearly fixed.

Evil Spawn: No, she doesn't. Trust me, Wilde Woman, you need someone who can play dirty. That's not Blaire. Never has been. If it was, you'd have higher bonuses on the back end.

Me: I don't have bonuses on the back end.

Evil Spawn: Again, I know. Wilde, you've done decent up until now. But you've got Hollywood salivating. If I'm dirty, they're downright unsanitary. You need me. Me and my intel. Like the real reason Riley Moore is coming all the way to the frozen Chicago tundra to moderate a romance panel.

I didn't even know Riley was moderating until I arrived. Which means Blaire didn't know. Christ, it better not be for Hartley.

Evil Spawn: Hollywood loves a scandal. Your tirade piqued her interest. And her husband's. Best-kept secret in Hollywood: you want a producer willing to shell out big bucks? Get their partner obsessed with being the star. I get it, you and Blaire, twelve years… Do you know what twelve years is in dog years?

Me: If you're trying to get me to sign with you, calling me a dog isn't the way to do it.

Evil Spawn: Then what is?

I set down my phone. My hands are slick with sweat. I'm not doing this. I can't do this. Even the suggestion of it is a betrayal. Blaire believed in me when no one else did. She's my biggest cheerleader. She puts up with my shit. No questions asked. If Max Donner is going to even attempt to go up against Blaire, he needs to prove he can do what she can't.

Me: Stop Hartley West.

Evil Spawn: Me? How could I do that?

Me: You represent her.

Evil Spawn: Do I? 🙄

Me: Clock's ticking, Donner. She takes that stage, it blows up.

Me: Get me my keynote back. And we'll talk.

Evil Spawn: 👍

A wave of nausea roils my stomach. I push through and gesture to Clarice to continue.

A young woman with freckled cheeks wearing a T-shirt with my face on it rushes forward as if shot from a canon. "Natalie," she says, though the blue sticky she shakily hands me reads "Natuhlee." You need a license to reel in a fish but any goofball with a phonetic dictionary can name a child.

"ThankssomuchIthinkyou'reamazing," floods out of Natuhlee's mouth.

"Aw." That pleased-as-pie feeling that never gets old isn't enough to counteract the churning in my gut. "You're amazing too. I'm nothing without my readers."

Natuhlee flashes crimson from neck to brow to ears. "Ohmygodyou'reeverything."

I gesture for her to sit in the chair beside me, but she's too nervous. She rocks back and forth on her heels before pushing a small box of designer chocolates into my hand. All white, my favorite, as anyone who has ever read or listened to an interview with me would know. A staple in the lightning round, more trite than Fiona's plotting. Except remember that thing about lying? I despise white chocolate as anyone with taste buds would. Fans gifting me white chocolate ensures I will never be tempted to eat it. As a child of the eighties, accepting food from strangers will forever be synonymous with razor blades in apples.

I slip the chocolates into my pocket beside my phone. The box is damp with sweat, reinforcing my life choices.

Natuhlee clutches her phone and continues cramming syllables together, asking for a photo. We don't allow them during normal signings. They hold up the line, that's the convention's justification. But the real reason is this right here: it's a perk. Part of what you get when you pay extra.

Natuhlee glues her cheek to mine. The smoked salmon of her

Jam Session breakfast infuses her breath as she says, "Iforgive-youforVance."

All the air leaves my lungs. "What did you say?" She begins, and I interrupt. "Take a breath first."

Then it comes, still hurried, but unmistakable. "I forgive you for Vance."

My face is firm, despite the life draining from it. "I don't know what you mean."

"Oh, 'cause you wrote it so long ago? Heard you say that at that festival in St. Louis where you sang 'Paperback Writer' during karaoke."

Oh, Lacey, the things you make me do.

"You're lovely, and thanks so much, but . . ." I gesture to the line, where those clustered at the front are leaning in to listen.

"So you remember?" Natuhlee says.

My smile is so forced that it hurts my jaw. "Yes, well, thanks, Natuhlee. Enjoy!"

"I'll try." A tear slides down her ruddy cheek. "I will. I mean, I will, course I will, but it'll be hard when he dies."

What. The. Fu—udge. Fudge, fudge, fudge.

"Safe travels, Natuhlee!"

"Who?" says the woman next in line in a Team Callum tee. "Who dies?"

"Dies."

"Dies."

"Dies."

Like a game of telephone in which nothing is actually distorted, "dies" ripples through the room.

I stand.

I grab Natuhlee's arm.

I yank her toward the exit behind me.

"Let's get you a T-shir—"

"Vance!" Natuhlee cries. She hoists the book above her head. "Vance dies!"

At the back of the room, Hartley crosses her arms in front of her chest. And smirks.

KILL YOUR DARLINGS

MURDER. I CONTEMPLATE IT FOR A MOMENT. A VERY, VERY LONG moment. If you're going to commit a felony, go big or go home, right?

Proving she's the one who orchestrated this, Hartley nods triumphantly at Cooper-Brad and slips out of the room.

A chorus of "Sofie's" and "Not Vance" and "She's lying" mix with the sound of pages turning, the entire room desperate to learn the truth.

I spring from my chair, barreling through the confused and sobbing readers, ignoring Clarice's high-pitched, "But Ms. Wilde," my body in motion with a singular mission of destroying Hartley West.

An acidic taste burns at the back of my throat. I power through the pain in my foot, moving, moving, moving like a shark. My feet hit the gold carpet, and I see her halfway down the corridor. I'm on fire like I've swallowed molten lava, and she must sense the heat radiating off me. She turns, sees me, and bolts. Pure rage fuels my short legs and my gait catches up with hers.

My phone beeps and flashes like a radio control tower, and I can picture Lacey and Blaire fuming as their Google alerts ping them with what's just happened.

The hallway is empty, with attendees and authors at their events. I'm grateful for no witnesses. I lunge forward. Hartley whirls around. The ends of her long silver hair tickle my arm. The smooth fabric of her flowered dress slips through my fingers, but the shock stops her just long enough for me to seize her wrist.

The door to our right marked "storage" opens, and out comes a hotel employee pushing a cleaning cart. I tighten my grip on Hartley, and we're over the threshold before the door shuts behind us.

It's pitch-black. My heavy breathing betrays me as it finds a rhythm with hers. I finally release her wrist, setting off the motion sensors and engaging the automatic lights.

She's smirking, still. For the first time in my life, I wish I knew how to throw a punch. It's true that anyone can develop a penchant for violence. Just takes the right buttons to be pressed. Hartley has not just pressed, she's pummeled mine. Again and again, but this is the worst. She couldn't hurt me anymore if she tried. She was, though, trying—wasn't she?

Here's the thing: I don't virtually gush over other authors' releases or artfully taken bookstagram posts. I do not squeal and tackle-hug when we meet at events. I am not part of the author "in crowd." And still I know there's a code. A line one doesn't cross. Hartley West set that line on fire.

"Why?" I say.

Shoulders sheathed in silk white peonies rise. Her blue eyes have those hints of silver. Even with that hook at the end of her nose, she's pretty, prettier than I realized. There's no rule that a devil can't be attractive.

"That's it?" I mimic and exaggerate her shrug. "Ten years. More than that. Fifteen—twenty really, if you count all the time spent learning how to do this. It's not blood, sweat, and tears, it's headaches and carpal tunnel and back spasms and saying no to two-for-one margarita girls' nights, and your mom's sixty-fifth birthday party, and goddamn pickleball leagues." (Roxanne. Texts me twice a week.) "This is my entire life. I don't need the trappings others do. These books are my children, my sales numbers are what keep me company, appearances on bestseller lists are my comfort food. Records have been broken. Numbers topped. All to get to this very place. This is the moment designed to make me a legend. And a fuck-ton of money. You just annihilated my life's work. *My life*. And all you can do is . . ." I ram my shoulders against my ears so hard it hurts.

Hartley gently sets her hand on my shoulder, slides it down my forearm, her cool skin a contrast to the fever of mine. She trails until she ends at my hand. She winds her fingers through mine, a surprising if sweet gesture. "Oh, honey, that's just so . . . pathetic."

She drops my hand.

And that's it. My fist lands in her face.

Okay, so more like her ear lobe. The right one. If it matters. Which, turns out, it does. As she defensively jerks her body back, her left shoulder smacks into the pole of a mop, flipping the bucket it's standing in. Dirty, foamy liquid pools under her feet. She backs away from me. And slips.

Her arms flail. Her legs do the cancan. She's going down. I'm elated and then—

Thwack!

Her head smacks into an industrial-sized can of liquid soap. The sound reverberates through my bones. I still. I wait. She doesn't move.

"Hartley?" I say.

No response.

Her light hair blends in with the long strands of yarn from the mop. I bend over and gently sweep a wet clump off her forehead.

"Hartley?" I nudge her shoulder, and the strap of her small purse slips off.

Oh, god—is she dead? She can't be dead. (Though what a way to script a solution to my problem.)

I shake away the thought and try to think. *Think, think, think!* But the only thought I have is to google how to get away with murder. (And that's how set in my ways I am, because the better bet would be to ask AI to write me a way out of this.)

The filthy liquid from the mop begins to seep into the fabric of her dress, turning it slightly see-through. Even she doesn't deserve to have her breasts outlined in the photos the police will take of her dead body. I grab a bath towel from the shelf beside me to cover her. As I do, her chest inflates.

Bodies twitch postmortem. They do not breathe. This any self-respecting author has researched. I haven't been this relieved since my fifth book hit the list (proving that the one before it wasn't a fluke).

I sit back on my heels and tuck her purse into my lap, continuing to stare at her boobs until I'm (1) sure of what I saw and (2) mildly uncomfortable. My phone dings in my pocket. I pull it out to see texts from Lacey, a missed call from Blaire, and an email from my editor. I'm surprised to see a text from Grace until I remember that Rosie made us all exchange numbers. Grace texted me from the store, asking me to call her, smart enough to at least not put anything in writing. I don't want to respond to any of them. The only person I want to contact doesn't have a phone.

So instead, I call Rosie and ask her to find him.

Two minutes later, a knock on the door. "Housekeeping," he says, like it's a good time to be joking. And then I wonder if maybe I'm wrong, that it's not him, that it truly is housekeeping, but why would housekeeping knock and announce itself to the storage closet?

I'm losing it.

I open the door.

Cooper-Brad stands before me with one of those gigantic orange crates.

"We're not," I say.

"Oh, but we are." He taps his chest. "Snatching this volunteer shirt was truly one of my more brilliant ideas."

He steps closer, and my nose crinkles. "If only you stole two."

"I didn't expect to wear it for two days straight."

"Right, you just expected to take me down in a single day and fly back home with your manatees fully represented by Max Donner."

"No."

"No?"

"No. Hartley paid for my room for the full three days. She does respect you. She assumed it would take the entire convention to truly tear you down."

"Do I want to know what else she had planned?"

"I would say no except . . ." He gestures to the crate. "It'd certainly make you feel better about this."

Cooper-Brad did actually steal two red volunteer shirts. I unwind my aquamarine scarf and tug the red shirt over my button-down. He's also brought me a hat that's going to completely destroy my two-hundred-dollar blow-out. Read or Bleed, the hat says, which I find disturbing. Still, I put on this disguise that wouldn't fool a toddler.

Hartley hasn't moved, hasn't made a sound.

"What if she's hurt?" I ask.

Cooper-Brad raises an eyebrow. "If?"

"I mean like really hurt. Like hospital-doctor hurt."

He crouches beside her and feels for a pulse.

"Strong?" I ask.

"Sure, let's go with that." He hovers his palm over her nose and mouth.

"Normal? Not ragged or shallow? Because that could indicate a collapsed lung."

"She didn't fall on a spike."

"Are you sure?"

"Reasonably. Seeing as we are in a hotel in Chicago in the twenty-first century and not Camelot or Harrenhal."

Those short eyelashes of his don't take away (much) from his dark eyes, which are looking at me as if we're back in that mod-glam lounge, this time sipping Manhattans. He's working me. He sees a middle-aged woman with pancake breasts and gray pubic hairs (well, not literally on that last part), and he's working me.

I clear my throat. "Yes, well, no spikes, then."

"Highly improbable," Cooper-Brad says.

Still, he lifts her torso and feels under her back. As he does, she releases a soft gurgle. He freezes, but she doesn't open her eyes. He tells me to check her head for blood, and I press a towel against her skull first, then shine the light from my phone.

Her silver hair makes it easier to see the absence of blood. "All clear," I say.

"Then just a nasty bruise awaits."

"Says the glacial manatee scientist?"

"Do you want to call a doctor?"

I twist the towel in my hands. We could do just that: call a doctor, leave this as an unfortunate accident, trust Max Donner to get my keynote back. Say I'll only sign with him if he gets Hartley to stand down. For good. Two birds, one very guilty stone. No need for this felony or any others. But that means leaving Blaire.

"No," I say with hesitation.

"Thought not," he says. "Time to move."

"Room key?"

"Uh, negative, Apollo Creed."

"What do you mean? We made a deal. You promised to help."

He points to the orange crate. "I am. But I didn't sign up for this. I'm not holding an injured public figure hostage in a hotel room that's in my name."

"She's not a public figure."

"This comes out, she will be."

"So what, then?"

"We could pull the plug," Cooper-Brad says. "Head back down to the bar for a Manhattan?"

I both like and do not like his apparent ability to know what I'm thinking. "It's ten thirty in the morning."

"Right, so with scrambled eggs on the side, then."

A small laugh breaks through, but the talk of Manhattans gives me an idea. "I need to make a call."

EMBRACE THE DARKNESS

"LIFT WITH YOUR KNEES," COOPER-BRAD SAYS AFTER I END MY quick call to Fiona.

"The day my knees sprout opposing thumbs is the day that expression will make sense to me."

"Writers," he mutters. "Watch me."

Cooper-Brad squats and tosses his empty arms out in front of him. He stands. And does it again. It's like he's riding an invisible pogo stick.

"Like this?" I bend my knees an inch.

"Sofie, come on." He squats. "Like." Again. "This." And again. And once more. "If twenty years of oyster farming have shown me anything, they've shown me how to lift with my—"

"Knees, got it."

He rights himself. "You're messing with me."

"You're right."

"I deserve it."

"Right about that too."

I unlock the tabs of the orange crate, and my lips thin. "This one, really?"

My own face stares back at me. Minus the crow's feet and haphazard white hairs in my eyebrows. I reach inside and fold over the end of my banner.

"I didn't exactly have time to choose the perfect vessel to transport a dead body."

"She's not dead."

"I didn't know that, then, did I?" Cooper-Brad stages himself at Hartley's head, gesturing for me to take her feet. We bend like synchronized criminals. He counts down.

Before he hits three, I say, "You really thought she might be dead?"

He shrugs. "Rosie was cryptic. And your face when you left the room . . . My surfboard and I met with a shark off Wellfleet and it was less angry than you. So death? Maybe? Maimed, for sure."

"And still you came."

"I came." He rakes his hand through his curls. "Deal's a deal, right? All we have is our word."

The texts from Evil Spawn weigh heavy in my pocket.

I take Hartley's feet. I restart the count. On three, we heave her off the floor and into the crate. Cooper-Brad's stronger than I am, and her head lands inside first with a thunk.

"Cooper-Brad!" I cry.

He cocks his head. "That's sticking, then?"

"Not now."

He grabs the aquamarine scarf I dropped on the floor and my heart pinches as he bunches it under Hartley's head. I settle her legs in the crate, tucking her feet beneath her because she's half-giant.

What am I even doing here? This woman is passed out.

Probably concussed. And I'm stuffing her in a storage bin? This isn't real life. This isn't *my* life. Especially not here, not now. Not when I've just left a room full of arguably my most dedicated fans.

My aching joints creak as I bend beside the crate. This woman wanted success. Success in this wildly glorious and confounding industry. Just like me. I rub the bump on my ring finger. I may have my grandmother's engagement ring back, but I gave it up. Without hesitation. I should be embarrassed to admit it, but it's who I am. All or nothing. That's always been me. I didn't want one Smurf action figure; I wanted the entire village. Why bother reading one *Sweet Valley High* if you weren't going to read them all? If I was going to study for a test, I was going to S-T-U-D-Y. Flash cards and handwritten notes and highlighters and practice tests. And if I couldn't have what I wanted—straight A's or a dozen cookies or the friend I thought wanted me too—I'd get by without any.

I never wanted to just be *an* author. I wanted to be *the* author.

Cooper-Brad begins to lift the lid. "Ever wonder why she picked you?"

"Not until this moment." I look closely at Hartley. She lacks the lines around her eyes and sagging jowls that usually accompany a woman's shift to gray. Her hair is so smooth, so uniformly white, and I scan from the tips to the roots, admiring the sheen. But the roots . . . I once again use the flashlight on my phone and press my face too close to hers. Her roots are red. I remember her standing at ease before Brad in a completely different persona with her hair haphazardly piled above her head wearing that bomber jacket. Hartley West is an excellent liar.

Her eyes snap open. The shock of it makes me gasp, and a few drops of my spittle fall onto her face.

"Queen Bee," she says, her voice a little pained but clear.

"Hartley." I swallow my surprise and hefty amount of guilt. "I'm sorry. I didn't mean—"

She fixes her gaze on me. "Unseat the queen, and you become the queen."

I shake my head. "I'm sorry?"

Hartley touches the back of her head and winces. "You hit me."

"No, no, you fell. There was a can of soap. Metal and—"

She bites her bottom lip. "Sofie Wilde came at me with a mop. My scream died in my throat. I couldn't move. I could barely breathe. And then . . . everything faded to black."

"That's not—"

She smirks. "No one stages a coup of the second-in-command. Take down the best, you become the best. Voila."

She got one thing right—I am the best. And I'm picking up that goddamned sword.

"Cooper-Brad? Find me an extension cord."

Wheeling a squirming body in a gigantic book crate down the halls of a sold-out hotel during the largest romance readers' convention in the world while trying to go unnoticed turns out to be exhilarating. This is how I imagined Callum felt when kidnapping Torrence the first time. My writing was spot-on. No surprise, after all, considering I am a great author.

I laugh out loud. Suggesting that I may very well be a great author who is losing her marbles from an overdose of adrenaline.

"There. The north elevator bank." Hartley's purse bounces against my hip as I direct Cooper-Brad to follow the signs. Fiona said it was the north elevator bank that led to the underground speakeasy—or the south. Grace grumbled in the background, then her voice came over the phone, saying, "North, north, north—details, Fiona, you never pay attention. This is why your settings lack authenticity." A squabble ensued, with Fiona calling out Grace's *trite character arcs* and I hung up the phone.

"Clarice, nine o'clock," Cooper-Brad says.

I swivel my head to the right.

"Nine o'clock," he says with urgency.

"Can't you just say left?" I lower the Read or Bleed hat and peer out from beneath the brim. Clarice's cheeks match the color of her red volunteer shirt. Her hands flail as she animatedly speaks into the Bluetooth headset that's situated in her ear.

"Disappeared, what do you mean *disappeared*? It's the party for her own book. Of all the things Sofie Wilde would do, she'd never abandon her fans."

My brain seizes on *all the things she'd do* before shifting to *abandon her fans*. That's what they're going to think, isn't it? After my pity-fueled tirade, my fans are going to turn against me, aren't they?

A thunk comes from inside the crate, and I quickly toss Cooper-Brad my phone. I duck behind a cardboard cutout of a heart with a Band-Aid across it. Cooper-Brad raises the volume on my phone, and out comes Rosie's voice. *"Not that we needed the boost, considering we're the top-selling genre across all books in every category."* Cheers from what sounds like a full house. *"But, yes, certainly, the pandemic caused people to turn to what we romance authors have been delivering for decades: happy endings."*

This is our cover for when Hartley thumps the crate. Cooper-Brad and I have been role-playing as such hard-core fans that we listen to the livestream of the panels while doing our volunteer duties. We (and by "we" I mean Cooper-Brad) stuffed a washcloth in Hartley's mouth and tied her hands with my scarf and her feet with the extension cord. But that hasn't stopped her from smacking into the crate. A lot.

"Obviously," Clarice says. "I know that. It's not going to help us in our argument to get her keynote back."

Clarice, dear Clarice. I knew you were my biggest—

"Lacey might be posturing. But she's the publicist to more than a third of our authors. If we don't get Sofie Wilde that keynote, and Lacey isn't bluffing, we can say goodbye to nearly all of our most popular authors next year."

Oh. *Oh.*

Well, thank you, Lacey. Whatever it takes, right?

"The timing for all this is horrific," Clarice says. "Riley Moore's on her way, and I haven't even had a chance to make sure her toilet flushes properly, let alone stock her room with orange Starbursts and peppermint-scented soap."

And I couldn't get my hand sanitizer disguised as lotion?

"Let's do this," Clarice says. "The flu has been going around. If she doesn't show in twenty minutes, that's what we say. She's sick. Then we end the launch party and give them passes to cut the line at Hartley West's Beautiful on the Inside panel this afternoon."

Hartley's Beautiful on the Inside panel?

Cooper-Brad continues on to the north elevators. Clarice is too distracted to question the crate that's hopping like a jacked-up car. When the elevator dings, I run despite my attempt at keeping a low profile. Cooper-Brad and the orange crate are positioned at the back of the elevator behind two readers, probably mid-twenties, dressed as goth vampires—Tara Kara must have a Q&A or an author talk soon. I slip in, head down, not making eye contact.

A young woman holding two fake fangs beside her leg says, "The hotel next door has a high tea."

The other, legs covered by black fishnets, responds, "Perfect, I could go for a scone."

Goth vampires at high tea. Such an unabashed generation, one has to admire it.

Fake Fangs scrolls on her phone. "Wait, what? Vance? Megan, are you seeing this?"

Fishnets says, "Heard it in the bathroom from a woman dressed as Anne Boleyn talking to a woman who I think was supposed to be Theodosia Burr. Sofie Wilde truly is a brilliant author."

I feel a smile creeping in.

"Crappy person," Fishnets adds.

"Megan! She did a crappy thing. That doesn't mean she's a crappy person."

"But it might."

"It might."

And just as quickly, my smile fades.

The elevator doors part as we reach the lobby. As the two vampires exit, I sneak a peek at Fake Fangs, who wiggles her phone. "Apparently Sofie Wilde had to leave her own event. Flu, they think."

Cooper-Brad steps forward and extends his arm out to stop the doors from closing. "Don't believe every tweet you read."

Fake Fangs and Fishnets whirl around as if noticing him for the first time. I face the back of the elevator and cough to cover Hartley's whack against the crate.

"Oh, yeah?" one of them says. "And you are?"

Cooper-Brad slaps his chest. "Volunteer."

"Can you get us tickets to Hartley West's keynote?"

"Sofie Wilde's doing the keynote."

"Not according to this," says the girl, presumably Fake Fangs with her all-knowing phone.

Cooper-Brad sighs. "What did I just say?"

"No offense," says the other—Megan. "You're our elder and

everything, but you're also, like, just one person. Why would I believe you over the hundreds of people posting about this?"

Hundreds are saying I've lost my keynote?

Cooper-Brad says, "More people believing a lie doesn't make it true."

Fake Fangs says, "Doesn't make it not true. So, no tickets, then?"

"No," Cooper Brad says. "Because it's not Ms. Wilde who's under the weather. It's Hartley West."

The doors close, and I spin back around.

"More than living up to my end of the deal," he says.

"Long way to go, Cooper-Brad. But it's a start."

The elevator sinks to the underground level, an apt metaphor for how low we are now going. But it's true, this is a start. One that will give me some breathing room to figure out what comes next. Fake Fangs and Fishnets will spread the news that Hartley West has the flu, not me, and it will become fact. Her absence at all her events explained without us having to do anything more. The internet will make her disappear. The same way it made her appear in the first place. The reach of social media is both terrifying and extraordinary.

I suddenly feel very, very tired. And by tired, I mean old.

I open my texts without reading the new ones from Lacey. I fire off a quick message, instructing her to contact Clarice and tell her that I had an emergency. I cannot alienate my readers. Not when they have "the next Sofie Wilde's" book just ready to be added to their to-be-read lists, and not when I need them to be not only willing but eager to follow me from Jocelyn's world to the new stories I want to tell. I text Lacey and offer to buy my entire backlist for everyone at the event if they wait for me to return in twenty minutes. I suddenly wonder if we should have drilled air holes in the crate.

I hesitate, then angle my phone away from Cooper-Brad.

Me: Headway, Lord of Darkness?

Evil Spawn: Oh, now I'm royalty? To what do I owe this change?

Evil Spawn: Wait, let me guess. Blaire's burning sage and meditating on this.

Blaire. The Blaire who paid for me to go to my first festival and sends holiday cards on my behalf because she wants to stave off my carpal tunnel.

Me: Forget it, this is a bad idea.

Evil Spawn: Truthfully, I love sage. And meditating? The lifeblood of my negotiating tactics. Stay the course, Wilde Woman. Hold tight.

What am I doing, like *what am I doing*?

"Pantsing" leads to this: unrealistic events and weak characterization.

"A little help, Sofie?" Cooper-Brad says from beyond the open elevator door.

I tuck my phone back in my pocket and position myself behind the other end of the crate. Together, we guide it past ladders and cans of paint. The construction detritus spreads down the hallway like breadcrumbs. We follow the trail until we reach the end. A sign reads Pardon Our Appearance While We Work to Bring You a New Clandestine Experience!

Behind streams of yellow tape, an ornate door gleams with fresh varnish. Either the door is original or a well-done replica, with long cracks and knots that make the wood appear aged.

"Is that—" Cooper-Brad points to a small indentation at chest height "—a bullet hole?"

"Is it wrong that I hope so?" I assess an even larger groove. "Bat?"

"Or a nightstick."

A muffled cry accompanies a wild thumping from inside the crate. I feel a little bad. And then I remember her taking my hand and calling me *so pathetic.*

"So, Sof, how good are you at picking locks?" Cooper-Brad says.

"Not something I've had to research, *Coop.* You?"

He shakes his head. "Not a lot of time for such delicate work during an apocalypse."

"YouTube?" I reach for my phone.

"Leaves a history."

Another muffled cry and then "it."

Cooper-Brad says, "Did you catch that?"

"No. Do you think she's okay?"

"Pathetic" or not, she can't stay in there much longer. Though at least she wasn't bumped along her majesty's pitted road and floated across white rapids like Fiona's potato farmer. Still, it can't be comfortable.

"What if she swallowed the washcloth?" I say.

Thump, thump, thump.

"I can do it!" Hartley's voice is both raspy and shrill. "Let me out of here, and I will do it!"

"If she did swallow it, it doesn't appear to have done any harm." Cooper-Brad gestures toward the lock. "Well?"

I hug my arms tight to my chest. Common sense says this ends in mug shots no matter what we do. But if we give up now, that happens before I get the chance to stand on the stage as headliner of the Romance US convention—if I get nothing else, I at least want that. I bend to open the crate.

I nearly bite my tongue in surprise. Hartley is a fright. Sweat from her forehead has bled into her mascara, and black rings line her eyes like a raccoon. Her hair is matted to her head. White fuzz from the washcloth sticks to her lips.

"Rosie Gardens," she says, kneading my Photoshopped face between her hands. "Why didn't I choose Rosie Gardens?"

I yank my banner out of her grip. "Yes, why didn't you?"

Rosie would have never had a viral tantrum. Rosie would have opined a thoughtful and powerful op-ed in the *New York Times* in defense of art. Rosie wouldn't have responded to Max Donner's texts. If Hartley had chosen Rosie, I'd still have my keynote. If Hartley had chosen Rosie, I wouldn't be committing a felony. Because even if Rosie had come up with this scheme herself, I wouldn't be helping her. Odds are, she wouldn't have asked.

"Sofie, don't you see?" Hartley says. "I am both repulsed and in awe. This is exactly why I chose you."

And then Hartley hawks a glob of snot-filled spit directly into my eye. (The left, in case you were wondering.)

FORCED PROXIMITY

Two failed escape attempts and nearly ten minutes later, the lock to the speakeasy clicks open.

Hartley hands me back my earring, bent beyond recognition. "If this has all been an elaborate ruse for a surprise party to celebrate my success, you should know I hate surprises."

"Me too," I say.

Cooper-Brad raises a hand. "Love 'em, myself. The unpredictability of life is a gift."

"One I require a gift receipt for," I say.

He laughs. "I can't wait to read Tucana."

"Says the turncoat." Hartley's nostrils flare, but I can see her wandering eyes, once again checking out the path to the elevator. This is the only reason she agreed to pick the lock. Her chance to escape is much higher outside the crate. She faces Cooper-Brad. "We had an agreement. I gave you everything you wanted."

"No," he says, "you gave me only what you were in a position to give. Sofie and friends happen to be in the position to actually give me everything I wanted."

"Nice try. Sofie doesn't have friends. Another reason I chose her."

Holes or no holes, we should have left her in the crate. I don't have time for this.

Hartley glares at Cooper-Brad, tightening her jaw. "Doesn't your word matter at all?"

"You didn't just say that," I spit out. "*You*. You're a fraud from that silver dye job to this prairie-bohemian-whatever look you've got going on. You're Frey level, Hartley."

"Actually I'm not," she says, though she touches her roots. "He presented his memoir as fact when it wasn't and never intended the truth to come out. I always intended this truth to come out. This wasn't done on a whim. I planned every piece of this. Perfectly."

Cooper-Brad tips his chin at her. "Current circumstances notwithstanding."

Hartley keeps her dirty look squarely on Cooper-Brad, but her feet shimmy to the left. I nudge him to block what's clearly another escape attempt.

"Inside, now." I check the time on my phone. Clarice is afraid of Lacey, which surely delights my publicist to no end. But it also means my launch party remains full of readers waiting for me to return. I'm due back in just over ten minutes. Rosie or Fiona or Grace have less than that to get here. With his own words, Cooper-Brad has proven he's committed only to the best offer that comes across the table. And while I'm pretty sure if Hartley had more to offer, she would have already, I'm not risking leaving them alone together. They need a babysitter. "And hurry."

Bravado in her gait, Hartley enters first, followed by Cooper-Brad and the crate, and then me. It's darker than the black hole Vance uses to travel between realms. I fumble for a light switch.

(Clandestine better not mean lit only by candles.) When I finally find something that feels like a dimmer, I tap until the room is bathed in a soft dancing light.

"Cooper!" I shoot my hands in the air. "Drop!"

A line of policemen holding nightsticks scowls at us from the other side of the bar.

Cooper-Brad's face pales. His Adam's apple bobs. "This isn't what it looks like," rushes out. "We're writers."

"Authors," I correct, and Cooper-Brad pulls a face. What? It's more professional. It legitimizes us. "Research. We're doing research for—Hartley, no!"

She rounds the bar, putting her makeup-smeared face an inch from the first officer. She lifts her hand, places it on his chest, and shoves. The officer falls to the floor without a sound. Except the whisper of cardboard grazing the floor. She pushes each of the officers, and one by one, they go down, wafting a slight breeze through the room.

"Course, course," Cooper-Brad says. "Knew it. Just having a laugh." He saunters to the bar where he takes a seat beside a cardboard cutout of a flapper. Pearls, feather in her bob, silver cigarette holder—the whole kit and caboodle. "Come here often?"

Hartley gives a small shake of her head.

In our defense, they're quite lifelike. High-end, for sure. They make the lobster in the restaurant window across from Harbor Books look like a paper doll.

Hartley stands between two mafioso, one holding a pistol and the other a bottle of unlabeled alcohol. "Underground, I presume? No windows, maybe even soundproofed, if this place is actually original. Again, repulsed and in awe. So, this is where we are. And this is what I'm going to do. I'm going to skip the indignation, the how-could-yous, the crocodile tears, the wait-until-the-police find out, the wait-until-social-media-finds-out. We're here. Let's be here. What do you want?"

Fire ignites under my skin. I'm not letting her take control of this situation. "You make a statement that you were misguided. That you have come to realize using AI to imitate me was wrong and an insult to the great author that I am. You leave the convention. Recall your books. Discourage writers from doing what you did. And never write anything that has even a whiff of my voice again."

If this place isn't soundproofed, the decibel level of Hartley's laugh will bring half the hotel here.

"Okay then, have it your way," I say.

I never expected her to agree, but she doesn't even make a counteroffer. Instead, she circles the bar until she finds the hinged piece that flips up to allow her through. She enters the horseshoe and stoops to search the lower shelves.

Cooper-Brad slaps the bar top. "Woman after my own heart. Never too early. But for appearances sake, make it a mimosa. Bloody Mary, but only if that's all you've got." He looks at me. "Not the biggest spice fan."

My resting bitch face is on full display because this isn't the time for jokes. This has spiraled, already, and we've barely started. Hartley's fall and threat to say I *intentionally* hit her, followed by that hideous thing with the crate, and now this hidden speakeasy feels much more serious that the original plan of simply locking her in a hotel room. I flip off the Read or Bleed hat and dig my hand into my pocket, finding the damp box of chocolates beside my phone. I yank out the disgusting box, toss it on the bar, and text Grace a non-incriminating question about their ETA.

The clink of glass against glass, and Hartley's head pops up from behind the bar. "Nothing. Just barware."

"That's disappointing," Cooper-Brad says.

"Understatement. Not even a dried orange wheel, and I'm starving." Hartley comes out from behind the bar. "Wait, chocolates? Can I have those? Sofie?"

Grace and Fiona are still at the store, at least twenty minutes out. My heart threatens to stop beating.

"Sofie? I asked you a question? You've kidnapped me, the least you can do is answer when I'm speaking to—"

"What?" I start calling Rosie.

"Chocolates. Can. I. Have?"

I flick my wrist. "Whatever, yes. Assault your taste buds, what do I care." Rosie answers, and I lower my voice to explain where we are and how we got here.

Hartley lifts the box lid. "Why is the box all wet? Did you lick it or something?"

I march away from the bar, hoping the thrumming in my foot isn't from a broken toe. Apparently, decades of healing slows down recovery as we age, which I learned from my dermatologist when a simple hangnail festered and I had to use some ointment made of silver for weeks, like I was fighting a werewolf bite.

"Sofie, do you have a map?"

"What? She doesn't need a map." I press the phone harder against my ear. "No, not you, Rosie. Just follow the ladders to the end of the hall."

"Here, let me see," Cooper-Brad says. "Sometimes it's underneath."

I hear the tumble of chocolates on the bar and then spin around to see Hartley two feet from the door. "Cooper!"

"What?" he says. "Oh, no."

"You're supposed to be watching her!"

"You never said that."

"Implied, it's *implied*."

"Sorry, it's my first kidnapping." He sprints past me, three chocolates in hand.

"You're eating? You're actually eating while she's—"

"Trust me." He sticks a chocolate between his front teeth and says around it, "Hazelnut."

Hartley stills.

"And pecan. Almond too. A tree nut bonanza."

She spins toward him. "You're bluffing."

He's close enough to grab her wrist but instead says, "Try me."

Her lips part and her brows rise. She's not angry. She's scared. She retreats from the door.

"So you're really that allergic?" I say. "If he actually bit that in half would you—"

Hartley's face pales. She looks woozy. I turn and see Cooper-Brad chewing. He actually ate the chocolate? Either he isn't really her friend—even a craft-fair friend—or he really, really wants to impress me. Hartley shrieks, and I rush to ferry her across the room. I'm starting to hyperventilate. I don't want to go to jail or kill her—*right, or kill her*—and then Cooper-Brad smiles.

"Have I mentioned I used to be a professional poker player?" He chews loudly. "Mint. Surrounded by white chocolate and something gummy. Caramel, I think. A rather disgusting combination in actuality. But the only flavor in the box, so if you still want them, they're all yours."

I'm currently hugging Hartley's waist beside a stack of jazz records. She's shaking. I let go.

"That allergic?" I ask. "Even encased in chocolate?"

"Maybe?" She expels an almost hysterical laugh. "I don't actually know."

I give her some space, and she migrates to a booth filled with cardboard customers. Her head drops to the table and she wraps her hands around the back of her neck.

Cooper-Brad wasn't joking, was he? Or wrong? Could there actually be nuts? I hurry to the bar and scoop up the box. No ingredients listed on the outside. My gluten intolerance means I can't risk testing them myself. I drill my eyes into Cooper-Brad's.

"Mint, I swear," he says.

He hands over the product information, and I scan each and every ingredient twice. No nuts, no gluten, just lots of chemicals, making me reconsider the young Natuhlee's affection for me.

All gluten does is make me best friends with a toilet for a day and a half, but still I understand her fear. I return to Hartley and pass her the sheet. "They're safe," I reassure her, knowing how meaningful it is for me to hear the same. Sweat still dots her forehead, and her eyes have a far-away look in them. "Is it something else? Are you, uh, feeling okay? Was the crate un-comfortable?"

Her lips curl back like a rabid possum.

"I mean, overly so? As in are you hurt or do you need medical attention? Food, you need food. Right, we can—"

"Sofie, stop, just stop. You trying to be nice is making me want to hurl." She sucks in a breath. "It's a phobia, all right? Go ahead, spread it all over social media if you want. Hartley West is nuts! Pun intended. I don't even care."

"I wouldn't do that."

But Lacey would.

"I am allergic. My first and last tree nut was Nutella on toast when I was three, but my mom instilled the fear of every god in me. She blames herself to this day. Makes me text her photos of my EpiPens in my bag."

"Sounds . . ." *obsessive?* ". . . nice."

"She's my biggest cheerleader and the smartest woman I've ever known. My inspiration for Addie."

"I thought that was Jocelyn?"

She straightens her spine. "Certainly, Jocelyn too. Mostly Jocelyn. But my mom's in there too."

The expression on her face unnerves me, but whatever this is, we're done. She's gotten something from me, but I've gotten something more, without even having to crack open her book. Something that's going to end her escape attempts. Something that's going to lead to her voluntarily giving my keynote back. Maybe even make all those memes disappear. This new information changes everything, and now I'm all in. The high that comes when puzzle pieces fit together envelops me.

I take out my phone to call Grace. "Change of plans," I say as she answers. I'm about to open the door when there's a knock from the other side. I gesture for Cooper-Brad to keep his eyes on Hartley, and he gives me a thumbs-up.

As I open the door, I greet Rosie and join her in the hall. She listens as I explain my incredibly brilliant and mildly unhinged idea. I have Grace's breathing in my ear and Rosie's face before me. Rosie laughs, thinking I'm joking. When she realizes I'm not, her eyes widen. But then, the wheels turn in her mind.

"Certainly increases the stakes and consequences, doesn't it?" Rosie says.

Hartley's purse is still draped over my torso. I open it and find the sleeve housing Hartley's hotel room key. I hand it to Rosie.

"Someone needs to put the Do Not Disturb on," I say. "Quickly."

Rosie nods, her long silver earrings grazing her shoulder. "Your instincts are enviable, Sofie. It does all center on food."

YOUNG AT HEART

I DON'T HAVE ENOUGH TIME TO WIND MY WAY THROUGH THE hotel to the author green room, outfitted with the requisite La Croix, Kind bars, and most critically at this moment, a private bathroom. My own room all the way up on the twentieth floor is out of the question. I slip into the restroom nearest my event space, grateful that the other panels are underway. I wouldn't want to have to use my status to cut the line. (Well, *wouldn't* is a strong word.)

My appearance shocks me. It lacks the mascara runoff of Hartley's (thank you, kind Sephora clerk), but the bags under my eyes wouldn't fit as carry-ons. I swear there's a new streak of gray on the left side of my part. I even think the hair's grown back on my freshly waxed upper lip.

I wet a paper towel and pat my blotchy skin before slipping Hartley's purse off my shoulder and tugging off the red volunteer shirt. Stray threads and red lint stick to my white blouse. My scarf. It's still in the crate. My chest constricts. I've worn a scarf matching the color of my latest release as far back as book one. I was setting up a persona even then. It's my signature. It's what people expect. And somehow, maybe, what I needed to slip into this role I wasn't actually born to have. A girl who would rather throw up than give a book report before the whole class doesn't scream "entertainer."

For years, I thought it was hereditary, skipping a generation with my mom. My parents are the most sociable people I know. Still. That I welcome disappearing into a story world instead of ungluing my feet from a tacky dive bar floor or inhaling the hot alcoholic fumes of a crowd belting out "Auld Lang Syne" on New Year's remains unfathomable to them. I'll never forget the avalanche on my father's face when I told him I couldn't come to my mother's sixty-fifth birthday party because I had a deadline. He'd already checked my schedule with Blaire. He had never caught me in a lie before. Or at least admitted that he had.

My grandmother was more like me. She couldn't even call for her own haircuts. My grandfather did everything for her, which was sweet when I was eleven. But the older I got, the more I saw. "Everything" included telling her how to cut her hair. How to roast a chicken. How to water down her wine so as not to embarrass him at firm dinners. How to look the other way when he brought one of his mistresses to the guest room in the home they shared for sixty years and then sat reading the newspaper while she cooked the young woman steak and eggs the next morning.

The day my grandmother showed me her engagement ring and explained she was leaving it to me when she died was the day I realized she wasn't like me—a shy, self-conscious girl convinced everyone was laughing at her behind her back. My grandmother had simply married an asshole and was too stubborn to admit her parents were right. She wouldn't leave him. Unless it got "really bad." Fortunately and unfortunately she died before I ever found out what might meet that definition.

If it had gotten "really bad," the ring was her way out, a way to fund a new life. My grandmother routinely skimmed off the top of the allowance my grandfather gave her for groceries and household supplies. Each time she amassed enough, she'd take the ring to get reset, changing out the diamond for one with more carats and clarity. By the time she died, it was as clear as a summer day and weighed down her small hand. He never even noticed.

She had wanted me to have the ring so I'd have the same security she had. But it also gave me something she hadn't intended. I loved her, I admired her will, but I vowed I'd never be like her. I'd never let anyone or anything hold me back from what I wanted—including myself. So I faced my fears. I broke out of my shell and no longer care if anyone is laughing at me. A crocodile's skin is thick enough to stop a bullet. Mine too. You can't self-publish half a dozen books and search for a literary agent otherwise. Or you can, but it'll break your heart.

I drop the red shirt next to the sink and dust off my chest. A spot of pink peeks out from beneath my arms. Plural, both of them. The dye ran. Christ. I can't sign books like this. But I can't *not* sign books.

It feels like I've stepped into some writing prompt gone astray: here I am, pink armpits and all, about to sign hundreds of copies of the culmination of my life's work while Hartley West is being held hostage in a booth beside a cardboard gangster, a flapper, and a newsboy.

A text lights up my phone.

Lacey: Tell me you have a Sharpie in hand.

Shit.

Me: Tell you when I have one in hand?

Lacey: Sofie, WTF? I'm expending all my capital on you, and you can't even sit at the goddamn table? You live for this.

Which is why my armpits are Barbie pink. Think this defense would stand up in court?

Lacey: Don't let the keynote get in your head. Blaire's being too diplomatic. I'm handling it.

My fingertips hover over the keyboard. Max Donner and Lacey would be unstoppable together. Lacey's been my publicist since the beginning, but her relationship with Blaire predates mine. Blaire said she's working on it. Maybe she's right. Maybe a little positive energy is truly all we need. Especially with Hartley locked in the basement.

I whip off my button-down and put the Romance US T-shirt back on. When I get home, after making history by receiving the longest standing ovation this convention has ever seen, I'm resizing my grandmother's ring. Because this goiter on my finger can go fuck itself.

The restroom door opens with a squeak. I snatch up Hartley's purse and duck into the stall behind me. For some bizarrely unsanitary reason, fans who are also writers see toilets as the perfect setting in which to pitch their story idea. I have three minutes to get back to my event before Lacey sends a search party for me. Carrying pitchforks. This goddamned kidnapping will not ruin this convention for me.

"Tara Kara are hilarious! They literally finish—"

"Each other's sentences. Ha!" The woman's voice is slightly nasal, like she has a cold. "Told you. Their Insta feed is just like that. Tips for WIPs is awesome."

"Whips? Kinky."

Nasal voice laughs. "Works in progress. Super generous to spend time giving us newbies advice."

Cleverly disguised self-promotion. Tara Kara have a really good coach.

"That's why I'm psyched they're going to be on the Beautiful on the Inside panel. The two of them and Riley Moore together will be *a-ma-zing*!" A zipper opens and there's a clatter of various items hitting the counter. "Here, mascara. Let me borrow your lipstick."

"Don't forget Sofie Wilde is on it too," says the first woman in an excited (rightly so) voice.

"Did you hear—"

"No! Lalalalala, not listening. I know something's up, but I do not want spoilers. Whoever leaked whatever it is they leaked should be tried for high treason."

Hear, hear!

The excited woman adds, "I do so love her."

The nasal one says, "But that video . . ."

"She only said the truth. Unlike Hartley West. And, like, why isn't she in jail? Isn't what she did stealing?"

"But *technically* it wasn't her. AI wrote the book."

"Which it wouldn't have been able to do without Sofie's body of work. I don't care what lawsuits have said or will say, Sofie should, like, get every cent of what Hartley West makes."

I should be recording this. This is what should go viral.

"Hmm," says nasal voice. "I don't know. Hartley did have to edit it. It's not like it came out perfect. It sounds like she actually did a ton of work. And by herself. Without an editor.

I'm keeping an open mind. I'm curious to hear more from Hartley herself."

Water rushes from the faucet and I can hear the sound of a bag being zipped closed.

"Whoa," the woman with the nasal voice says. "Anika, you've got to see this."

"I said no spoilers, Liz."

"It's not a spoiler. It's worse. For you. And probably for Sofie Wilde."

I halt my tapping foot.

"I thought her having the flu was just a rumor?" Anika says. "They're hashtagging the crap out of her appearance on the Beautiful panel. I can't miss her! If only we could have afforded those launch party tickets!"

"One, my eardrums," the nasal one her friend called Liz says. "Two, seems like she's going to be there. But it's Hartley who has the flu. She's pulled out."

"Of the panel?"

"Of everything," Liz says.

"Karma."

"Maybe . . . or . . ."

"What?" says Anika, her excitement morphing into frustration.

"You don't want to know."

"Is it a spoiler?"

Liz says, "Not of the books, but maybe of Sofie."

"This is bananas," Anika says, and I make a mental note of her quite good use of the code word. "Just say it."

"See for yourself." The sound of something, presumably a phone, being set on the counter. "According to Twitter, Hartley West isn't sick. Sofie gave the convention an ultimatum: either Hartley West goes or she does. Hashtag #WildeWestShowdown."

Seriously? How do these rumors even start?

Goth vampires. Can't be trusted.

Liz adds, "No surprise who Romance US chose. It's all about the bottom line."

"*Or*," Anika says, "about supporting the better author—the *actual* author. Maybe what Sofie said about this not being a meritocracy is starting to change things. Still, even I can say, it's not exactly the high ground. *If* it's true."

"True or not, they're calling her a bully. And jealous. #SourSofie is starting to trend."

"How is her agent letting this happen? Remember what Tara Kara said about their agent? He'd never let them be so disrespected."

He being Max Donner.

I retrieve my phone to text Blaire but can't stop myself from rereading the last text from Max: Stay the course, Wilde Woman. Hold tight.

I write to Blaire: Any progress?

Three little dots appear, then disappear. Then nothing.

But a message comes in from Lacey.

#SourSofie? You're killing me. Full on, ice pick in the heart, machete to my neck, arsenic in my matcha latte. Now get to your goddamned launch party.

I suck in a breath. #SourSofie will only bolster the worries of the bookstores on my tour. I cannot lose them or the chance to plant seeds with my fans for the next version of me. Hartley has to be on that panel. I push open the stall door. The two women see me in the mirror and gasp.

"So awful about Ms. West, isn't it?" I say with such sincerity I almost fool myself. I begin washing my hands at the sink.

"I'd have been bawling on the bathroom floor if I had to miss my first Romance US featured panel. Fortunately, technology truly is a lifesaver. Where would we be without Zoom?"

"She's joining remotely?" says Liz, who's borrowed her friend's coral lipstick (which totally clashes with her skin tone, by the way).

Anika bounces. "So she's actually sick? I knew she was! You're not sour at all, Sofie. I mean, Ms. Wilde."

"No, it's Sofie. Please."

"Sofie." Anika beams. She then nods at my red shirt. "Love it. Your scarves rock, obviously. But supporting the convention? You're a fan at heart, like us."

"Exactly like you," I lie. I'm taking control of this. Social media is not going to win. "I don't mean to overstep, but I'm on my way back to my sold-out launch party. Would you two care to join, on me? Front of the line?"

The two of them exchange a look of awe.

Liz wiggles her phone. "Photo?"

"Perfect." I point to the stalls that would be our background and likely incite some "Sewer Sofie" hashtag. "Maybe the other direction?"

We swivel around, and they flank me.

Just as the photo clicks, Anika says, "Ooh, Liz, why don't you tell Sofie about your book! You've got to hear this. It's incredible. You should read it!"

I fight through the gritting of my teeth. "Why I'd love to."

Red flames up Liz's neck and she gives an embarrassed, "Uh, wow, thanks." Then she clutches her phone and starts tapping. "Photo uploaded. Hashtag #SweetSofie."

GET INTO COSTUME

I AM TRULY A GREAT AUTHOR. I SEIZED THE REINS AND TOOK CON-
trol of the narrative, plotting my way out of an attack by an an-
tagonistic force. Not just by turning the tables but by setting
them with elegant china and gold-plated flatware. No more
#SourSofie. It's all #SweetSofie from here on out. The words
were repeated to me in a never-ending chorus throughout the
rest of my launch party, hashtagged in the hundreds of photos
uploaded, and even cited by Clarice as she closed out my record-
setting signing line. We let everyone in—not just those who'd
purchased tickets for the event but any attendee who saw the
missive I had the convention send out: anyone with a purchased
copy was invited to form an additional signing line and receive
VIP treatment from Sofie Wilde, complete with velvet-armchair
signing and exclusive launch swag until we ran out. Social media
has just become my best friend. I finally understand the appeal.
It is a weapon to wield. And much lighter than a sword.

As I emerge from my shower and dress for the day in a brand-
new souvenir Romance US tee gifted by a fan, I am not just

cleansed of a sleepless night but of the vitriol of trolls and haters. This is a Sofie Wilde who embraces her status as not only a great author dedicated to her fans but as the leader of a vanguard. One remorseful for how the truth about this industry came out, but not that the truth is out. She holds this industry dear, she prizes being a part of it, though it is not without its flaws, often deeply entrenched ones that will not be conquered in a single post or by a few publishing hires or a reimagined mission statement. Voices need lifting, systems need revamping, the dollars redistributed so as to promote all. Needed now more than ever because we face a common enemy. One without a beating heart, without a soul, without the understanding of what it is to feel and to infuse those feelings into thoughts and observations that speak to the human experience.

AI is not a creator. It is a parrot. And that bird must remain caged.

I hit stop on the record button and take a breath. And then I release the laugh I've been holding in. I grab the coffee—hazelnut—that's been brewing in the kitchenette in my hotel suite as I send my video to Lacey. If Fiona is right about my account gaining followers, Lacey will do all she can to keep it going. I don't have to instruct her to post this video far and wide with the #SweetSofie hashtag. She's better at this than I am. I learned what I know from her.

As I wait for my coffee to cool enough to sip, it's almost as though this is all I have to do: interact with my fans, sign my blockbuster series, and take advantage of these breaks in my event schedule to recharge.

Except I have to do this *and* continue to mastermind a kidnapping. Fortunately, lying is only a step above multitasking in the list of skills I excel at.

I signed *Light As* with a pen in one hand and monitored the hostage situation on my phone with the other. Exhilaration over my launch party combined with the constant terror of a SWAT team—or, even, maybe, Special Forces?—raiding the speakeasy sent my pulse soaring. Now, my body craves rest, my mind aches to return to *Pick Me* or Palladium, but neither will get what it wants because of Hartley.

The panel needs to go forward with its original slate. Meaning we aren't just holding Hartley hostage, we're holding her hostage and forcing her to participate in the featured multi-author event of the convention, made even more momentous by the addition of Riley Moore.

We are now not just performers without safety nets but performers without safety nets trapped in a pressure cooker that nobody even knows how to work. (Seriously, all those buttons? No wonder people blow their fingers off.)

For our plan to work, we have the added complication of needing Hartley's laptop. Fiona's on it, while Grace stays with Hartley and Rosie is off commanding the room at her solo author talk.

I blow on my coffee, which is like trying to cool the surface of the sun. Short on time, I plunk in a few ice cubes from the bucket on the counter and down the lukewarm watery mess. I pop two Advil for my aching foot and drop the bottle in my tote, which I retrieved from my launch party, being sure to hide Hartley's purse at the bottom.

On my way out the door, I unearth my phone to check my messages and some masochistic part of me opens Twitter instead. With a swift, but not attention-grabbing pace, I make my way to the elevators, trying not to trip as I type. I search for #WildeWestShowdown and brace myself.

@daenerys4eva writes: Sofie Wilde **better** not bring a knife to a gunfight. We know the Wicked Witch of the West plays dirty. Time for a mud bath. (Shoutout to #Spas: Available for promo, DM me.) #SweetSofie #NoHeartInHartley #WildeWestShowdown

@RomanceIsLife responds: @RomanceUS, are you going to acknowledge this offensive characterization and degradation of an entire class of people?

@daenerys4eva: People? Hartley West admitted to being a robot! She's not even real! #WestNotBest #OnlyHumansAllowed

@RomanceIsLife: I meant witches. #IgnoranceIsBliss #SourSofie #WildeFansSuck

I close Twitter.

It is in these moments that I don't feel embarrassed that my mailbox is cluttered with invitations to join AARP.

As I reach the elevators, a text comes in from Roxanne, must be some middle-aged telepathy, as if she can sense my need to be surrounded by people who stash tissues up their sleeve to combat a constant postnasal drip.

Roxanne: Book It to Books?

Me: If you're having a stroke, you should really call 911.

Roxanne: Charming. Insensitive as hell. But that's its own kind of charm.

Roxanne: It's a bookstore. In Austin. On your tour. You've been before, haven't you? How was the turnout?

Me: You'd have to ask Lacey, why?

Roxanne: Just curious.

Me: Since when do we casually text about curiosities?

Roxanne: Since I'm doing you a favor by not stocking your nemesis's book.

Oh. She's missing out on revenue by not selling *Love and Lawlessness.*

Me: I honestly don't remember. But I can ask Lacey, if you want.

Roxanne: Don't bother. I was just being conversational. What I'm actually curious about is how they shelved their YA. They report steady sales.

Me: I can take a look.

She sends me a thumbs-up and a martini-glass emoji.

The elevator doors open, and I make a call.

"Are we ready?" I say as Fiona answers.

She replies, "Affirmative. Mission WildeWestShowdown a go."

"Don't call it that."

"It's creative. And this is all about supporting human ingenuity, isn't it?"

"Human ingenuity?" I say as I enter the speakeasy, a flutter of nerves tickling my throat. It was somehow morally and ethically easier to be the mastermind of this without actually being here.

"Exactly." Fiona issues a satisfied smile and tips the Read or Bleed baseball hat she's now wearing at Grace.

"More like insanity." This is sick. This is twisted. This is absolutely working.

Fiona and Grace have taken my simple if mildly (moderately) cruel directive and exploded it. I suggested a bag of shelled peanuts. Instead, big-box-store-sized containers of nuts of all varieties are spread throughout the room. On the bar, in the booths, on top of the vintage record player, on a cocktail table by the door. And behind each and every one is a circulating fan. If Hartley tries to escape or if she even begins to cry for help while on Zoom, the bags will be cut and the spinning fans will release tree-nut particles into the air.

She sits on a barstool, twisting my aquamarine scarf in her hands, looking like she's going to throw up. At least it won't be difficult to sell her having the flu.

"You let her do this?" I say to Grace.

Rosie had left Grace and Fiona to put the details into place since, unlike them, she had convention programming this morning. I have to believe if Rosie had been here, she'd have never let it get this far. Though a part of me—one I'm not all that proud of—is relieved she wasn't here.

"Proof you don't know Fiona," Grace says.

"She doesn't know any of us," Fiona says.

Grace rotates her tall frame as if she's the subject of a photo shoot. "True," she says to Fiona. "But what's relevant in this circumstance is your tendency to embrace the grand-gesture trope. The unwinnable joust, the boom-box serenade, the sprint through the airport—that is our Fiona. Go big and then go bigger. And bigger."

Hartley attempts a scoff, but it dies in her throat as Cooper-Brad sets a bag of almonds beside a laptop already situated on a table in the middle of the room.

Fiona follows him, her tiered, ruffled gown swishing, and I

shudder at the thought of her shopping in that absurd fuchsia costume, captured in store security feeds throughout downtown Chicago.

She opens the laptop. "Nothing wrong with a trope. Enemies to lovers. Mistaken identity. Locked room. It's all in the execution, my friends. Our job is simply to entertain. To give readers what they want."

A soft "Exactly," from Hartley, whose eyes widen as Fiona sets a pair of scissors beside the almonds.

"Which you will all do on this panel," Fiona says. She looks around the room, ensuring she has everyone's full attention, before continuing. "Just so we're clear, Hartley joins the Zoom with a cough and a sneeze, pretending to be under the weather. Maybe a sore throat? Sofie, what do you think?"

I'm a little stupefied by all these nuts. "Maybe we don't go overboard."

Though clearly it's far too late for that.

"Gotcha," Fiona says to me. To Hartley, she says, "Quick answers. No elaborating, just like we said. Otherwise . . ." Fiona taps the scissors against the almonds. "Snip, snip, snip."

Hartley, eyes tinged with fear, nods.

One thing is certain: they really did think this through.

Grace walks toward me, her eyes scanning my body. "You should go. Change now. You can't be late for the panel."

I smooth down the front of my Fictional People Are My People souvenir convention tee. "I'm wearing this. Makes me relatable." I look at the pink bra strap peeking out from her off-the-shoulder sweater. "Not that you understand that."

Grace follows my gaze and tugs on her sleeve. "You think I dress like this because I want to?"

I look to Fiona, who's smirking and not going to help me.

"Why else?" I say.

Grace snorts. "Sure thing. The same way I like to pose naked in my bathtub holding a carefully placed book. You've seen my feed?"

I haven't.

"Sofie," Fiona says condescendingly. "*Relatable* is what they ask for when they *don't* want you posing naked in a bathtub. Grace, on the other hand—well, let's just say her advances benefit from it."

"You're playing with me," I say, wishing it to be true—this apparently being where I want publishing to draw the line.

"They won't verbalize it anymore," Grace says. "But during the marketing meeting for my first book, my appearance was part of the strategy. My agent said my *modeling career* added 50K to the advance."

Fiona drags a chair to the table with the laptop. "Code for that gorg face and body I'd literally kill for. Not you, Grace. I wouldn't kill you to get it. But if you were already dead, and there was a shady body-swapping syndicate, well . . ." Fiona twiddles her fingers before pointing at my shirt. "You? You're nailing relatable. And in comparison, the pink color makes your eyes look less bloodshot."

"Thanks, Fiona," I say. "Helpful."

She shrugs. "Anytime." She sits in the chair, a stunt double for Hartley. "Password," she asks over her shoulder. "Hartley?"

Hartley sighs. "Hartley West."

"Your password is your name?" Grace says. "Sofie-level vanity right there."

And what's wrong with that? Wait . . . did I just prove her right?

Grace adjusts the laptop to better position its built-in camera. As she and Fiona bicker about the lefts and rights and how many records to stack under it to perfect the height, I gesture for Cooper-Brad to walk with me to the door. "How is she?"

"Fiona's a riot. You should see her whittle a pair of lips out of a potato. Apparently, her dad bought her an actual potato farm in Ireland for her research. And Grace? Do you know she did a commercial for adult diapers? When she was nineteen? She has a PhD in psychology. Her insights on character arcs have been a true MasterClass."

"I meant Hartley." Though I didn't know any of that about Fiona or Grace.

"You care how Hartley is doing?" He pauses, then starts nodding. "Ah, #SweetSofie, right? Getting in character before the panel. True dedication."

I don't bother to correct him. I shouldn't care how Hartley's doing. I shouldn't care about the defeated look on her face. She set out to destroy me, she admitted as much. This twist in her story is deserved and entirely necessary for me to get what *I* deserve. I picture myself on that stage, on all the stops on my tour, with Hollywood offer upon offer rolling in, writing whatever I want for the rest of eternity. It plays out like a story, one whose ending I am sure of, one whose beats I must remain in control of.

"You got me," I lie, "it's not only actors who can use the method approach."

"Maybe . . . except, and don't take this the wrong way," Cooper-Brad says, "but you don't seem like a felon."

"Are there people who would take that the wrong way?"

He gestures at the cardboard cutouts in the speakeasy. "Half of these guys, probably. Considering how I'm feeling surrounded by their one-dimensional versions, I certainly wouldn't have wanted to run into them in the flesh."

"Really?" My brow lifts. "You wouldn't have come here, back then?"

"To an illicit club with banned substances and fashionable young women flouting conventional standards of behavior?"

"That's admirably specific. So, would you have?"

"No."

"No?"

"No, unless perhaps as him." Cooper-Brad points to the newsboy.

I cock my head.

"Does that surprise you?" Cooper-Brad says.

"Some. You haven't exactly shied away from taking risks."

"Out of desperation. None of this is my usual scene. I won't even go to a farmer's market on a Saturday—too many people."

"And no bathroom," I say.

"Porta-potties are for the Coachella crowd." He pauses. "Did I say that right?"

"I think so. Yet, I'll admit to still not being entirely sure what that is."

"Same."

Hartley might know, considering the red roots of her hair. Together, we watch as Fiona settles Hartley in front of the laptop and dabs the end of her nose with bright red blush.

"How about you?" he says.

The profound resignation in Hartley's eyes slows my response. "Me what?"

"You? Would you have come here? Been a fashionable woman flouting conventional standards of behavior? Ah, of course you would have. You are confidence personified."

This rankles me. His automatic assumption does a disservice to all I've gone through to become the person I am today. A person able to do this. (Granted "this" particular "this" might not be the achievement to tout, but still.)

My posture stiffens. "Then perhaps you need to deepen your character studies."

He folds his arms across his chest, and the compass rose

tattoo that speaks to a life integrated with the sea faces me. His lips part, but he hesitates, perhaps unsure why his sudden flippancy offended when all that's come before didn't. "You're right," he finally says. "Perhaps I can pick your brain on that when all this is over?"

This is in lieu of an actual apology and magnitudes more meaningful to me. That he knows or intuited it suggests he's not so lacking in the character development department, after all.

He rakes his hand through his curls. "And see—this right here—this is why I would have only come here as the newsboy. I feel a kinship with him. Despite my Puritan roots, or perhaps because of them, my family wasn't flush. I had an actual paper route, bike, messenger bag, tiny little bell. But more importantly, I would have never come otherwise because I'd have swallowed my own tongue trying to talk to a girl. Something I outgrew. Mostly."

There's nothing about him to suggest a shyness, evidence that his present doesn't necessarily reflect his past either.

He lowers his head toward me, one of those curls dusting his eyes, and the expectation is now on me to share, to explain what would have stopped a 1920s version of me from slipping into a fringed flapper dress and painting my lips candy cane red.

My inclination to share matches that of a toddler deep in the terrible twos. And yet, it's that lingering look of defeat on Hartley's face that makes me say, "I would have wanted to be here, but I would have figured that no one here felt the same."

Cooper-Brad doesn't say anything. He simply tucks his chin, as if he understands. And there it is—the thing that truly bonds every author. We may not have all been tortured, but we've been wounded. And unlike the rest of the population, for some reason, we feel the need to sort through those wounds by sharing them with the world—even if sometimes they're masked by alternate dimensions and accompanied by killer manatees.

Before us, Fiona adds a tissue to the crumpled pile in front of Hartley, already high enough to be in the camera frame. Earlier, Fiona must have had Hartley change into the orange Bears sweatshirt and red beanie I bought on the street. The knockoff Burberry scarf is draped across her shoulders like a shawl. Better way to sell her "flu," and I have to admit, Hartley does look miserable. Scared too, understandably. But perhaps not only because of the copious amount of nuts—this is her first true Romance US panel, which also happens to be the convention's featured event. Last night's impromptu panel had an eighth of the audience who will be in attendance this afternoon. To be included on the convention's flagship panel, surrounded by the best authors in the genre, moderated by a mega movie star, is a big deal for anyone. (Truth be told, even I'm a little nervous— though that could be more from the whole masterminding a kidnapping thing.)

My phone lights up with a text from Lacey.

Your video lighting was terrible, but Maddie fixed it. Otherwise, delighted to discover you *have* been listening to me. Stellar work, Sofie. Your Instagram is an explosion of hearts and "death to parrot" comments. Keep. It. Going.

I look at Hartley, who has no idea the tide is now trending in favor of #SweetSofie.

Questions live in Cooper-Brad's sympathetic eyes, but I push forward. I'm no longer in the past. That tide can't change. I have to work with what I have in the present, and right now that means moving ahead with our plan. I can't let Hartley drag me down into the muck.

"#WildeWestShowdown," I say, causing Hartley to direct her attention to me. "That's what they're calling it."

Cooper-Brad whispers, "What are you doing?"

I shush him and say to Hartley, "They're expecting fireworks."

"Guns blazing," she says. "So as not to mix metaphors."

What a good tutor AI must be. "But we won't do it on the panel. We won't feed the trolls. I won't so long as, unlike last time, you don't. If you do, you won't only have me on the other side, you'll have every person on that panel coming after you as well." *I hope.* "This is bigger than just me." *So Rosie says.* "You may not have felt that yet." *Because they're being petty.* "But you will. We stay professional." *Technically,* start *being professional, but all the same.*

Her gaze is firm. "Fine."

"Good." I holster a fake gun and have perhaps never felt so awkward in my life. But ensuring she doesn't try to rile me up means the audience will hopefully continue to rally behind me and bookstore owners will have no reason to cancel any future appearances.

Fiona and Grace begin arguing about which fake background to use: beach or desert or space ship.

"Desert," Hartley huffs. "Obviously. I mean, Wild West?"

She's got a decent sense of humor. You wouldn't know by looking at her, at least in those sad prairie dresses.

I beckon Cooper-Brad closer and lower my voice. "Stage yourself by that laptop. Any hint of her revealing anything, you shut it. Make sure she sticks to her script. She's sick, highly contagious, flu, COVID, maybe the plague."

"Passerfly fever?"

I attempt to cover my surprise. "You got that far?"

"Past it. I'm in the second book. But Jocelyn choosing herself at the end of book one? Leaving Torrence at the altar and Callum still in the medical bay having fever hallucinations? A gamble."

"One that paid off."

"It did make me dive into book two."

"Risks were easy then. No one cared except for me."

"And now everyone cares. But you're still taking risks. Vance? You didn't have to do that."

"Actually, I did. It was always his destiny. He was brought into the world because Jocelyn wasn't able to fulfill her own fate. She didn't have the strength. Mothering Vance gives her something to live for."

"And die for."

"Exactly. She became stronger than she could have ever imagined. Vance served his purpose. But he was also holding her back. Her love for him meant she would never put him or any of them in danger the way she must if she were to prevail. She needed to lose him in order to save the world. Vance made the ultimate sacrifice so Jocelyn could do the same."

"And he's really dead? Guts of steel to kill off a little boy."

"Right." I give a wry smile.

"Wait, is he not dead?" Cooper-Brad tugs at a tuft of hair.

"You need to read for yourself."

"But that's eight and a half books away."

I tip my head toward Hartley. "The benefit of being a baby-sitter. Now if you'll excuse me, I have to go try to be beautiful on the inside."

"Shouldn't be too hard, considering the outside."

SLOW BURN

THE ELEVATOR DOORS CLOSE, AND I FLOP AGAINST THE BACK WALL.
"Oh, okay, cool."

That's what I said. The words fumbled out before I could stop them. This is exactly why I prefer to live in the worlds in my head. Real life offers zero opportunity for revision.

Cooper-Brad was being Cooper-Brad. Trying to manipulate me. Angry static buzzes inside my head because despite how very much I see right through him, I let him see a piece of me. Revealed a little of my own truth. This is what getting close to people does: it gives them ammunition. It'll be used against me if he gets the chance. He's doing this because it's an adrenaline shot to his career. And maybe a little because he's a writer and understands what it would feel like to have his work stolen. Nothing more. Which is good. Great. I don't need more.

I dig out my phone and open my favorites. Blaire, Lacey, my carpal tunnel massage therapist, my chiropractor, my local wine store, Roxanne, Mom, Dad. In that order.

The elevator opens onto the fifth floor. I casually saunter out, wait for the doors to close, then immediately press the button to go down. The time this will take is worth the risk of not being seen coming up from the basement.

As I step into the next elevator, I scan Lacey's most recent text, listing five more ways to keep #SweetSofie going. But the best way to do that is to get on stage and put a stop to *Love and Lawlessness* before it becomes anything more than a novelty.

With a soft ding, I arrive at the ballroom floor. As my ballet flats burn a hole in the carpet, I hike my tote higher on my shoulder and double-check my messages. Nothing new from Blaire. Logically I know that if she'd made progress on reclaiming the keynote she'd have been in touch. But still, a part of me needs to hear her voice, maybe even hear her give a positive spin on the situation, so I tap her name and call. It goes straight to voicemail. I hang up without leaving a message because there's nothing I can say that won't make her feel worse than she likely already does. Yet the silence speaks volumes, and the voice in my head whispers one thing and one thing only: Max Donner.

If I said yes, this could all end now. As Hartley's agent, Max could use his leverage over her to stop her from issuing that absurd call to action, here or anywhere. She wants success. She wouldn't risk losing Max for some publicity stunt. Besides, she wouldn't even need that stunt with Max behind her. We could release her, let her join me on stage for the keynote (part of it, an introduction, maybe?), perhaps even spin it so I came to her rescue with some mega-strength cough syrup or all-natural echinacea-elderberry-ginger-hemp remedy. Help me attract some of the Goop crowd. But achieving all of that comes at a cost: Blaire.

I lengthen my stride, the Advil having done its job and dulled my foot pain. Blaire has always believed in me. The same hasn't necessarily been true in return. I've questioned her confidence—not in me but in herself. In her own power as a negotiator, in her restraint in making demands other agents would make in a heartbeat, in putting courtesy and respect above all else. Maybe that's fine for some authors. But publishing doesn't know what it wants until you tell it what it wants. And then you make it think it came up with the idea in the first place. That's never been Blaire.

She's not out there promising to have the convention director's car hand-washed or threatening to have her authors boycott this event for eternity like Lacey's surely doing. I shouldn't be surprised that she's still playing the good cop. But what if this is something that can only be fixed by a bad cop?

"Sofie," Rosie says as I enter the green room. "We were just talking about you."

I tug on my ear. "And here I thought I was coming down with an ear infection."

Rosie laughs heartily and the other Beautiful on the Inside panelists, which include Tara Kara and Lake Nolan, appear confused. They've never really seen us (mainly me) engage in this kind of lighthearted banter before.

Kara finishes her can of sparkling water—not something I would have advised, unless she wants to learn the dangers of overhydrating before a panel the hard way.

"Your video wasn't bad," Kara says.

"Not bad?" Tara says with the enthusiasm of a cocker spaniel on speed. She pumps a hand in the air, miming something I can't quite make out until she adds, "Nailed it! Woot! Woot!"

The disdain on Lake Nolan's face is impressive, which is saying something coming from me. Born in a small town in South Carolina where she still lives, Lake is a warhorse in this industry. Her books covered my nightstand as a kid. They were the first romance books I ever read, starting at way too young of an age. But my mom read Lake Nolan, so I wanted to read Lake Nolan.

Tara checks her teeth in the mirror beside the coatrack.

"With any luck, it starts trending and the keynote falls right back in your lap!"

Lake doesn't look up from her knitting. "What happened to Sofie's keynote?"

"Lake! Where have you been!" Tara cries. "It's all over the socials. They're pulling it and giving it to Hartley West. Because of the whole . . ." Tara now flings her hand out in front of her, presumably imitating me sweeping the bestsellers off the table in Harbor Books. "Ten bucks says Riley asks her about it on the panel."

Christ, she probably will.

"I remain blissfully ignorant of all of this." Lake's metal knitting needles scrape against one another until she finishes her row. "Sure as rain and my children fighting over my will at my funeral, I know you kids don't want to hear what an old lady has to say, but—"

"Kids?" Kara says. "Sofie's nearly sixty!"

I grind my teeth, knowing if I get through this, I'm definitely going to need that mouthguard my dentist has been trying to force on me for years. "I'm forty-nine."

"Really?" Tara Kara say at the same time.

Rosie stands beside me. "I'm fifty-three."

Huh. I make a mental note to ask Rosie for her brand of skin cream.

"Infants, you all are," Lake says. "Still, even with your spry metabolisms and robust bone densities, I wouldn't want to be young now. The internet's good for one thing and one thing only: Ina Garten recipes. Cauliflower toast, trust me."

"No disrespect, Lake," Kara says, "but not understanding how something works doesn't make it inherently bad."

"Who said I don't understand it? Twitter, Instagram, even TikTok. I understand them all, better than you."

"Sure," Kara says, flippantly.

"Here, answer me this," Lake says. "Any idea why I'm still around?"

"Cryogenics," Kara says.

"Ooh, I was going with hologram," Tara says.

They high-five, and a piece of my soul dies. The more creative answer would have been an ancient publishing contract that has no term limits like the Supreme Court.

Lake simply says, "Typewriters. I have never written on anything but an old clickety-clack."

Kara screws up her face. "Not very environmentally friendly. All that paper."

Tara taps her chin. "But no electricity. Probably comes out even."

Lake picks up her knitting, which is either a tan heart or a set of breasts. "Never mind, then."

Rosie catches my eye. We only have a few minutes before the panel, and we need to circle up on Hartley. And yet neither of us wants to see Lake's feelings hurt. If I opened the door for most of these authors, there's no denying that Lake opened it for me. I give Rosie a nod and a subtle thumbs-up to indicate we are solid, or as solid as one can be in a kidnapping.

"Tell me," I say, crossing the room to sit at the table with Lake.

Lake glances at me over her reading glasses. "Tell you what?"

"Typewriters. Why are they the reason you're here."

Her knitting needles scrape faster. "I don't need your sympathy."

"Sympathy? Have you met me?"

She laughs. "Dammit, girl, you made me slip a stitch." She wiggles the point of her needle into the row below, and like a magician, extracts a single thread of yarn that she weaves back into place. "You really want to know?"

"We all do," Rosie says, with sincerity, claiming the chair beside me. "Please, Lake, you truly are an inspiration. I learned what *gyrating* meant from your books."

"Buttering me up like a slice of whole wheat, aren't you?"

"I'm serious," Rosie says. "My mom tucked your books under her mattress after she finished them. It wasn't until I was thirty with my first novel published that I confessed to sneaking in and stealing them."

I don't realize I'm smiling until Lake says, "You too?"

Rosie turns to me.

"Same on *gyrating*," I say. "And *engorged*."

"Oh, yes, that too." Rosie laughs. "And how is it that I'm suddenly as self-conscious as I was at thirteen?"

Lake lights up. "Sofie, were you a thief too?"

I shake my head. "My mom just started handing me the longest books we had in the house. She got tired of taking me to the library twice a week."

"Three here," Rosie says.

"First step in becoming a writer," Lake says. "You two should be on a poster."

I watch Rosie's face shift.

We were on a poster once. At that event where no one came. The bookstore had gone all out. They asked if we wanted to take it, and I said no, I hadn't wanted a reminder.

"So, clickety-clack?" Kara says, and I refocus on Lake.

Lake huffs but sets down her knitting needles. "One word: *precision*. Something you kids don't even think about. You strike those little buttons and vomit onto the page without taking the time to think through what you want to say. You write and delete and write and delete and spend so much time rewriting that you could be spending writing something new. If only you slowed down and put some brainpower into it." She taps her temple. "The mantra I live by: I write while standing up and I type while sitting down."

"Well," Rosie says. "Fifty books over forty years. You must be onto something."

"And all without any *socials*." Lake clucks her tongue. "Only encourages the fast fingers. Fire off a tweet you don't like? Delete it. An Instagram post with a typo? Click *edit*."

Kara's eyebrows lift in surprise.

"Told you I understand it," Lake says. "Understand it enough to know it's toxic. Why do you think you're all at odds? Maybe because you can't keep your damn eyes on your own damn paper? And how could you, what with this one gushing about this deal at auction and that one flashing a pretty picture announcing their fifteen-city tour. No offense," she says to me.

I shrug. Technically, Lacey posted it, not me.

"You all are inundated with each other's successes. You all hide your failures. This is a business where someone's always at the top. Ergo, someone has to be at the bottom. No one wants to be at the bottom. Me included. But in my day, we didn't really know how anyone else was doing—or how they appeared to be doing. We met at these events and dressed up like maidens and queens and borrowed each other's corsets and drank too much whiskey and skinny-dipped in the pool at midnight. We had fun. All these best-of-this and best-of-that lists and this many followers and that many likes can make you dizzy. You only win when others lose, and that's not a world I want any part of. And so . . . clickety-clack."

Lake slides her knitting needles between her fingers and picks up where she left off. Tara pulls out a lipstick, and Kara retrieves another sparkling water, both trying not to admit the loud ring of truth in Lake's words. Rosie looks at me and we hold each other's gaze. We haven't been doing this as long as Lake, but we've seen the changes. We've been part of the changes. Or at least I have. Authors pulling at one another like pieces of a Jenga, not wanting to be the one to fall. Maybe Lake's right. Maybe we are all just little shits out to prove we're better than someone else.

I look more closely at Lake's knitting. "What is that you're making, if you don't mind me asking?"

She holds up the swathe of knitted yarn that I now see are two ball-shaped sacks. "Modeled after my husband of forty-five years. Wrinkles are the hardest part to get right."

I laugh, picturing Lacey trying to turn this into swag. "You're a lucky woman."

"That I am."

Kara cracks open her water as she heads toward us. "Hey, Sofie," she says, looking at her phone. "Aren't you heading to St. Louis after this?"

Lacey texts me my travel information the morning of. I can't keep every real-life detail and every fictional one in my head at the same time. "Maybe?"

"Love Me Some Books? Cutest store."

The shelves are heart-shaped. The register a pair of red lips. A mural of romance heroines adorns the back wall. Lacey loves it for Instagram. Maybe I should tell Roxanne to check it out. "Sounds right. Why?"

"Oh, nothing." But she passes her phone to Tara.

"Hand it over," I say. She hesitates and I add, "And a tip for you: bathroom, now, or you'll regret it."

Kara opens her mouth for some quip, but Tara takes her phone and says, "She's right. Go." As Kara hurries to the bathroom, Tara sets the device in my hand. Her eyes linger on the dark sunspots on my skin as if she's making a mental note to wear more sunscreen. "Remember what they say about the messenger."

The letters on the screen are as tiny as a flea. I pinch my fingers across the glass to zoom in. It's an email from Tara Kara's publicist asking if they might be able to fill in last minute at an event at Love Me Some Books after the convention. There's no mention of me. That it's my event. That they'd be taking my place.

My tour. Lacey's tour. One we built together after years of making contacts and currying favor with booksellers and showing them how many fans my events could draw. It *is* being "tweaked." If Blaire thinks she can sell me being replaced as simply a "tweak," she has no business being my agent.

My heart drums in my ears as I set Kara's phone on the table. Heat flushes my body like a feral hot flash. Social media did this. Social media will undo this. Lacey said to kill it. To smother the internet trolls. I am #SweetSofie. And I am ready to pick up a goddamned metaphorical pillow.

The door to the green room opens, and Clarice calls us to the panel. She sweeps her eyes around the room, "Lake? Is that?"

"A scrotum, you betcha." Lake nudges my shoulder. "This one's not the only one that brings a little life to this party."

I give my #SweetSofie smile.

Clarice bites her bottom lip. "Well, let's not bring that particular party to the panel? The drama here is matching that of your books."

Tara squeals. "Drama, what drama?"

Lake shakes her head.

The tablet in Clarice's hands shakes as she says, "Riley Moore's airport pickup didn't show. Max Donner, on the other hand, just arrived at the hotel unannounced and is demanding a suite. We're nearly sold out of Sofie's books. And—" she sucks in a breath "—Hartley West is missing."

FRIENDS TO ENEMIES

NEARLY SOLD OUT OF MY BOOKS. IF THE SAME HAPPENS ON MY tour, I'd hit the list—the top half. Balance would be restored. The full tour must proceed as is, with all the press coverage and bookstore Q&As and fans who will see me in person and see that I am still me, with everything to give for this book and all the ones to come.

"Sofie, did you hear me?" Rosie tugs on my arm.

"Yes."

"And?"

"Well, what I meant is that I heard you ask if I heard you."

Rosie gives a forced smile, letting Lake and Tara Kara proceed to the auditorium ahead of us. She pulls me aside. "Missing? They must know she's not in her room."

"How would they know that? That's not what Clarice said."

"It is. You weren't listening. They were worried, ostensibly about her well-being, but also about the tech for her to Zoom in. So they sent someone to check her equipment, bring her a mic, that sort of thing. They had hotel management open the door. The place was trashed."

"Did someone break in?"

"No, we *let* someone in." I give her a quizzical look, and she says, "Fiona? To get the laptop? We should have sent Grace. Fiona has always been a snoop. And proud of it. After staying at my house a couple of years ago, I found little notes from her in every nook and cranny. My medicine cabinet. My shoe closet. Even my vibrator drawer."

The fact that they socialize outside of events shouldn't surprise me. Or make me feel the way it's making me feel. "You were all there when I outlined that part of the plan. Nobody said anything. I didn't know."

"You not knowing is the root cause of everything, isn't it?"

"Fiona's the one who turned our simple plan into an episode of *CSI*. This isn't about me."

"Everything's about you, Sofie!" She bursts like a dam unable to withhold the pressure anymore, putting me on the defensive.

"Only because it's my work she's copying. It's my career on the proverbial chopping block. You're the one who said it affects us all."

"I don't just mean this. Everything Lake was saying in there, don't you see? You've always made it all about you. From before you were you and I was me. When no one had read our books and being struck by lightning was more likely than having a bestseller. That day when no one showed up to our signing, you acted like it only happened to you. But it happened to me too, and I have the poster to prove it."

"You took the poster?"

"I wanted to remember the moment I swore I would never treat another person the way you treated me."

"But I didn't do anything."

"Exactly. And that includes being a friend."

"But I didn't need a friend."

"What if I did?"

Her words hit me like a one-star review grumbling about the level of "fantasy" and "romance" in a book billed as such. Because Rosie was Rosie Gardens—confident and self-assured even then, before she was *Rosie Gardens*. I didn't think about her needing a friend that night because I had no reason to think she was anything like me.

She shakes her head. "You are your own moon and your own sun and you don't revolve around anything but yourself."

"Then why are you helping me?"

"Because I don't hold grudges. Because we are both here because of Lake Nolan, and we owe it to her and our fellow authors and everyone else who cares about what we do to stop this. Because I believe what we do matters, and we have an infinitesimally small window to prove that. And because Blaire is my friend. And so loyal to you that when my agent retired and I reached out to her for representation, she declined. She wouldn't risk the conflict of interest even though the commission could have bought her a small island. When she told me about the bonus you gave her after Max Donner tried to poach you, she had tears in her eyes."

I shuffle my feet.

Rosie shakes her head. "Look, I like you, Sofie. We could have been actual friends if your ego didn't make you the most grotesquely judgmental person I've ever met. I don't have Grace's degree in psychology, but I've been creating character wounds and wants for nearly half my life. I understand you're coming from a place of hurt. It's all over your books. I know you believe that barreling through life like a Whac-A-Mole keeps you safe. But we aren't out to hurt you. Me, Grace,

Fiona—we never have been. We're here doing this with you. We're giving you a chance, and maybe it's time you do the same. Otherwise—" she juts her chin at my Fictional People Are My People shirt "—you won't just live by that, you'll die by it too."

Rosie turns on her heels and strides toward the auditorium. I trail behind, listening as she calls Grace and explains that we have to stave off the filing of a missing person's report, giving instructions to relay to Hartley.

At the entrance to the auditorium, I squeeze my eyes shut, my head spinning from Rosie being hurt all those years ago and her fictional-people-will-be-my-only-people threat right now. But Blaire isn't fictional. Blaire has been there for me. Her lack of response isn't because she no longer supports me. She hasn't responded because she wants to be in touch when she has good news. But there is no good news. She hasn't found a solution. Or pushed hard enough for one. Not because she doesn't care, but because it's not who she is. It's not the power she has. Unlike Max Donner.

I pause and take out my phone. Blaire's happy, supportive face stares up at me from her contact photo. This time I don't bother to tap it. Maybe this is it. Maybe this is as far as we can go together.

The thought hammers my heart and an overall sense of frustration seizes my brain. This is my turf, where I feel most like myself, and Hartley and Rosie and all of them are making me sweat so much that if I were attached to a rain barrel I could fill it with ease. No more. I smooth the front of my shirt, feel my heart beating beneath it, and head high, take my seat.

Hartley's ruddy face looms above us on a gigantic screen—counterproductive to our goal of minimizing her presence. But the threat of nut particles swirling in the air seems to be working. She's just finished calming a frantic Clarice. Per Rosie's instructions, Hartley said she switched hotels. Her suite's windows let in too much light, and she was having trouble sleeping. She promised she was feeling well enough to participate in the panel. She even slugged some of the cough syrup that Fiona and Grace had staged before her as a prop. Together, they excel in world-building.

Despite Hartley repeating Rosie's instructions nearly verbatim, I feel like I'm on a tightrope strung between skyscrapers as we wait for Riley Moore. Clarice had to send an Uber from her own account. Apparently, Riley Moore has never downloaded the app.

I balance on the edge of the seat, my toes skimming the floor. Tension as thick as coastal fog has replaced the momentary lightness of the green room. Rosie won't look at me.

Grotesquely judgmental.

Honestly, hasn't she just done what she's accusing me of? So what if I'm not the group mani-pedi type. If I were, I wouldn't have five bestsellers to my name, a sixth on the way, and Riley Moore's interest piqued.

Except Rosie has just as many bestsellers and still finds time to host slumber parties for her author friends.

I roll my neck. Writers have two highly annoying traits: correcting everyone's grammar and fancying themselves armchair psychologists. The former is ingrained, the latter learned. To create a character who lives and breathes despite being made of ink and dried pulp requires a compelling backstory. Their hopes, dreams, fears, wants, needs, and most importantly, their motivations for it all.

Rosie doesn't have to psychoanalyze me. I know who I am. And I know why.

While I refuse to give Sandy with a *y* and Sandi with an *i* full credit, I did shy away from making friends, letting my introverted self dominate, becoming more and more the polar opposite of my extroverted parents, who lived and breathed "the more the merrier." Our house was so full on birthdays and Thanksgivings and random Tuesdays that I wasn't missed. I never had reason to change. I could stay in my room, head in a book, and escape to a world full of characters who I knew weren't friends but who still kept me company. It's not that I didn't want friends, but my tendency toward "all or nothing" that's served me well in my career didn't translate into understanding how to be a good friend. I was either too clingy or not clingy enough. I shared too many secrets or too few. I told too many secrets or too few. I remember wishing my parents had socialized me when I was little the way they did our poodle.

I was a quirky only child who wrote my own plays and acted them out alone. The one time my parents coaxed me into performing in front of a small group of their friends, I threw up for so long that I disturbed the acid in my stomach and had to eat only fermented foods—sauerkraut and pickles—for weeks to restore it.

Needless to say, I was never part of any "in crowd." I had a few friends here and there, always the misfits, and I was too self-conscious to let go of the judgment of others and accept them for who they were—and myself for who I was. So I grew up an awkward, lonely kid who became a less awkward, less lonely teenager who found the love of her life at a summer job restocking shelves at the library. He was into *The Lord of the Rings* and *Star Wars*, and we met when he used his lightsaber to help him retrieve a Latin dictionary from the top of the references shelf and knocked the whole thing over.

He went to a different school, one where no one knew I didn't fit in. His friends became my friends, and we spent our last two years of high school pretending we were Han and Leia, not knowing the characters we imagined ourselves to be would get a future and a family, albeit troubled, in stories and movies to come. Still, they got more than we did. My Han died in a car accident our junior year of college. We were still together. We thought we always would be.

After, I was both more and less awkward, profoundly lonely at times, but something had opened—a desire not to be, even if that was through the characters I created. My Han taught me what I needed to know to write the books that have given me this career: Love. Lust. Desire. Yearning. Hope. And heartbreak.

The pounding of footsteps against the wooden platform draws my attention. Riley Moore scurries across the stage in a pair of tall UGG boots. She's so California that the air actually warms as she claims the moderator's chair from a relieved-looking Clarice.

"Oh, hey, hey, all you beautiful people. On the inside and the outside!" Riley claps, spinning toward the auditorium, which is empty. Her face resets. "Um, this is . . . unusual. Are you sure you used my name in the description?"

Clarice scurries forward. "We haven't opened the doors yet."

"Stellar. If we have time, get me a glass of ice and a splash of apple cider vinegar with the mother."

Clarice's brow crinkles. "Not sure what that is . . . but we can send someone?"

"Forget it." Riley sighs and slugs something from a metal bottle dangling from her YSL hobo bag. She faces the panel and smiles as Clarice introduces us. When Clarice gets to Rosie, Riley says, "Hey, hey, girl! One of my few double picks for a Riley Read."

Rosie raises an eyebrow. "What can I say, you have excellent taste."

Riley tosses her head back and laughs a hearty laugh that's probably fake but I can't tell. She is a very good actress. She drags her hair over one shoulder, her usual bleached blonde a couple of shades darker. And longer—her hair seems longer than it was in her post announcing the latest Riley Read.

(Which, yes, I watched despite how green with jealousy it made me.)

When Clarice introduces me, Riley saunters across the stage and extends her hand. I try to sit up straighter, and my goodness, this is what "presence" feels like. I accept her hand, noticing the bracelet that hugs her wrist, a series of interlocking figure eights, the symbol for infinity. Jocelyn wears the exact same one.

"I had it custom-made," Riley whispers, fluttering her long lashes, drawing attention to the colored contacts she's wearing that have turned her eyes a light blue-gray. "Let's talk after?"

I nod, and all the puzzle pieces click together. Riley's hair, her eyes, the replica bracelet, shaking only my hand . . . Her interest is more than piqued. She wants to play Jocelyn, and my word, she should play Jocelyn. She *has to* play Jocelyn.

The door to the auditorium opens, and I quickly slip on my event smile. But it's not the audience. It's Max Donner. He slithers in, long sandy brown hair, feathered over his ears, five-hundred-dollar distressed jeans, custom-made blazer with the contracts of stolen souls peeking out like a pocket square. He's a Hollywood agent trolling in the literary waters and entirely comfortable in the mud. Prefers it.

Tara Kara whisper to each other. He's their agent. They must think he's here for them.

Riley waves to him, and he meets my gaze, pointing to himself, claiming responsibility for bringing her here, as he takes a seat up front. I slide my phone out of my pocket and text Blaire as a final attempt.

Just met Riley Moore. I think she might have interest on the film/TV side. Have you heard anything?

I hold my phone, waiting for a reply that doesn't come. Blaire has absolutely no idea. Unlike Max.

He's a snake. As crooked as this arthritic hump makes my finger. And yet Max Donner has pull. Max Donner has power. Max Donner can use them both to put me back where I deserve to be.

Guilt weighs down my fingers as I pull up my last text chain with Max.

Me: Riley Moore. You actually got her to come here?

Evil Spawn: Need any more proof of my prowess?

Me: Keep your dick in your pants, Donner.

I hesitate, staring at his smug face, knowing this is the moment when everything changes. One way or another. Staying with Blaire doesn't equal status quo, not with Hartley to contend with. Blaire represents the past, but there's no going back.

Me: Three conditions.

Me: Make that four.

Evil Spawn: I don't date clients, sorry #SweetSofie.

I wish for a middle-finger emoji.

Me: 1. Keynote is mine and mine alone. 2. Tour is rock-solid. 3. Hartley West apologizes for using AI. 4. Riley Moore plays Jocelyn. I want to see a signed contract in a week.

Evil Spawn: Keynote, tour? On it.

Me: That's only two.

In his seat across from the stage, Max grins, and an email notification flashes on my phone. I tap it open and skim. It's an offer from Riley's producer husband. Dated this morning.

My heart thrums at the same time as it falls to pieces.

Me: And Hartley?

Evil Spawn: I'll do my best.

Me: Best isn't good enough.

This is Blaire. I'm doing this to *Blaire*. A knife slices my veins.

Evil Spawn: I can, but only if I represent her.

Hartley West and I will be represented by the same agent. Equals. A heavy dose of salt in the wound.

Me: I'm in. Don't fuck this up, Donner.

Heat burns the backs of my eyes as Donner sends a barrage of celebratory emoji. I click off the screen and pocket my phone.

This is business. Blaire will understand. She'll be happy for me. I mean, I didn't stop her from signing Rosie. (But you would have.)

Christ, I suddenly wish I were back in Palladium or tumbling down Vance's black hole—anywhere but here. Where I've just betrayed one of the only true friends I have. Make that *had*.

DAMSEL IN DISTRESS

RILEY MOORE MANAGES TO BE THE CENTER OF ATTENTION AND yet not steal the show. She wears the concentrated face of a brain surgeon as Lake describes the blocking she and her husband do to ensure her sex scenes are true to life.

"Of the many things I'm blessed with, flexibility is at the tippy top," Lake says. "If I can't do it, my readers can't do it, so damn straight my characters won't do it."

"Ooh, the things we artists get to call *research!*" Riley winks, inciting raucous applause. She waits for it to die down before turning serious. "I truly love that. Authenticity is the foundation of all extraordinary art."

Riley doesn't direct this to the packed auditorium. Instead, she fixes her gaze on the screen. She leaves the statement hanging. So far, Hartley has answered each question she's been asked with brevity, like she can't wait for this to be over. There's been no mention of #WildeWestShowdown or AI or anything that might incite a shootout. My nerves had begun to settle, thinking we might actually pull this off. Now, with the way

Riley's fixated on the screen, it's like I'm three car lengths back, watching as the brake lights flash up ahead, with no time to stop what's coming.

"Hartley?" Riley's tone is soft but commanding. "Would you care to weigh in?"

Hartley's eyes drift, presumably to Fiona or Grace or Cooper-Brad who are likely wielding a pair of scissors. Hartley wipes her nose with a crumpled tissue. "I'm sorry. My ears are clogged. I'm not sure I heard the question?"

Riley takes this as a challenge, one she greedily accepts. "What do you think is the key to creating extraordinary art?"

Hartley tugs on the folded cuff of the beanie on her head. "A lot of time and hard work and attention to detail."

The response is not just short but tragically trite. Maybe this is more than just Hartley being under duress. At both Harbor Books and the meet-and-greet panel, Hartley maintained control over the questions. She'd had time to prepare. She'd had time to ask AI to write her responses. Here, she's on her own, and it shows.

I sit up straighter, already feeling the heat of her crashing and burning.

Riley presses, "Certainly, but is it actually *your* attention to detail or Sofie Wilde's? Stealing itself has been called an art form, but do we really consider the thieves who pilfered pieces valued at more than five hundred million dollars from the Isabella Stewart Gardner Museum to be artists? You'll be able to decide for yourselves when Netflix drops my new series next month." Self-promotion ingrained in us all. "I play a Harvard art professor. Emphasis on *play*. I don't pretend to be something I'm not." Riley looks at Hartley expectantly.

"Is there a question?" Hartley says. "Because if not, I have one. I was wondering how Tara Kara decided to make their vampires goth instead of punk rock or emo or—"

Tara or Kara clears their throat, but neither speaks. We are all waiting for Riley's next move.

She crosses her long legs, revealing the red soles of her expensive heels, which she changed into before the audience flooded through the doors. "We'll get there," Riley says, "but let's live here a little longer. I find it fascinating." She spins her head to the audience. "We all do. I mean, this is a first."

"That we know of," Hartley says under her breath as if it just slipped out, but I've seen Hartley in action before. My hackles rise.

"Excellent point," Riley says. "Half the books at this convention might have been written by AI."

Murmurs from the audience.

"One hundred percent might be next year," Riley continues, and the murmuring grows into whispers and a few "noes" and a couple of variations on "ridiculous."

Riley glides off her stool and saunters to the edge of the stage. "I'm sorry, are we taking issue with that?"

"Of course!" someone shouts.

A few woots in support. Several wave aquamarine scarves above their heads.

Riley places her palm on her chest. "Excuse me if I'm a little confused. I only just arrived at the convention, but my understanding is that Ms. West's books have been flying off the shelves. Her signing lines are as long as anyone's. Am I mistaken?" An eyebrow ticks up as she looks to a terrified Clarice, who shakes her head off-stage.

I've never met Riley Moore before. She's never chosen one of my books for her book club. And yet, she's defending me. I need to believe it's because of Max. So I do.

Riley's heels click as she casually strolls across the stage. "It appears as though I'm not mistaken. Hartley West is being embraced by readers inside and outside this convention center. For something to take hold, it requires a tipping point. This is it." She points the microphone at the audience. "You, lovies, are it."

A woman in the front row stands. "Ms. Moore?"

"Well, yes, hey, hey, lovie."

The woman blushes. "First, I adored you in that movie where you played the first female dentist! My goodness, how you made cavities sexy."

Riley nods appreciatively. "Real-life inspiration is a gold mine. Lucy Hobbs Taylor made it easy."

"Plus, all that leaning over your patients." The woman curves her bosom forward. "Anyway, with all this, I've been following online, but I'm honestly wondering what all the fuss is about. I read books for the books they are, generally not for the authors. Half the time, I don't know who wrote what and a month later, if I knew, I certainly don't anymore. Isn't this what we're supposed to be doing these days? Being more inclusive?"

Rosie draws her microphone closer. "A concept we should be discussing, but inclusivity refers to those who have not had equal access to resources or opportunities. Those being humans."

The woman shrugs. "Does it matter?"

"Yes," Rosie says firmly. "It does."

From off-stage, Clarice whispers, "Goth vampires, Ms. Moore."

Riley hears Clarice, holding up a single finger in acknowledgment. "Let's run with this a sec. Does it matter? Does it matter where your art comes from? Does it matter if, say, I play Lucy Hobbs Taylor or if an animated version of me plays her?"

Tara clears her throat. "Like when they mapped your body so you could play Rapunzel?"

"Motion capture, yes," Riley says. "That's how we did the animated version of Rapunzel. Even though it wasn't live-action, they wanted to be able to say *starring* Riley Moore. But what if they didn't care about having my name attached? Right now, actors are being paid to have their likenesses captured. They're signing away the rights to how those likenesses will be used. They become AI, able to be adjusted and distorted to play any character that can be dreamed up. Why, someday, you'll be able to munch away on kale chips, call up *Titanic*, and plonk your face where Leo's or Kate's once were. Is it still *Titanic* then? Does it matter?"

"So this is it?" Hartley's voice descends from above. "You're afraid of losing your job? For the first time, white-collar workers are in danger of being replaced, and the world is going to stop and take the time to engage in an intellectual debate?"

Tara Kara remain still, Lake seems completely out of her comfort zone, and I cannot engage.

Rosie is the one to say in a measured tone, "This is a varied and complex issue with tentacles that extend from copyright and financial compensation to the very real dangers of bias and disinformation to what it means to be a member of our society. But I believe it starts here. With us. Because if humanity is exhibited anywhere, it is here. In art."

Riley plants her hands on her hips. "Sofie Wilde is on the front lines, but we can't let her stand there alone."

I'm fascinated by Riley, the whole room is. It's almost like we've forgotten Hartley's face is even on that big screen above us. Until a thump echoes through the audio system, and I look up to see Hartley's hand flat on the table in front of her. She drags her chair forward.

"Seems we're still without an actual question from our moderator," Hartley says. "If the panel is over, then—"

"You want a question?" Riley says. "Don't you care about art?"

"I wouldn't be here if I didn't."

"But you're only here because of Sofie Wilde."

"And Sofie Wilde is only here because of Lake Nolan and Diana Gabaldon and Nora Roberts and Danielle Steele and Charlotte Brontë and Jane Austen and all the way back to Shakespeare and Homer."

"It's not the same."

"But it is. We're all building on what's come before. The only thing that's changed is the technology."

"The technology that allows you to actually not create anything."

"Bullshit." Hartley rips off the red beanie, and the audience gasps. She's no longer scared. She's pissed.

I power through to maintain my polite half smile despite the confetti cannons exploding behind my eyes.

Hartley steadies herself with a deep breath. "I apologize. My current situation has me on edge." Her eyes float to the side—surely to Fiona or Grace or Cooper-Brad—and she says, "The Wi-Fi here is dicey." Hartley fluffs her hair and reclaims her measured tone. "Riley, is it all right if I call you 'Riley'?"

She flutters her fingers. "Certainly, lovie."

"Perfect. I'm happy to respond, Riley, but I realize I'm not the only creator on this panel. I don't want to have this result in any Hartley Hog hashtags." She covers her face with her hands. "Oops, well, now that's out there. Consider it a gift."

The audience titters, unsure if it's okay to actually laugh.

Hartley continues. "If you use that hashtag, at least make it clear that I tried to defer to my fellow authors, but that I also couldn't risk offending Riley Moore. I mean, it's *Riley Moore*."

Now the audience is in it. They clap and hoot and someone shouts, "You got this, Hartley!"

A prickling goes up my spine watching how it lifts her.

She physically grows in the chair. "I've already explained

this." She looks pointedly at Riley. "I am the creator of *Love and Lawlessness*. It is simply the words I did not create."

"I'm sorry, Hartley, but that sounds like double-talk."

"And I'm sorry, Riley, but that's only because you don't actually know what you're talking about."

The audience "oohs," and I'm really glad the #WildeWest-Showdown is being run by Riley and not me.

Hartley adds, "I don't mean that as a slight. But it's not like you hit the *generate* button and out pops a book. It's not a toaster."

Lake slides her chair back for a better angle. "Then what is it? Since you all refused to let me keep my head all warm and cozy beneath the sand, explain to me how it's not a toaster."

Hartley seems to focus directly on me, as if asking permission. I don't know if Hartley saying more will help or hurt me. I give a noncommittal shrug, which she takes as a yes.

"This AI can do tremendous things," she says, "but as everyone has repeatedly reiterated, it isn't human. If I just let the AI churn out a book, it wouldn't be a book anyone would want to read. There'd be inconsistencies with characters introduced and forgotten, plot points repeated, and conversations that go nowhere. And twists or surprises? Either none or ones that make no sense. For this to work, I had to be in control."

Lake snorts. "Then why use it at all? If you're in control, be in control. Just do the thing."

Silence. Then, Tara says, "Easy for you to say, Lake, you've been doing the thing—"

"Since dinosaurs roamed the earth," Kara quips.

Lake ignores them both. "Hartley? Go on. Curiosity officially piqued."

Somehow, this is becoming exactly what we were trying to prevent: Hartley getting a platform. I feel Rosie's eyes on me and turn to face her. But I can't shut this down. Not if I want to keep my #SweetSofie. Maybe *she* could pick up the god-damn sword? Oh, wait, was that too *grotesquely* judgmental?

Hartley's smile exudes humbleness. I've seen this before. She's exactly where she wants to be. "I didn't know I wanted to do the thing. All I wanted was more Sofie Wilde in my life. So I asked for the same light that is Vance, the tragic loss of a best friend like Triana, a love that would endure like Callum and Torrence. But it grew into more. And soon I wasn't alone." She takes a long breath, and her eyes well with tears. "It became a partnership, but still, I coaxed every scene. I'm the one who understood when we needed to dial up the tension, when to slow it down, when the pacing lagged. Sentences came out fully formed, but I massaged each line into its final form. I created the rhythm, shorter and longer sentences, pushing the style to be a little more Jocelyn here, a little less Tucana there, to be my version of Sofie Wilde."

The audience is silent. Hartley's eloquence combined with her display of emotion is winning them over. Riley has the patience of a kindergarten teacher as she waits out Hartley, dabbing at the corners of her eyes with one of the crumpled tissues.

Riley then seeks out Max Donner, who gives her a subtle nod of encouragement. In a softer tone, Riley says, "At the end of the day, it's still not the same effort, amount of time, or skill."

"And yet, it is still effort, time, and skill. Just applied in a new way." Hartley's jaw clenches. "Painters once had to grind pigment and mix it with oil to make their own paints. To make a tapestry, you had to spin your own fibers into yarn. Art is not stagnant, and its definition cannot be either."

Riley's lips part, but no sound comes out.

It is Rosie who engages. "What do we become, then? If we no longer write? If we are no longer authors?"

"You are still an author," Hartley says. "Just with a new tool. The same way new software and electronic readers and tablets were the tools that brought about self-publishing. Evolution, that's all this is."

"One that makes us simply idea factories. That's what we become."

"And there's nothing inherently wrong with that."

"You want me to be a puppeteer?" Rosie balks.

"I want you to recognize that for every con, there is a pro. Just because something is new, doesn't mean it's bad. But I get it. Change is difficult because change is loss. We mourn, but we must move on. A shift in mindset, that's all this is."

Rosie shakes her head, vehemently. "I do not believe that. Our books are our hearts on a page. The ink may as well be our blood. We write to process the world and our place in it, and readers read for the same reason."

Rosie is well past resting bitch face. She's angry and she's not bothering to hide it.

Hartley presses closer to the camera. "That doesn't have to change."

"No disrespect," Rosie says, "but that's naive, Hartley. Emotions are what make us human. Sympathy and empathy and the lack of both."

We've lost the Jocelyn thread, what this means for me—my keynote, my tour, my future books. Rosie better find a way to bring it back. That is why we're doing this.

She continues, "A machine cannot imbue words with the experience of being human, with *my* experience, no matter how much data it draws from. It will never truly echo life because it is not alive. Readers will not see themselves in it."

"You're purposely ignoring what I said—that I had a role to play in crafting the end result, the same way your editor does.

But I can do it much faster than your editor and than you. Think of it: we are a binge culture. AI means we authors can do what we do and give our readers more of what they want in weeks, not years."

I hadn't thought of that.

Rosie pushes her gold-tipped hair behind her ear. "Quantity isn't the issue. I don't know a single reader who has conquered their TBR list, do you? Let alone watched everything they favorite on their zillions of streaming apps. We're inundated with entertainment options. We don't need or want mass production in art. This isn't a bag of Doritos."

"But it is a product," Hartley says. "One AI might even make better, if we give it a chance. Let's be honest, a lot of our entertainment right now, created solely by humans, is mediocre. AI will evolve, the same way I know your very first book wasn't the masterpiece that your current one is. We all learn, we all improve. One day, AI will strengthen all art—and do it faster and cheaper."

"Cheap is the only part you're getting correct. AI will cheapen all art. AI *does* cheapen it. You can't teach taste."

Hartley grows more animated, gesturing with her hands as she speaks. "But that's your subjective opinion, isn't it? Of what is or feels *cheap*? Most people will never see the *Mona Lisa* or Monet's *Water Lilies*. But they can hang a poster of both on their wall. Is that wrong?" Rosie starts to protest, and Hartley holds up her hand. "If a story is well written and well told, so much so that we can't tell if it's created by a human or AI, does it truly matter how it was generated? Or is this simply a case of not wanting to believe the thing you spent your life learning to do is so easily done by a computer. Is this ego?"

Rosie sits back in her chair. She looks down the line of authors. "Maybe," she says. "But AI can only do what it does because it's able to process massive amounts of data—data that is made up of the stories we've created and the words we've used to do it. Years, lifetimes' worth of the work of human beings boiled down to algorithms. *Insert commercial success here.* Is it ego? Some. It's also a fear that in amalgamating everything art becomes generic. We lose creativity. We lose experimentation. I don't want art that is all trope."

Lake taps her mic. "And I don't want it all owned by a conglomerate."

Hartley pushes herself higher in her chair. "But it already is. Books are products, paid for in all the same ways as Sofie so eagerly pointed out. This would at least level the playing field."

Oh, no, you don't. You're not dragging #SweetSofie into this. You're all doing fine on your own.

Harley's eyes brighten. "All of you so intent on hating on AI shouldn't do it until you try it. Because then you'd see that apart from all of this, using it is fun. It just is."

Rosie stares at me intently. When I don't say anything, she lets out a heavy sigh. "Fun? Maybe. In the way it's fun to teach a toddler how to slide open a barn door until she slams the thing back and forth so many times it comes off its hinges. But let's say that it doesn't become as destructive as my niece. For me, this is about awe. Life has so little. We know how every sausage is made. Art might be the only source of wonder left in the world. It allows us to live in another person's mind, for just a little while. Even if the quality is the same, even if the work is indistinguishable, I will forever marvel at the depth of another *human being's* creative soul. I read the works of these authors beside me and dozens like them and am inspired. I am in awe. I will never be in awe of a machine."

I am a great author. Rosie is better.

"You're the one who buys a sixty-dollar candle," Hartley murmurs.

Riley cocks her head. "I'm sorry, I think I missed that."

Hartley freezes. "Oh, nothing. I didn't mean to interrupt."

Rosie says bluntly, "You didn't."

Silence shrouds the stage. Hartley shifts in her seat. Finally, she says, "Spending sixty dollars for a candle from Target seems ridiculous. Even if it's by Joanna Gaines. But at a pop-up market, sold by the woman who poured the wax and mixed the essential oils to create her own salt-of-the-sea scent? Wallets open like the mouth of a baby bird."

"So you agree," Rosie says, warily, as if fearing she's being led into a trap. "We value artisanship."

Hartley's jaw clenches. "Exactly. And that is what *Love and Lawlessness* is for those with less restrictive perspectives, which includes the thousands of readers who have found me and are finding me still." Hartley's chair jerks back, and the surprise in her eyes indicates it wasn't of her own volition. She covers with a cough, rolling it into a full-on coughing fit. "If you'll excuse me—"

The screen goes black as the laptop clicks shut.

A MARRIAGE OF CONVENIENCE

THE SPECTER OF THAT BLACKENED SCREEN HAUNTS MY *BEAUTIFUL* on the Inside signing. I tap to wake my phone after every *hearts never part*, and *love traverses universes*, the signature phrases that accompany my *SW*. Every book in the series gets its own catchphrase, though today I'm lamenting the number of letters in the ones I created for this release: *There is no better vice than that of self-sacrifice.*

I write letter after letter, strain to follow the spelling of names like "Carrie" as "Karee" and "Jenny" as "Jaenni," while simultaneously bantering about the frigidness of Chicago and which Riley Moore movie is my favorite. All the while, I continue to check my phone. I don't bother to hide it. Being the mastermind of an ongoing hostage situation is more stressful than one would think.

I need to talk to Fiona or Cooper-Brad. I need to know if Hartley is okay or if this haunting feeling is not just a feeling but Hartley's actual ghost.

When a pause in my signing line comes, I flex my fingers, trying to loosen the arthritic cramp that I tolerate because it means an abundance of book sales. Finally, there's an incoming text. It's from Cooper-Brad. Someone must have decided he'd earned getting his phone back.

That panel was surely a thing of beauty.

He must be writing in code.

All the authors did fine and are fine now too. Still. ALL FINE.

He *is* writing in code, even if it is rather poorly. But at least he's confirmed that Hartley hasn't been offed by a jumbo-sized bag of Brazilian nuts.

Beautiful on the inside and the outside. Cool. Super cool.

Now he's mocking me in code.
I signal to Clarice that I need a break and text back: What is this?

Cooper-Brad: I believe it's called a "text" but I can verify with my niece.

Me: You know what I mean. This. Inside and outside stuff.

Cooper-Brad: It used to be called flirting but probably is called something else now. Should we group text with my niece?

This is definitely banter. Which I shouldn't be enjoying.

Cooper-Brad: I'm not doing it well, then? Though in all fairness, it's hella (again, as my niece says) intimidating to be flirting with the woman responsible for the Jocelyn-Callum-Torrence triangle. That has more tension than a fishing rod that's hooked a six-hundred-pound tuna.

Me: You're actually still reading? I didn't think you were a romance fan.

Cooper-Brad: I'm not. But I am a Sofie Wilde fan.

Cooper-Brad: How's that? Any better?

My fingers hover over the keyboard. The amount of cheese in Cooper-Brad would kill someone lactose-intolerant. My red pen would be bleeding all over these pages if I were critiquing it. And yet I find myself writing back: Get through another book and we'll talk.

He gives a string of thumbs-up emoji, and I wipe the cloying grin off my face. I still have a few more eager fans in front of me. Instead of individual panel signings, there used to be one mega signing at the end of the convention. But the practice was stopped to be fair to fans who couldn't stay for the full three days, as well as in response to authors who complained about their hands cramping too much to lift their margaritas. (And no, by "authors," I don't mean me—at least, not *just* me.)

As I press my ultra-fine-tip Sharpie to the page, I can't help watching Riley Moore. She has stamina. The whole time we've been signing, she's been here, preening in an endless string of selfies. She drapes her arms around the shoulders of nervous fans, gives the rock 'n' roll salute with the confident ones, and when asked, utters her iconic line, *"I put the whoa in woman,"* with the same enthusiasm from the first fan to the last.

All the while, Max Donner has been gesticulating wildly,

Bluetooth headset protruding from his ear, either actually working on my conditions or making a show of doing so.

As I sign an *SW* for one of my last remaining fans, the auditorium doors open. The convention director enters and walks purposefully in Max's direction, a look of disdain on her face. She clasps her hands together, perhaps to stop them from entwining around Max's throat.

When my signing line is finally finished, I push back from the table. Anika and Liz, the two young women who created #SweetSofie, linger near the merchandise, waiting to catch Tara Kara, who are packing up their swag: IV "blood bags" for beverages. Lake has already gone, but Rosie is still here, talking with Clarice.

The room is heavy with the absence of Hartley. Disappointed fans have been giving their names and addresses to a volunteer who will make sure they're sent personalized bookplates. The line wasn't short but hasn't been all that long either. I wonder if the same would have happened without Riley Moore.

I'm about to call Fiona to tell her I'm coming down when Riley plants herself in front of me.

"Hey, girl," she says, enveloping me in a limp-noodle hug.

It's then that I remember what I said during my viral rant. "About that whole Riley Read thing. I didn't mean to disrespect you or your—"

"You did, but I don't give a flying fig. Neither does my husband. You've got every author's agent battering down our door, begging for us to produce their adaptations. If only you'd done it sooner, I wouldn't be stuck costarring with a furry hot dog."

She's referring to the Riley Read pick about the woman and her dog hiking across the country to forage for mushrooms. The one that I mocked in my now-viral rant. "I'm sure Wiggles is a worthy—"

"Wiggles is a little shit. Little cretin's going to steal the show, I just know it. Choosing it was my husband's idea—some stats about box office receipts on movies with animals." She flits her wrist, and the replica of Jocelyn's bracelet gleams. "But that loss is our gain. I've been after him to option Jocelyn for an age. Production expenses be damned."

I've caught her in a lie. "That's lovely to hear, but we weren't accepting offers until the final book released. That's been the plan all along."

She pauses, and I can see her eyes calculating her next move. "You weren't on our radar," she says flatly, not bothering to keep up the pretense. "Fantasy romance? Rather niche, right?"

"If niche buys you oceanfront property, then sure."

"Not on Nantucket."

"Damn straight it will after the movies come out." Max Donner sidles up to us, a conspiratorial grin not eliciting a single line on his tanned and frozen face. "As Sofie will soon discover, my clients live by a certain *maxim*."

He wiggles his bushy brows, drawing out the inevitable.

Finally, I say, "You're going to make me ask?"

"Money."

"That's a word. Not a maxim."

Max cocks a fake gun at me. "You'll see, babe."

"No," I say at the same time as Riley says "Nuh-uh."

Max exhales a puff of air. "I miss the nineties. Hell, I'd even take the aughts."

Beyond him, fans clutching their unsigned copies of *Love and Lawlessness* leave the auditorium.

Riley catches me looking. "It's unsettling, isn't it? I admit, taking advantage of all this free press is what got me here. But hearing Hartley and seeing all this, I'm going to play the shit out of Jocelyn. I told your agent, but she didn't seem all that interested."

"Blaire? You talked to Blaire?"

"Not directly. I have people. But the sentiment was relayed."

"And?"

"And it was Max who promised he could get me a meeting with you."

Max cocks another gun, then slides his hand into his front pants pocket. "And delivered."

Tara Kara wave to Max after taking selfies with Anika and Liz, who clutch blood bags and syringes filled with candy apple red liquid. They notice Riley and begin to head toward us.

"Super," Riley says. "Our people will talk?" She wags a finger between Max and herself, and I nod through the roiling of my stomach. "And keep an eye on your socials. I'm announcing a surprise extra Riley Read pick for the month." She winks. "You're welcome."

I feel as cheap as a pair of imitation Crocs.

Still, Riley Moore is exactly who I need. Younger fans like Anika are the exception. I skew white-haired. Something Riley as Jocelyn would change. It's part of what makes Hollywood so seductive—the opportunity to introduce the universe I've created to more readers, younger readers, readers who will make Jocelyn the attraction not just at romance readers' conventions and country club author luncheons but Comic Con and Hollywood premieres. (Jocelyn, and, well, yes, me by extension.)

Riley puts her back to the approaching Anika and Liz. "My smile's off duty, and I'm meeting a friend across town. Do either of you have money for a cab? All I have is my ID. I never travel without my assistant who carries everything else, but there was something about a wedding—his, I think—or was it a funeral? Either way, I gave him the time off."

"I don't do analog," Max says.

I start to shake my head. I gave all my cash to the vendor in Millennium Park. But then I realize Hartley's purse is still in my tote. I retrieve it, find the slim case that serves as her wallet, and pull some bills from the center. (What? You think I'm not going to pay her back? One kidnapping, and suddenly I'm some kind of degenerate?) I get a glimpse of the photo on her license and quickly shove her wallet back into my bag, hoping no one else noticed the picture of a younger woman with red hair.

Riley manages to take the two twenties I hand over and duck out before Anika and Liz reach her. They quickly pivot, setting their sights on Rosie, apparently very comfortable with the special guest status I've bestowed upon them.

Max saunters over to one of the audience seats, his face as transparent as the weave at the crown of his head. That feathered David Cassidy is clearly a toupee.

"Riley Moore is the tip of the Max-berg," he says. "I'm going to assume we have a deal?"

Even though securing Riley Moore is a bigger win than Romance US, Max still has conditions to meet if I'm going to do what I'm about to do. So I ask, "The keynote?"

"Delivered. With an extra honorarium." He extracts an envelope from his coat pocket. "They're getting your banner rehung as we speak."

My heart sinks despite what I've done to achieve this. Or because of it.

"And the tour?" I almost want him to say he couldn't fix it. To give me a way out.

"Your unmentionables should remain packed. And if they're not, I can help." My insides cringe as Max pops out of his seat. "Let's document. I'll tag you as collaborator."

"No, that's not—" His arm loops around my waist.

"New client selfie. A Max Donner rite of passage."

Footsteps bound down the stage just as Max lifts me straight off the ground. "A what?" Rosie says with disbelief. "You're not doing that. You didn't do that. Sign with Max Donner? Sofie, please tell me you wouldn't do that. Does Blaire even know?"

Max points to the front of the auditorium. "She does now."

I have never shot a puppy, but if I had, I imagine this is what it would feel like.

Blaire enters the room with a pained gait. She moves with a heaviness despite her lithe frame. Tall with a long neck, dark brown eyes, and light brown skin, Blaire wears cream wool pants and an aquamarine blouse in honor of me. She carries a copy of my book with a blue sticky attached. The copy she wants me to sign for her, a tradition she started, one we were supposed to continue on my New York City tour stop. She is, as always, the definition of elegance.

A sharpness hitches a ride on my next breath. This is why my call went to voicemail. She was on a plane. She was coming here. To me.

I feel a tug on my sleeve, and Rosie yanks me aside. "You leave me with no words and yet with all the words, Sofie. How could we have underestimated the depths to which you will descend?"

"It's not what it looks like."

"But it is what it sounds like. I heard you. We all heard you. You want to know why I was helping you? I needed to prove that someone I think so highly of couldn't be wrong for thinking the same about you. All I did was prove myself right." Rosie releases my arm as if touching my flesh would taint hers. "I'm done helping you. You're on your own."

With determination in her step, Rosie marches out of the auditorium. She pauses at the door and clasps her hand over

Blaire's. No words are exchanged, but the intimacy of the gesture stings like a slap to my face. I watch as Rosie pushes through the door, lifting her phone, presumably to call Fiona or Grace.

Panic quickens the beat of my heart. I whip out my cell and dial Fiona.

"Don't leave," I rush as she answers. "No matter what happens or what anyone says. Stay."

"Hi, Sofie! I'm well, thank you for asking."

"Fiona, I don't have time—"

"I am in fact missing the sculpt-your-favorite-heroine-out-of-mashed-potatoes contest. That I did in fact suggest in honor of my spuds farmer. And I am in fact pissed."

"I'll be there as soon as I can."

"The panel killed, by the way. Thanks to Rosie." A pause. "Speak of the gorgeous angel. Calling me now. Gotta go."

"No, Fiona, wait—"

"Sorry, Sof."

My phone beeps with the ended call. Max is wiggling his phone and asking me what my Instagram handle is, and I don't even know.

"TheSofieWilde, no spaces," Blaire says. "I named the account."

I can barely look at her. "Blaire, I have to go."

"I understand," she says.

I'm three steps past her, but this makes me turn around. "You do?"

Blaire nods. "Do you remember that trip I took to Nepal?"

I hesitate for too long. I really need to pick up acting tips from Riley Moore.

"It's fine." Blaire waves her hand. "I wouldn't expect you to. While I was there, I signed up for a tour to seek out the snow leopard. If I'd had the business instincts you do, I'd have realized it was designed to empty the wallets of naive tourists. The snow leopard doesn't want to be found, even by its own kind. It can kill prey up to three times its weight and patrols hundreds of kilometers alone. It prefers a solitary life and is profoundly good at it. Its talent for doing what it does best, unmatched. That is you, Sofie. But I still go looking for you with every book. With every one of my emails that goes unanswered, with every text you demand an urgent reply to, whether I'm mid-meal or mid-orgasm. *The* Sofie Wilde and I built our careers together. I am indebted to you. I have been indebted to you. And because I am who I am, despite all this, I always will be."

"Blaire, I . . ." My eyes dart around the room. To the stage where Tara Kara sip red liquid from IV bags and watch all this like it's a play. To the door and the orange crates being brought in. To Max Donner ordering each one opened in a fruitless search for my banner. "I don't know what to say."

Tears brew in Blaire's eyes. "You do, Sofie, but for some reason, you don't know how to. For the record, I'm sorry too."

DARK NIGHT OF THE SOUL

I EXIT THE AUDITORIUM A BEAT AFTER ANIKA AND LIZ. I WATCH them walk down the hall and try to remember how to breathe. I hurt Blaire. I knew I would, of course I knew. What I wasn't expecting was how much hurting Blaire would tear a hole in my own heart.

I bend at the waist and try not to hyperventilate. This had to happen. It was the only way to not lose all I've spent a lifetime gaining. But it should not have happened here, like this, in front of her peers and mine. And fans. Fans too.

I jerk upright. *Anika and Liz.* They must have seen everything. Heard everything. Maybe even filmed everything.

Shit, shit, shit.

I clutch my tote bag tight to my torso and propel my short legs to catch up to Anika and Liz. All around me, readers lug heavy bags and excitedly squeal at the author notes in one another's books, and I'm about to call out to Anika and Liz when I realize they aren't my highest priority. Even if they do post a video, I will simply be a bold career woman making changes to secure my future. Lacey can spin any-thing.

But will she? After she finds out I've left Blaire?

My heart thumps. I truly had no choice. Objectively, I prob-ably should have done it long ago. This keynote shouldn't be my first one at this convention. I *am* this convention. Same as I am the creator of a series wanted for a high-profile movie adaptation with a megastar attached. That I wasn't told any-thing about. Why didn't I see it before? Blaire has been hold-ing me back.

This is my moment. That Fiona and Grace releasing Hartley will destroy. If it comes out that I kidnapped Hartley West, that's the end. I'm too old to start over. My liver can't take it. (Alcohol, not unbridled hope, is the best way to soothe rejection.)

I pump my arms as I pass Anika and Liz on the way to the north elevators.

"Sofie!" Anika cries, her voice three notches higher than usual.

I smile my #SweetSofie smile but don't reduce my speed.

"That was a total blast!" Anika says.

Liz impersonates a catapult and falls in line beside me. "That debate was super eye-opening. I mean, I'm not sure I should say this, but before it, I thought AI sounded, like, really cool. Writing's hard, and if AI could help . . . I'm not going to hand-write a book because I'm afraid of a keyboard, right? I've been trying to write for a long time, like six years, ever since I was a junior in high school."

This isn't happening.

"So I was going to try AI." Liz isn't even breathing hard to match my pace. "What could it hurt? But when Hartley said that thing about the sixty-dollar candle, I was like, huh,

I *wouldn't* buy a sixty-dollar candle at Target. But at Anthropologie? Maybe. Probably. Fine, I have."

"That's so not the point," Anika says, appearing at my other side. "Hartley proved once again that she's such a copycat. She didn't come up with that analogy. It was in a book I read. One of those free ones on Amazon. Was a decent read though."

This makes me reduce my speed. Fiona wouldn't have let Hartley use AI during the panel. "Are you sure?"

"Definitely. The book was about a glassblower. Vases and lamps and wineglasses. The main character fell in love with the sand delivery guy. Did you know you melt sand to make glass? So, like, climate change and all that, there's all this sand erosion, and if it continues, will we have no glass? Just plastic? And then that's horrible for the environment so it's like a total cash-22 situation."

I pinch the bridge of my nose. "Catch-22. From the book?"

Anika's brow furrows. "No, I don't think that was in the glassblower book."

My brain cells are dying. We're nearly at the north elevators. Hartley could pop out any second.

"The book, summarize. Quickly—just the candle part." I hold up my phone by way of apology. "Sorry, packed itinerary."

Undeterred, Anika says, "Well, you already heard it, really. The character, the glassblower, she had the same analogy when she was explaining to the dreamy sand guy why she bothered to blow glass when machines could do the same thing faster and cheaper. The human element. Artisanship. It's like my mom's apple pie. It tastes the same as the one from McDonald's, but my mom's is still better. Because she made it. Plus, I don't have to pay for hers."

The candle can't be a coincidence. We reach the elevators, but Anika keeps talking. "I totally related to what Jocelyn was saying about my face on Kate Winslet's though."

Liz wobbles her head in agreement. "Could be cool—only for like a second though."

"Maybe," Anika says. "If I could kiss Leo! Young Leo. Because old Leo . . ." She shudders.

I hit the button for down, then realize my mistake as I can't lead them to Hartley. I press the up button several times.

Liz says, "But, Riley Moore, *a-m-a-zing*! You must be so psyched for her to play Jocelyn."

I stiffen. "Yes, about that . . . if you want to be a writer, I'm sure you know how this industry is?"

Liz gives a half shrug.

"Negotiations can take forever. Deals aren't deals until they're signed. And even then!" I let out a hearty laugh. "So whatever you heard, it can't leave that room." I gesture around us. "Or these elevators."

"All we heard is you getting the representation you deserve," Anika says. "Tara Kara said they wouldn't be here without Max Donner. If he's your man, you'll be epic, Sofie. I mean, even more so than you are now."

Anika seems genuine, but as she's speaking, Liz is trying to hide her phone. I pluck the device from her hand.

"Hey!" Liz cries.

On it is a video of me, Max, and Riley. I strike the screen and hit Delete.

"First tip of being a writer. Author friends. Get them. Now, send me your manuscript so I can pass it to Max Donner. And not a word of this to anyone. Ever."

With appreciation in her eyes, Liz nods. "Your author friends are really lucky to have you."

"Damn straight they are."

I really am an exceptional liar.

"Now, one more time," I say to Anika. "Are you sure the

sixty-dollar candle analogy wasn't in *Love and Lawlessness?*"

"*Love and Lawlessness* doesn't have Targets." Anika pulls out her phone. "Wait a sec."

Liz grins with pride. "She writes down every book and every author. You're on there, many times. And now we're in front of you. I mean, life doesn't go where you expect does it?"

"Surprising but inevitable," I say. "Like the best plot twists."

Liz opens an app on her phone to write that down. My back arches the tiniest bit. Knowledge may be power but it also makes you feel powerful. Maybe Lacey and I can start some writer tip reels after all this.

"Here it is!" Anika says. "I add little notes to remind myself. Right here: glassblower and dreamy sand guy."

"And the book?"

"*Transparent* by Genevieve Lily." Anika taps her phone, eyes glued to her screen. "That's strange. No website. No author photo attached to her book either."

She flips her phone around for me to see, backtracking to the cover of the e-book, something that's either designed to be blurry and opaque or just appears that way to my tired, strained eyes.

"Ooh, maybe she's already a famous author!" Anika says. "And she wants to be judged on her words, not her name."

"Maybe," I say, feeling a foreboding that only comes with having plotted a dozen and a half books.

My phone buzzes—an incoming call from Grace. My heart beats hard and fast. "I need to take this," I say to Anika and Liz. "My publicist. I'm surely late for something. That packed itinerary and all."

I give a little wave that's more of a shooing gesture, desperate to appear calm despite my imagination picturing Grace and Fiona waltzing into the ballroom, arm in arm with a freed

Hartley. I hurry to answer just before the call goes to voicemail. "I'm coming," I say with a rush. "Grace, listen, please don't—"

"Now you say *please*?" Grace says. "If you've also learned *thank you*, warn me before you use it. I'll need to sit to prepare myself."

I ignore her jibe and push the down button of the elevator, rotating my head to ensure no one's close enough to be tracking me.

"I'm on my way," I say.

"You better be. Otherwise Fiona gets the go-ahead for her release plan." Grace's voice lowers. "It involves squirrels, Sofie. A horde."

The line goes dead.

I burst through the door of the speakeasy.

It's empty save for the cardboard police officers, the flappers, and the mafioso.

"No," I whisper.

My breathing grows rapid and shallow. I'm lightheaded.

Please no.

My legs quake as I enter the room. And then, I see her. Hartley is curled on a banquette in the far corner, the Read or Bleed hat propped to conceal her face. She's still wearing the Bears sweatshirt and has my aquamarine scarf looped around her neck. A perimeter of nuts surrounds her.

I hear a screech and whip around. Rosie stands behind a small round table beside the door. Laser-focused on Hartley, I blew right past them. But they're all here: Rosie, Fiona, Grace, and Cooper-Brad.

My heart beats a single flutter of relief, thinking maybe Rosie changed her mind about being done. But then I see the tightness of her lips. The firm cross of Grace's arms. Even Fiona's nose is turned up, like she's just performed an embalming. The only one not looking at me like I've sprouted devil horns is Cooper-Brad.

Tonight is the fan-appreciation dinner, which always follows the featured panel. We only have a short break in between, and I'd hoped to use the time to change back into my standard event attire. Instead, I'm here with a group of self-righteous women who wouldn't invite me on a hotel tour of a speakeasy let alone a slumber party where our thin-walled bladders would have kept each other up all night as we took turns getting up to use the bathroom.

Grace purses her bright red lips. "Donner? Sofie, this is next level. When I said Fiona's philosophy is go big and then go bigger, it wasn't an invitation. You're acting like a petulant child whose favorite toy was taken away."

"Who then breaks the rest out of spite," Fiona says. She shifts her chair to face me, and the tiered ruffles of her silk gown cascade to the floor.

Rosie simply remains standing. As if her presence is judgment enough.

It is. But also, it isn't. Because I didn't get here alone.

"You asked me to do this," I say calmly. "Demanded, actually."

I turn away from them and walk deeper into the room, trying to gauge if Hartley is asleep or pretending to be. Either way, she's still surrounded by nuts and there's not a furry-tailed creature in sight. This hasn't all fallen apart. Yet. Thanks to me.

But instead of appreciation I get judgment from these women who only gave me entry into their little club because they each wanted something from me, something for their careers. And yet me putting my career first by signing with Max Donner is somehow unacceptable.

I understand it's a bold move, but that's how I got here in the first place. I wanted this: success, adoring fans and book signings and my name on a banner and money, yes, the money. I'm not ashamed of it or to say it. And yet, none of it is why I started writing. I started writing in order to be someone else. It's why I keep writing. Jocelyn isn't me, but at the same time, she made me who I am. She gave me an outlet I desperately needed, a way to socialize and fall in love and have adventures and a life that felt full and lived. She made me feel a part of something bigger than myself before my fans did the same. That's my community now, but I had one before them. With Jocelyn, I was never awkward or lonely. I belonged. Because she never made me feel like I didn't.

"You took the poster," I say, turning back around to face Rosie.

"Poster?" Fiona brushes back the red curls of her wig. "What are you talking about? Your banner? Because it's right there."

She points to my banner on a nearby table, neatly folded as if it were a flag previously draped over a casket. But Rosie places her hand on her throat. She knows what I mean.

I glance at Hartley. She's still, her chest inflating and deflating with measured breaths. No sign of being awake. But she's an expert at faking it. If we're doing this—if Rosie and I are doing this—we're not doing it in front of "the next Sofie Wilde."

"Not here," I say, and head for the doorway.

Rosie's on the move without a moment's hesitation. She marches past me to leave the speakeasy first. Chairs scrape the floor, and Fiona and Grace pop to their feet. They join Rosie in the hallway. The awkwardness of Cooper-Brad being here makes me want to avoid looking his way. Yet when I do, I see genuine concern in his eyes. He nods, giving me the encouragement I didn't know I needed—or wanted.

The instant I enter the hallway, the atmosphere shifts. It's like walking into a sauna and being smacked in the face with a wall of heat. I inhale a sharp breath and take in the three of them, an irritated Grace leaning against the wall, an impatient Fiona beside her, and a stoic Rosie front and center.

Behind her is the now-ironic Pardon Our Appearance While We Work to Bring You a New Clandestine Experience! sign.

Fiona gathers the ruffles of her dress out from under her foot, resting it on top of a paint can. "We didn't touch your banner."

Rosie shakes her head. "She's not talking about her banner."

"No, I'm not." My voice trembles, and I curse my body's betrayal. "I'm talking about the day when not a single soul came out to support me and Rosie." I step forward, my indignation building, and address her directly. "It was our first time meeting. You wanted us to go out, drink away our sorrows and shame, pretend like it didn't matter."

Rosie holds up her palm. "I never said that."

Grace cuts in. "Wait, what is she talking about?"

"Nothing," Rosie says quickly.

"Everything," I say, my tone clipped. "If I'm a snow leopard or a lone wolf, I didn't become one all by myself."

Grace stares at me, frustration etching the tiniest lines around her mouth. "I'm waiting for the relevance. This century."

Maybe I should let this go. Be done with them. It's bad enough that I broke down and defied my better judgment to ask them do this with me in the first place. I should have found a way to stop Hartley on my own. Or the opposite—just let her implode all by herself. Maybe the attention would have eventually died down without us going all *Ocean's Eleven* (and if we are all *Ocean's Eleven*, I'm totally George Clooney and definitely not Elliott Gould). But we did go all *Ocean's Eleven*. And like Danny Ocean, I started this with a team.

I steel myself and lock eyes with Rosie. "You judged me then the same way you are now."

"Hold on," Rosie says, shoulders rigid. "That was a disaster of a night. I wanted to get a drink with someone who understood how I was feeling."

"No, you wanted to get a drink *with me*. But you didn't know me and you didn't take a single second to try to. You assumed we were the same." All these years, Rosie thinks I wronged her. Her role in it never even a blip on her radar. "Do you remember what you said?"

"I asked you to go for a drink."

"But do you remember how you asked?"

"What does that have to do with our current predicament?"

"So that's a no."

"I guess it's not seared into my memory."

"Well, it's branded into mine. You said we should go out and show all those readers who didn't show up that we didn't need them anyway. Except, I did. I needed them. I wasn't strong like you. I felt like I'd had my wisdom teeth pulled without anesthesia. I couldn't just laugh it off—put the blame on the bookstore for not enough advertising or the local high school for daring to hold a playoff game the same night. You could, you wanted to. You were confident and strong, and I was nothing like you, but I wanted to be exactly like you. Yet, I couldn't fake it, not back then. Sit beside you, sip Pinot Grigio, and create a war story? Done in a heartbeat now, but not then."

Rosie draws back, her face morphing into confusion. "You should have said. I would have understood."

"If I had been strong enough to say it, I probably would have been strong enough not to feel it."

Hiding my awkward, lonely self was such a deeply formed behavior that one invitation to drinks wasn't going to change it.

Rosie gathers herself. "I'm sorry you were hurt, Sofie, but I'm not a mind reader. And it was a long time ago."

"But feels like yesterday. Apparently to us both." My veiled accusation, that the hurt of that day wasn't all one-sided, messes with the narrative in her head.

Rosie stands in this hallway littered with ladders and paint cans and brooms, the detritus left from trying to improve upon something. Are we the same to AI? Simply the detritus left behind?

"Mistakes have been made." Rosie gestures to Grace and Fiona. "And yet, we're here together now—all of us. We chose to ride the wave of this tsunami with you."

"With me, really? Because what I heard was *pick up a goddamned sword*. That I alone owed it to everyone who ever scribbled a nugget of a story idea on a napkin to defend our profession."

Fiona twirls a red lock of her wig. "Which, truthfully, you didn't do much of on that panel."

Grace nods in agreement. "Thank the convention planners that Rosie was up there with you. She's the one who stopped Hartley."

Are they truly this myopic? "Not by herself. Riley Moore owned that stage. And that candle bit? It was Hartley who shot herself in the foot and her book square in the spine with that one. Which apparently she stole from some self-published book. We should leak it. Show whatever fans she has left that she's a thief through and through. Oh, and would you look at that, another way to actually stop Hartley coming not from you all, but from me."

Grace cocks her head. "Stole it? How do you know?"

"My fans," I say. "Who are actually behind me."

Grace puffs out a breath. "They don't know you like we do. You'll betray them the moment it suits you. Just like you did with Blaire. Just like you'll do to us."

I clench my fists. "Apparently not before you do it first." Though my fingernails dig trenches into my palm, my voice remains strong. "I didn't ask for any of this—that's the piece you all seem to forget. Maybe my rant didn't help things, but I didn't cause it to go viral any more than I caused what started all of this in the first place. Still, you all made it my responsibility. And I delivered. Whatever Hartley tries next, Max Donner will stop her. Because of me. Because of what I did and gave up and sacrificed. I did this for all of us. I gave in to all of your demands, and it's still not enough to break into this little clique."

I can't believe I'm here trying to justify myself to a group of women who don't know me and never made an effort to try.

"Break in? Oh, Sofie, that's not . . ." Rosie's face softens. "Will you just look at this? At how much we care about all of this, how deeply these feelings trail into our souls like tentacles, grabbing hold of the pain of betrayal and the sting of rejection from a lifetime ago. This is who we are and what we do. We're writers. We live and breathe emotions. We draw on our own hurt, conjure it on demand in the name of art. It's how we create characters who feel real. All to ensure our readers feel seen. Maybe us too. That's why this all matters and why we joined you, Sofie."

Grace adds, "More like dragged her kicking and screaming."

Rosie gives Grace an admonishing look before continuing to address me. "This was never about blurbs or cover designers."

Fiona scoffs. "It wasn't?" Rosie's scolding gaze turns on her, and Fiona adds, "Not all of it, naturally."

Rosie sighs, and something about her having to corral Grace and Fiona makes me think of all that Blaire has had to do for her authors, including me.

I allow myself to look at her, trying to let go of the anger. And the hurt. "Why are you even here?"

Rosie takes a deep breath. "Upstairs, I was in shock. But a part of me does understand your logic about Max. And maybe he will keep Hartley in check for a little while because he wants something from her the same way she wants something from him. But that's a relationship built on greed. It will fall apart. The only relationships that last are those built on trust. Something Blaire gave you. And you're not wrong that we never extended that trust to one another. Maybe this could have been a start. But we let ourselves get carried away. You feeling like the only option was to leave Blaire was a wake-up call for me. But it's not too late. We can still end this—together. But the only way to do that is to let Hartley go."

Let her go? Now? When I'm on the verge of getting back everything I lost and adding so much more? I think of the sadness on Blaire's face and imagine the anger on Lacey's and the disappointment on Roxanne's and can't have it all be for nothing. If we let Hartley go now, all the hurt will have been for nothing.

I steel myself and offer Rosie my best resting bitch face.

She shakes her head in disappointment and presses the up button on the elevator because there is no down from here. "Lone wolf it is. We're done."

My heart sinks, but I maintain my composure. "Good. I realized long ago that the life I had was the one I wanted. I don't need anything more."

Rosie stares at me, her arms crossed against her chest, her finger tapping her elbow. "Impressive, Sofie. You really are an excellent liar."

I slam the speakeasy door shut and press my back against it.

Cooper-Brad's head jerks up from my book. "Suffice it to say, they're not coming back?"

I shake my head and push myself off the door, straining my

neck to get a glimpse of Hartley to see if she heard. I point to her and the nuts caging her in. "Is she okay?" I whisper.

"Physically, she's fine," Cooper-Brad says in a low voice. "The tip of the scissors grazing the bag of Marcona almonds was enough, but mentally, it's taking a toll."

"The nuts?"

"The kidnapping in general, I'd wager."

"Yes, well, despite me having a tendency to be verbose, we've tipped into our third act, so I expect this is all going to come to an end soon."

Cooper-Brad gets up from the table and moves beside me. "Well, I'm glad you're back. If you hadn't returned when you did, they were going to have me relay a message."

"Which was?"

He exaggerates a brow raise. "I can't. I'm a fisherman, and even I've never heard language like that. Masters of their craft, for sure." He flashes me a grin that suggests he's joking, but even if he's not, I appreciate the intent behind it. To show me that someone is still on my side. "Okay, then. What's next?"

"Next?" I say. "How am I supposed to know when all I have is you?"

"Want to try that again without the tone? Because *all you have is me.*"

"I know."

"Now might be a good time to start trusting me."

"But I'm a snow leopard."

"A what, now?"

"Nothing, forget it." I hug my arms to my chest, trying not to replay everything that just happened, but that only makes me return to Blaire and the look on her face. I'm not the person she and Rosie think I am. I can't be. But perhaps I'm not a good enough liar to fool myself.

Shame and sadness and fear and self-doubt push me to slump in the corner and strap on a pity-party hat. Pity-party streamers and pity-party balloons—

That I pop one by one. I tear that pity-party hat right off. I just released the tenth and final book in my culturally iconic series. I'm going on a kick-ass book tour. I'm about to ink a movie deal with a major production company. There's a Riley Read on its way. I didn't ask for any of this, but it's happening. No way I'm swallowing these lemons whole. I'm juicing them into lemonade and boiling them down into essential oils and creating my own organic soap and body lotion line and I'm going to wear yellow from head to toe even though with these neck wrinkles it'll make me look jaundiced and I'll be known as the Lemon Queen from here on out.

I'm not a lone wolf. I *am* a goddamned snow leopard. I thrive on my own. I don't need them. I can solve this on my own. So I'm going to live the lesson Rosie was trying to teach me all those years ago. Push past. Laugh it off.

I smile what feels like a touch too widely and rein it in to what I hope is a notch below deranged. Cooper-Brad comes closer, his breath smelling of coffee, and I picture Fiona going on a coffee run, bringing them back whipped concoctions to sip while spinning a story about a love triangle between one of the cardboard cops, the flapper, and the newsboy.

"Let's try this again. Thank you for staying," I say, tamping down the jealousy my imagination has incited. His curls have more kink, and the skin below his eyes sags from exhaustion in the way it only does post-forty, but still, I feel my body reflexively angling toward him, craving a connection, something physical and uncomplicated.

Cooper-Brad fixes his gaze on me. Up close, those stunted eyelashes seem to fit his face just fine. He flutters his eyes and my woolgathering imagines them eliciting the gentlest breeze.

"No matter what the rest of them think," he says, "I'm honored to be of assistance to *the* Sofie Wilde."

A bubble of something unnamable—a mixture of fear and adrenaline and sadness and laughter—percolates inside me. "So this isn't about the spoils coming your way?"

"Oh, it is." A grin spreads across his face, a bit of a cat-ate-the-canary kind, and the clatter in my mind eases, giving my body the space to light up. "I was just being nice."

"Admitting that makes it less nice."

"But amps up the tension. Did you know enemies to lovers is one of the most beloved tropes?"

"Right up there with fake dating."

"And forced proximity," he says.

"You've learned a lot while in here."

"The best writing retreat I've ever been on."

"I can expand my offerings."

"Sign me up."

We're close enough for this to be an invasion of space but neither one of us draws back. I vacillate between feeling invisible to men and too visible, my author persona and the books I write slotting me into a category they're embarrassed to be tainted by. Serious relationships over the past few years don't even need one hand to be counted on.

The only men in my life I fully trust are my father, Callum, and Torrence. I don't trust Cooper-Brad. But I don't need to trust Cooper-Brad right now. I just need him to flirt and banter so I can feel the joy my readers do and inhale the dizzying scent of make-believe and escape real life, and just for a moment, wash away the betrayal that clings to me like the spray of a skunk.

He inches toward me, bending his neck until his lips hover

above mine. This is wildly inappropriate. And yet, I suddenly understand why people have affairs. The wrongness is intoxicating.

"Can I—" he starts, and I answer him off by pressing tiptoes into the ground and grazing my lips against his. He pauses, his eyes intense, his movements slow as he positions himself before me. Then his arms reach for me, his hands entwine around my waist, and he half lifts me off my feet. Our bodies meet, and the heady rush of smelling his sweat and digging my hands into the muscles of his back and feeling the growing engorging against my midsection makes me dizzy. We're kissing, not up-against-a-wall, can't-make-it-to-the-bedroom kissing. But definitely just-ran-through-the-airport-to-stop-you-from-boarding-a-plane-to-Singapore kissing. His lips are chapped, and as he drags them down my jawline and neck, the hint of abrasion causes my back to arch. My fingers disappear into his wavy hair and I almost forget where we are.

Until Hartley West barrels past and out the door.

HOW TO CHOREOGRAPH AN ACTION SCENE

SHE JAMS HER FINGER AGAINST THE ELEVATOR BUTTON. I SPRINT down the hall, nearly colliding with a giant metal ladder. My tackling knowledge comes exclusively from *Friday Night Lights*, and now I'm trying to remember if I duck my head or my shoulders or neither to avoid ending up in a wheelchair like Jason Street. I hear the elevator moving through the walls, and so I press my feet into the floor, ready to leap.

Hartley whirls around and juts a pair of scissors at me. "Don't come any closer."

She looks deranged, feet bare, eyes darting wildly, a bird's nest of hair on one side of her head from the banquette. She bounces in place, brandishing the scissors. The handles are pink, *Barbie* emblazoned across the blades, and I stifle a laugh.

"This is funny to you?" She swishes the scissors above her head and nearly drops them.

"Hartley!" I shout, because this has turned decidedly not funny. "Careful!" She looks from me to the numbers above the elevator to the scissors to me in an unceasing cycle, and I force myself to remain calm. "Listen, the panel went well. People loved you. Them thinking you were sick was even—"

"Stop, just stop." She gulps down a breath of air, as if relishing the lack of threat from tree nuts.

The elevator numbers tick down.

I inch toward her. "Just . . . Let's talk about this rationally."

"Rationally? You want to talk rationally? There's nothing rational about someone who kidnaps another person and uses nuts to hold them hostage!"

"Hartley, please. This will all be over soon. That's what I was coming down here to say. I've talked to Max, and he sorted everything out."

She flinches at his name, and I wonder if she actually signed with him or if she was bluffing with Cooper-Brad or Max was bluffing with me. If Max isn't her agent, he has no leverage over her. I cannot have left Blaire for nothing.

Hartley senses my hesitation and snorts. "Oh, honey, you are too cute. You think any of this ends with you leaving here unscathed? That you'll still be taking that stage when this comes out?"

"It's not going to come out."

The elevator dings as it counts down.

She lifts an eyebrow. "It's too late, Sofie."

It can't be. It can't end like this. She cannot get on that elevator. Fear pumps through my veins. "I don't think so." I need to stall, to keep her attention on me. "With what you said during the panel, your time here is done. You want to go out with grace not—" I flick my finger at her unhinged appearance "—like Wile E Coyote."

"I'm nuanced. People like nuance. I can turn what I said at the panel to my advantage like that." She snips the air with the scissors, and the sound of metal scratching echoes off the walls. "I don't need the keynote. I'll use every social media platform that exists and maybe even invent my own. My message on the benefits of AI and how it turned a pathetically insecure author into a felon will go far and wide, and everyone will turn against you, this time for good."

I underestimated her ability to spin a good story. "I'll admit that this has escalated in a way neither of us could have anticipated. But you've gotten attention, an agent . . ." I try to gauge her reaction to this, but she's so keyed up that I can't read her. "I have my release, my tour, my keynote. We both have what we wanted. You're on the way up, and I'm exactly where I was before." Just with a Sold! sticker slapped across my soul. I tentatively step forward.

She backs up. "Stop. I'm not going to say it again."

Cooper-Brad comes up beside me, hands outstretched. "Let's be adults about this. I found the storage closet for the bar setup. Aperol spritzes, what do you say?"

The elevator arrives with a cheery ting.

Hartley issues a smug smile that demands to be wiped away. "I say *arrest warrant.*"

Cooper-Brad looks at me. "Sofie, tell me the plan here."

He's willing to help stop her—for me. Or so he doesn't go to jail. But either way, I am a strong, intelligent, self-sufficient woman. This is my problem to solve.

I place my hand on his forearm. "I've got this."

My attention shifts back to Hartley. I wait until her eyes flicker to the opening elevator doors and then duck beneath the scissors raised in her hand. I plant myself between Hartley and her very real means of escape. "Go ahead. Do what you have to do. And I'll do the same. I'll prove just how little you care about stealing from your fellow authors." Her smile falters ever so slightly at the accusation. "The candle analogy you used in the panel? You plagiarized it nearly verbatim from *Transparent* by Genevieve Lily."

Her eyes widen in shock, and she hesitates. I take full advantage and lunge, wrapping myself around her torso and tackling her to the ground with a strength I didn't know I had. The scissors scatter beside a box of paintbrushes.

My heart rockets inside my chest as I scramble off her and reach for the scissors. *I did it.* I actually did it. I'm both impressed and truthfully a little nauseated. And I think I may have pulled a muscle in my groin. I turn to enjoy this moment with Cooper-Brad, but he's offering a hand to help Hartley up. She accepts, but then smacks him away as he guides her back inside the speakeasy.

I try to stop my pulse from echoing in my ears as I send the empty elevator back up. Christ, how did this happen? I was one elevator ride away from this all ending in a perp walk.

I follow Cooper-Brad and Hartley down the hall and lean against the wall just outside the doorway to catch my breath. The caution tape that had blocked the door curls on the floor.

My phone buzzes in my pocket. I pull it out, drawing back at the name on the screen: *Clarice.*

"Hey, you," I say with full-on Sweet'N Low in my voice despite how she spoke about me earlier. "Quite the panel, wasn't it? What a way to kick off the dinner."

"Which starts in fifteen minutes," Clarice says hurriedly. "That's why I'm calling. We're trending. The convention along with a new hashtag #MooreWildePlease. People can't stop talking about it. We caught a half dozen fans trying to buy dinner tickets off existing attendees."

I can't help but smile just the smallest bit. "Well, you know what they say about any press being good press."

"That may have been true once, but not anymore," Clarice says. "Not in this world of social media and crime podcasts and conspiracy theories. Everyone's an amateur sleuth, poking around."

I squeeze my eyes shut. "Looking for what?"

"Clues—answers. Any information about Hartley West. The way her screen went dark is apparently a sign on the dark web of nefarious activity."

"You're joking."

"I wish I were. But we need to find her before this gets out of hand. Which is why the conference director is having me contact all our authors directly to see if they've seen her."

"And has anyone?"

"You're my first call. Since you two have a history."

"That's a polite way of putting it."

"Which is why I said it that way."

I grit my teeth. "Yes, well, couldn't you just put out a statement building on her not feeling well? That should be enough."

"Have you ever met a conspiracy theorist? Nothing but an appearance from Hartley herself will stop them. And even then . . ." Clarice grumbles something I can't quite make out, followed by, "Anyway, if you hear anything—anything at all—about Hartley, call me ASAP."

I hang up, tension giving me shoulders for earrings. I need to get to the dinner. I have to plant my banner somewhere a volunteer can find it. I can't let any more red flags sail up. But Hartley has upped the stakes. From what she just said, it's clear—Max or no Max—she's not going to simply forget this little bout of kidnapping. (Honestly, bygones being bygones can be quite healing.)

Hair even more wild, eyes screaming with betrayal, Hartley falls into the banquette on the other side of the room. I quash the bit of guilt that's creeping in and wave over Cooper-Brad. But he's not quashing anything. The guilt on his face would get him picked out of any police lineup in a snap.

"Sofie, that was—"

"Intense, right?" I press my hand to my supersonic heart. "I know. All I could picture was winding up in the emergency room."

"You winding up, not Hartley?"

I hesitate a beat too long. "Guess it could have been either of us. Both, even."

"But in the moment you were only thinking about yourself." He stares at me until I begin to feel uncomfortable—and judged. "They were right, weren't they?" he finally says.

I don't ask "who." I know he means Fiona and Grace and Rosie, and I don't care what they think or don't think. What I care about is all of this ruining that perfectly distracting kiss.

Cooper-Brad releases a heavy sigh. "I get it, Sofie. Your career is important. I hoped to one day have a career I could feel the same way about. But, really, Max Donner?"

"He's the one securing my keynote. He's a means to an end."

"Or maybe he's just mean," Cooper-Brad says. "Look, I didn't tell you this earlier, but before you clocked Hartley in the broom closet—"

"I didn't clock—"

"I ran into Max Donner in the bathroom."

I still. "Tell me you didn't pitch your book."

"So, to be clear, you want me to lie?"

"I told you I'd handle it."

"I know. But I wanted to see if I could handle it on my own. One last attempt. And after everything with Hartley and Harbor Books, well, I didn't want you to think I was using you. That you were just *my* means to an end."

I hold myself still, embarrassed by how much I want to believe him. "Well, what did he say?"

"Not sure. He was laughing too hard for me to make out any actual words."

Blaire would never laugh in the face of a writer. Blaire wouldn't laugh behind a writer's back. Blaire wouldn't do a lot of things Max Donner would do. That's why I need him.

"I'll talk to him," I say.

"I was actually more interested in working with Blaire. She seems nurturing."

She was. Is.

"Maybe it's not my place," he says, "but when Grace heard you left Blaire for Max Donner, she was livid."

"And not Fiona?"

"She said sometimes you don't understand how wrong something is until you do it."

Maybe her morals aren't so loose, after all.

Cooper-Brad adds, "But then she said you were too stubborn to ever admit being wrong."

An angry scream lodges in my throat.

He looks at me, concern in his eyes. "Sofie, you do know it's only a speech."

"I know." Except it's not. It's validation. And it being taken away is the opposite. "But it's *my* speech. My chance to build on the momentum and end all that Hartley has started. I'll be able to make that rant up to my fans and prime them for all I hope to do. An expansion of my brand, did I tell you that I'm hoping to increase my readership by—"

Cooper-Brad frowns, giving my feelings whiplash. "That's still all this is for you? Your books? Your career?"

"I'm confused. Isn't that what's been at stake here all along? I thought I was crystal clear on what you signed up for."

"But the panel and everything Rosie and even Riley said, that hasn't changed anything for you? At all?"

"Of course, it did. Together they managed to get Hartley to practically admit that readers shouldn't value what she did the way they value what I do. Once I take that stage—"

He starts to turn away.

"I'm sorry, did I say something wrong?"

"No, not wrong. Grossly self-centered, but not intrinsically wrong." Cooper-Brad exhales a frustration I'm still not understanding. "It's just, you haven't been the one here. I've had a lot of time to think about how I ended up here, but I've also had time to talk with these incredibly inspiring, brilliant people, all these authors—"

"Does that include Hartley?"

"Don't say it like that. She's not a villain. Or if she is, then so are the rest of us. That's why Rosie and Fiona and Grace gave you this last shot to realize it too. But you still don't see it. You've been off doing what you love, and I've been here following orders and watching my friend cower in the corner of a room full of nuts."

"Your friend? Now she's your *friend,* not your *craft-fair friend*? How convenient."

"She is a friend, and more than that, she's a person." He points to her. "It's just the three of us now. Maybe if we talk as equals, she'll be more open to listening."

"I just tried. You were there. You heard her response."

"That wasn't trying. You have to be willing to give something up."

"Not yet." Because we're not equals. That's the whole point. And I may have signed with Max in order to get him to rein Hartley in, but I don't fully trust him. I need more than the plagiarized candle to ensure I have the upper hand with them both if I'm going to give my keynote in something other than an orange jumpsuit. "After the keynote."

Cooper-Brad stares at me. "Which you'll use to defend art, all art, not just your own." I don't respond quick enough, and he shakes his head. "Maybe I could keep doing this if I thought you'd come to understand that."

"I do understand that." Logically.

"But you don't give a shit. You're in it for you."

"News flash, Cooper-Brad, everyone's in it for themselves."

"No, not everyone. Not anymore."

I don't understand why he's doing this. I step closer and try to look at him the way I did before, to get him to look at me that same way, to go back to lips on lips and no judgment and no distance between us. But he won't.

"I'm sorry," I say, shaking it off, "but it's too late for a crisis of conscious. We had a deal. I'll live up to my end, but you need to keep living up to yours. Through the fan dinner. Okay? It's almost over. Just a little longer, and it will be over."

"But what does *over* mean? Please tell me you have a way out of this, even if it's one you just don't trust me enough to share."

I've treated this like writing a novel, studying my character (Hartley), understanding her strengths (relatability to the masses, arrogance) and weaknesses (nut allergy, arrogance), and formulating the major plot points (kidnapping) from the outset. I've allowed the twists (goth vampire fans, #SweetSofie) to bubble up and have run with the ones that made sense. The way out was to appear as we delved deeper. A road we'd pave into existence. But there's no more "we." There is just me. A great author. Who'd very much like to stop being tortured and instead be drunk. Very drunk.

"You don't have a plan, do you?" Cooper-Brad says with disappointment.

I want to tell him that I've plotted more than a dozen books. That I always stick the landing. The ending will come to me. It has to. But somehow, I can't form the words.

He rubs the back of his neck. "Here's the thing, Sofie, you can't live up to your end of the deal. Blaire's out. Max won't help me. Maybe this is the solution to my existential crisis about writing. That it's not going to happen for me. Or rather, there are some lengths I'm unwilling to go to in order to make it happen. So I'll stay with her through dinner, but after that, if you want to keep her here, you'll have to do it without me."

I want to argue with him, use my skill with words to get him to understand, but I have to get to the dinner. I can't be late.

Actually, I can be. I just don't want to be.

I turn from him, spinning toward the door. It is then that my eyes land on Hartley's laptop—holding the potential for dirt on her. This version of Cooper-Brad would never knowingly let me use it . . . but fortunately he doesn't have to know.

"I have to go," I say, fighting the unexpected spark of heat behind my eyes.

"Right," he says.

I grab my tote off the floor and snatch a bottle of water that's sitting beside the laptop. I hold it out to him. "She's probably thirsty."

His lips form a tight thin line, but he accepts the water bottle and brings it to her. He whispers something to her, and I wish Vance and his superpowered hearing were here.

As Hartley drinks and Cooper-Brad sits beside her, I use the distraction to silently grab Hartley's laptop and shove it into my tote underneath my copy of *Love and Lawlessness*. I close the door behind me and hurry to the elevators.

I feel a sharp pain in my chest, a betrayal of the life I've built, the one that's suited me well for the past forty-nine years. I miss my blue recliner with its custom wineglass holder and my ocean views and my king-size bed and my walk-in closet that my slim wardrobe could never fill. I miss the version of me that would have never, not once, imagined that a simple kiss could mean something more. Or wanted it to.

BOOKFLUENCING

Sweat still pooling in my bra from my sprint from the elevator bank to the ballroom, I eat an entire bowl of gluten-free ravioli in a rich cream sauce across from Fake Fangs and Fishnets.

(Roberta and Megan . . . Don't quote me on that.)

The goth vampires from the elevator are the special guests of Tara Kara, complete with eyes ringed with black liner and painted red teardrops dripping from their charcoal lips.

(And, yes, still being able to eat while sitting across from that proves how hungry I am.)

My own special guests are, naturally, Anika and Liz. They sit on one side of me with Riley and Max on the other. Our table of eight had to squeeze in an extra chair, and we're tight enough that I can smell the garlic from Fishnets's Bolognese three seats down. (It seems cosplay doesn't extend to avoiding the pungent herb.)

At the next table, Blaire picks at a salad. Rosie and Lake buffer her as they make small talk with a group of fans whose faces I recognize. These diehards come again and again, driving for hours, paying for expensive flights, staying in rooms that aren't comped on top of outlaying money for the convention fees. Still, they don't skimp once here. They drag suitcases from panel to panel, filling them with purchased books and souvenir tees and candles and potato peelers. (Fiona really goes for it.) Their loyalty is why we get to do this.

I've always appreciated my fans. Being in front of them. Absorbing their energy. Their elation at being in my presence gives me a high that nothing else can touch. I do not take these opportunities for granted. They matter.

"I haven't run it by my husband yet," Riley says, "but I'm thinking twenty-seven?"

Max squints. "Even twenty-five. Provided you do a little something . . ." He pulls back the skin on the sides of his lips. "There."

Riley says, "Work isn't my thing. I'd rather go twenty-seven. Sofie, what do you think?"

I haven't been listening. I reach to adjust my scarf, but I'm not wearing it. Hartley still has it. Another thing she's taken from me.

Riley bites her bottom lip. "Damn, you think I should, and you're too polite to say it."

Tara Kara snort, and I glare at them before putting down my fork and facing Riley. "Run it by me again?" I say with interest I don't feel.

"Twenty-five or twenty-seven? I personally don't think we need to push the believability. Twenty-seven feels solid."

Christ, I have no idea what they're talking about. My eyes roam the table, landing on Anika, who tilts her head as if asking permission. I nod.

She says, "I'm not sure you need to age Jocelyn down at all."

Age down Jocelyn? To twenty-seven?

"I'm twenty-four," Anika says.

Max points to Anika's cheeks. "Exactly."

Anika continues, "I don't mind reading about an older character. I actually like it."

Riley appears to consider this, though there's a touch of condescension in her tone as she says, "Reading isn't the same. A visual medium requires certain adjustments. If one wishes to be successful."

Max says, "Wishing doesn't make it so. T&A does."

Kara tosses a Parker House roll across the table. "Seriously, Max, are you trying to get canceled? Because we aren't sticking around for it."

Max holds up his hands—a telltale arthritic bump on his right ring finger belies all the plastic surgery he's had done. He's as old as I am—probably older. He too feels bad when he learns someone who used to be on *Happy Days* or *M*A*S*H* dies. "Everyone here knows I'm always of good intent."

"No," Fake Fangs says. "We don't."

Riley places her hand (younger, though clearly a decade past twenty-seven) on Max's forearm. "What Max here is trying to say is that movies and television need to reach the widest audience possible to recoup our significant investment. A key factor is the appeal of the main characters and the actors who play them. We all want to expose Jocelyn to an expanded audience. Aging her down is step one."

To hear what I want repeated back to me in this perverted way makes my jaw clench. "That implies there is a second step?"

Riley tosses her head back and laughs. "And a third and a fourth, and I'm pretty sure my husband's notes will reach a thousand before we even get out of development."

I push my empty plate toward the middle of the table. "Let's stick with step two for now."

Riley looks at Max, then back at me. "Surely Blaire told you?"

I wince at her name, resisting the urge to turn to see if she heard.

Riley trails her aquamarine nails through her Jocelyn hair. "Combining books one through four into the first film?"

"I'm sorry, I'm not sure I understand."

"Oh, right, it used to be just one through three. But Jasper and I—"

"Jasper?"

"My husband?" The crow's feet deepen around Riley's eyes. *Twenty-seven, my bestselling ass.* "Anyway, the synopses show we can drop the first four realm crossings and not lose anything."

"The first four?" An angry lump swells in my throat. "That's not possible. Once you read the final chapter, you'll see how vital it all is."

Riley flitters her wrist wearing Jocelyn's bracelet. "Oh, I never read the source material."

"I'm sorry?"

"Scripts are so much shorter." She cocks her head. "It's a good thing you fired Blaire. She knew all of this. Never re-layed a thing—such incompetence."

Blaire knew all of this. She knew the strings that an offer from Riley Moore and her husband would come with. Which is why she never mentioned anything about Riley Moore or this offer to me. She knew I'd never accept. But more than that, she also knew how much it would hurt. Make me doubt myself. Make me want to pull back from letting anyone touch Jocelyn. Exactly the way it's doing right now.

"More wine?" Max says to fill the silence. "Champers?" He snaps his fingers in the direction of a server in a I Have No Shelf Control tee.

He doesn't look my way. He has no idea how deeply this affects me, how it will spread like poison in my writer brain. Even if he did, I'm not sure he'd care.

Anika clears her throat. "Riley?"

Riley's neck swivels as if she can't figure out where the voice came from.

"Ms. Moore?" Anika says, her voice eliciting the tiniest tremble.

"Ever present, if thirsty." She taps her wineglass with her fingernail. "Are these things always this long?"

"It's been thirty-five minutes," Tara says.

"That long? And not a single server with a cart of smoked cocktails? We need to get the team responsible for the Globes on this." She remembers Anika and flashes her I-put-the-whoa-in-woman smile. "Did you need something, hun? A selfie?"

Anika swallows. "It's just . . . reading is this incredible bonding thing. Reading the same book is like sharing a secret. No two people who love the same book could ever hate each other—not really. Books bring us together. It's why book clubs exist."

Riley reaches for her empty glass. "I thought it was the wine."

Liz shakes her head, but Anika continues, "Anyway, if that's how it is for readers, I think it's double for writers. So, I was actually wondering if you could share your process for selecting a Riley Read. Because, well, Liz—"

Liz gasps.

"Liz is a writer," Anika continues proudly. "She's so good. Like so, so good." Liz squeezes Anika's arm to stop her, but Anika won't be deterred from helping her friend. "But it can't hurt to get some tips on what to incorporate to appeal to a brand like yours."

"Yes," Riley says. "Well, it is a brand. As such, there's a whole team that chooses."

Anika nods carefully. "But you must have criteria? Things you look for?"

Riley doesn't read the source material. Clearly, not even for her book club picks. "Hmm, let's see. It really depends on the genre. The story itself. What's the book about?"

Liz trembles like a field mouse cornered by a Bengal cat.

Max finally gets the server's attention, and she heads toward our table with a bottle of white wine. He holds up his glass without looking at the server. "Pitch it," he says to Liz.

"Here?" Liz blurts out, scanning the room.

"Often the best opportunities come when one is held captive," Max says.

I choke at his word choice. I clear my throat to cover, realizing all eyes are on me.

"Fine, so this dinner isn't quite on the captive level." Max takes a sip of his wine and winces at the taste. "But close," he mutters. "The things I do for clients."

Tara Kara beam, but Max is looking at me.

I tuck my leg beneath me to gain height, remembering how poorly Cooper-Brad's pitching went. "We don't want to put her on the spot. We spend days—weeks—rehearsing our pitches." I drill my eyes into Tara Kara's, begging them to help.

They misunderstand.

Tara says, "Oh, Maxie loves to foster new talent. Let's hear it."

I interject, "I'm not sure this is the right time."

"Sofie, that's rude," Tara says. "She wants to. Don't you, Liz? I'd have killed for this opportunity when I was starting out. You too, Sofie."

Blaire's table is quiet as if they've been listening. I reach for my empty wineglass. I haven't had so much as a sip. I raise it as the server passes, catch Rosie's disdain, and put the empty glass back down.

Anika nudges Liz, who says, "Right, well, it's in progress. I'm still figuring things out."

"Aren't we all?" Tara says with an encouraging laugh. "Kara and I are still figuring out the twist in our last book—too bad it's already published!"

Polite titters around the table, but the air is heavy with tension.

Liz inhales a breath. "Well, it's a bit of a mashup. Like *Pride and Prejudice and Zombies* but not exactly. More like *Heathers* with witches."

Max's bored face transitions into a yawn.

Liz sits up straighter. "Not like *Hocus Pocus* witches but Salem witch trial witches so it's period but also kind of otherworldly? And there's a *Romeo and Juliet* story but Sapphic, but no one really says 'Juliet and Juliet' so I'm figuring out how to pitch that part and I was wondering if—"

Max snickers.

Silence shrouds the table.

Oblivious, Max tugs on the hem of the server's shirt, which happens to be draped across her buttocks, and she stumbles, dumping wine all over his blazer.

"This is Tom Ford!" Max launches himself out of his seat, swatting at his lapel. "Goddamned amateurs." His eyes flicker to Liz. "Surrounded by them."

It isn't Liz who this hurts. It's Anika. One look at Anika's glistening eyes, and Liz rises to her feet. Heat radiates across the table.

And all I can picture is Blaire doing the same for me.

My phone vibrates. A flurry of messages from Lacey.

Lacey: Your tour is "rock-solid."

Lacey: But Max Donner? If that wildly glorious but egotistical brain of yours actually thinks he's responsible for fixing your tour, you deserve each other. And you don't deserve me.

Lacey: Roxanne did it. She called every bookstore on the tour and promised not a single copy would go unsold. Because she would buy what was left. At EVERY SINGLE STORE.

Roxanne. That's why she was asking me about that bookstore in Austin. She doesn't actually care about their shelving. She wanted to know about turnout. Whether it was so she wouldn't have to buy too many extra copies of my book or to use as leverage to convince the store to keep my event, it doesn't matter. She went to bat for me after I trashed her store. I left her a check for the damages. But did I apologize?

At the table, Max pats at his chest with a napkin. Anika, cheeks flushed from having encouraged Liz, stares at her cuticles. Liz continues to fume. If she launches into a tirade, Max Donner's rejection will be made public, broadcast to the far corners of the internet. The pressure on this generation is overwhelming. When readers laughed as I pitched Tucana, only the penguin candlemaker heard.

That's why my linen closet brims with candles. She gave me one, every time a reader dismissed me.

Without those candles, I wouldn't be here. They made me determined to craft a stronger premise, to create a better story, to write a more beloved character. I wanted to ensure I'd never be given another goddamned candle.

I've worked hard enough to be able to flaunt my success in every laughing face. And it is true that writers need to let go of their work. Once it leaves our hands and enters the readers', it is theirs. To enjoy or not to enjoy. To pass on to their friends, to treasure on their shelves, to line their bird-cage with. Readers have the right to judge our work, even if they do it harshly and tag us so we can see how clever their cruelty can be. What readers—what no one, even Max Donner, especially Max Donner—has the right to do is laugh without reading a word.

"Funny," I say, calmly. "What you said about amateurs, I'm starting to feel exactly the same way."

Max bobs his lunk of a head in agreement. I'm not surprised he lied about being the one to fix my tour. I'm surprised it bothers me as much as it does.

Entirely clueless, Max continues to swat at his chest with his napkin. But Riley eyes me with suspicion. She says carefully, "I've had my share of bad auditions. Rejection is always difficult."

Max tosses his napkin on the floor. "But necessary." He cocks a finger at Liz and says, "Life lesson. You're welcome."

Liz's jaw could be chiseled out of marble. "You think you're the first? My Twitter feed is a museum of agent rejections. Each one a mark of not how I'm failing but how I'm trying."

I would have never admitted such a thing early on. I wouldn't admit it now. Perhaps that same pressure on this generation of lives laid bare for public consumption creates a comfort with it. Or a projected one. Underneath, I'd bet we're all little kids watching as pools of strawberry ice cream drown the things we love most.

And yet what I will admit now, what I believe deep in my soul, is what Liz is getting at. That the surest path to failure is quitting. So many writers I started out with are no longer writing. There was a time when I wanted to join them, to just stop and put an end to the hurt and the pain of rejection and the self-doubt that cripples every thought, every decision, every hope. I no longer fear failure. But maybe I should. Because without fear, our egos grow. Hubris brought me here. To a place where I was willing to not only quit on Blaire but on the one person I owe everything to: Jocelyn. She deserves better than Max Donner and Riley Moore.

I gird my loins (though, honestly, I'm not sure if I'm doing it right, considering I have no idea what *gird* actually means) as I glance around the table. "We are a bit crowded. Max, Riley, I think you're done here?"

Riley's eyes widen, but Max still doesn't get it until she yanks off her bracelet and drops it in her marinara. She asked for the sauce, hold the pasta. "You're on your own, Sofie," Riley says.

"I don't fear the familiar."

Max's lips thin. "Our deal . . . ?"

"Come on, Max," I say. "You've been around long enough to know when you've been played. Figured you'd appreciate the art in it."

"I can make things hard for you, Wilde."

"But you won't," Tara says, getting to her feet. "Because I'm really good at making reels." She taps her phone and out comes Max's voice: "Wishing doesn't make it so. T&A does." She hits it again and holds it up for us to see Max's palm cupping the server's bottom.

"Since when are you on the same side?" he barks.

Kara juts her chin toward Liz. "We take care of our young."

Anika clutches Liz's hand, and I think back to Rosie's finger entwined in mine.

Tara steps forward to add, "And our elders, when they show they deserve it."

Tara Kara nod to me and a weight grows heavy in my chest (despite that unfortunate *elder* part).

As Riley and Max swipe up their glasses and a bottle of

wine from a passing server, my phone dings with a text from Cooper-Brad: I'm not staying through dessert. Clock's ticking.

I push back from the table. If he leaves, then no one will be monitoring Hartley. As I start to rush off, a hand reaches across me to fish the infinity bracelet out of Riley's sauce. Blaire lays it in her napkin and wipes it clean. She presents it to me.

"I should have told you," she says. "Keeping things from you was paternalistic."

"Appropriate considering my childish behavior."

"I can't take you back."

"I understand." A sharp slice through my heart.

"I'm not sure you do, but I hope you will try to." Blaire clasps her hands in front of her torso, and I can't help feeling as if holding her own hands is her way of stopping herself from reaching for me. But then she looks at me with a mix of sadness and resignation. "All these years we've spent together, and still our relationship is murky. It's not just us. The author-agent relationship functions on more levels than it should. Part employee and employer with confusing role reversals in concert with each one's success. Colleagues in a way, friendly but not exactly friends."

This stops me, and I can think of nothing but the kinship I've broken with her.

"Blaire, I . . ."

Have been rash, juvenile, inconsiderate, selfish, and entirely like myself.

She nods. "I know, Sofie. The truth of it is, if half my authors were as singularly minded as you, I'd have my own agency and work remotely from a beach in Bali—and only when I felt like it. But then half my authors would be like you. I don't want that for them anymore than I want it for you. You are all in on this, Sofie, you always have been. What I wish you would see is that you can be all in on more than just this. Wouldn't that be something? Imagine the success you'd have if you did that? With, I don't know . . ."

"Pickleball?" I say around the constriction in my throat.

"Sure. Or, you know, this." Blaire gestures not to this ballroom but to the authors bringing it to life. "You care about your books, but sometimes I wish you cared about yourself even a fraction as much."

I still.

Blaire continues, "It's not my job to teach you, as your agent. But as a friend, well, that would be something else entirely."

I'm confused. "Is that a choice? Are you asking me to choose?"

Blaire looks to Rosie, whose lips remain thin, brow creased, clearly disapproving, but Blaire returns to me anyway. "No, this choice is mine. Because I could take you back." She offers a dramatic, weighty pause. "With a significant hike in commission."

My head nods so fast I strain a muscle in my neck.

Blaire unclasps her hands. "I'm not done. No more unanswered emails, no more unreturned phone calls. No more conspiring with Lacey behind my back."

Lacey, you tattletale.

Blaire holds her ground. "No bull, Sofie."

The pit at the bottom of my stomach begins to release because her demands have just proven how alike we really are. Who taught whom no longer matters, we belong in this game together. "Absolutely to the commission. I'll hire an assistant for the second. The third? Lacey? Yes, and I'm sorry. I'm sorry about it all." I place my hand on hers, and she squeezes.

Blaire blinks back the moisture in her eyes but still says, "And the last one?"

"No bull? I can promise to try, but I will fail. Sometimes. Probably a lot."

"We'll work on it." Blaire looks to Rosie. "We all will." She says it as a question and statement combined with a command that makes my toes tingle and appreciate her negotiating skills anew. She then circles the table and offers Liz her business card. "Query me when it's ready. And to answer your question about what we're looking for? To care. Love or hate. Sometimes a little of both." Blaire doesn't have to look my way for me to know she's talking about me. "It doesn't matter. Just make us feel something, and you've got us."

Through the sound system comes an announcement for even-numbered tables to head to the dessert buffet, and a sea of sugar-addicted authors and readers launch themselves to the edges of the room like it's an Olympic event. Time's up. And now I'm going to have to fight through this throng to get to the exit and to Hartley before Cooper-Brad sets her free. I give Blaire a soft smile and then hurry toward the ballroom doors. I'm pushing one open when I feel a tap on my shoulder. I spin around, half expecting Hartley.

Rosie's stoic face greets me. "You did a selfish thing, Sofie."

"But I—"

"And then a less selfish thing. They don't exactly cancel each other out, but it's a start."

My feet itch to run to the elevators before they open to reveal a ragged-looking Hartley ready to hold a press conference.

Rosie crosses her arms in front of her chest. "Now, what do you need?"

I do a double take. "You want to help me? Now?" Here it comes. When everyone else was making demands, she never said what she wanted. She wants Blaire, exclusively, or my editor or maybe my house? Does she want my *actual* house? "What is it, then? What do you want?"

"Nothing, actually. At least, I didn't want anything earlier. I only pretended to. Incredibly fun to have it hanging over you. But now, I want your help." Rosie tips her head toward the table I just left where Tara Kara animatedly talk with Anika and Liz. The elevator duo, Fake Fangs and Fishnets, appear to be filming it for Tara Kara, probably for their writerly advice reels on Instagram.

"Doing that," Rosie says. "I want to give back. I want to create a community for them. Young writers need it, the same way we needed it. And when you have it, I think you're a god-damn sight less likely to steal from your fellow authors. Let's put a face on writing that fucking AI in any form can't come close to replicating."

Rosie truly cares about this. It's the first time I've ever heard her curse.

"Okay," I say.

"Listen, I know we aren't exactly friends, but not having friends made you a target and Blaire's complete lack of subtlety back there got me thinking and—" She cocks her head. "Wait, did you say *okay*?"

"To be clear, I'm not missing any deadlines for it. Or read-ing drivel. Actually, I'm not reading anything. But provided it matches my interests and my schedule allows, I'm in."

"You make it both hard to like you and hard to hate you."

"It's a gift." I shrug. "But now, if you'll excuse me, I need to figure out how to un-kidnap Hartley West."

Rosie pulls out her phone. "We'll help. Let me call Grace."

Writing has always been a solo endeavor for me. Here, I let collaborators in, but the ending is one I have to craft alone—for all our sakes. "Actually, this is something I need to do."

She doesn't criticize me for it—for once again being a lone wolf. She almost seems . . . proud, and I hate it that I'm proud that she's proud.

"If you're sure," she says. "But we'll be here as backup."

She's giving me something, and Cooper-Brad's words about having to do the same echo in my head. I shuffle my feet. "I'm not sure who's representing you now, but if you still want Blaire and she wants you, I don't want to stand in the way."

Rosie lifts a brow. "You don't?"

"No, actually I do. But I won't."

"Well, with the higher commission she's getting from you, she may no longer need me."

"Here's hoping." I cross my fingers. "But, Rosie? The industry is changing. We might have to accept that our way isn't the only way."

"Then we can help shape what's to come. I'm not done, and I suspect neither are you."

But I might be. It all hinges on "the next Sofie Wilde."

I exit through the ballroom doors, above which my banner has been rehung. I silently beg Cooper-Brad to give me a grace period. He will, right? He wouldn't just let her go? Or maybe he would and Hartley is already draped in a fluffy white robe in her hotel room. Maybe she's filming something right now to release online. I can't stop her. I'm not Vance. I can't change the future any more than I can change the past. Like Jocelyn, I can only move forward with the talents I have.

My phone rings with a video call from Cooper-Brad. I slip into a corner and hit Accept.

Then my screen fills with Hartley's face.

MISTAKEN IDENTITY

"ONE, A STEAK. RARE, NOT BECAUSE I LIKE IT THAT WAY, BUT because I'm ravenous." Sweat drips from Hartley's red roots into her eyes. "Two, a glass—no, a bottle of Pinot, because . . ." She twirls her hand above her head. "And three, a heavy-duty garbage bag for all these fucking tree nuts."

"Okay," I say, my heart thumping. "But what—"

The phone shifts, and her face is replaced by Cooper-Brad's. "Sofie, Hartley's agreed to talk with you. And I'm agreeing to stay with her."

If she's agreed to talk, that means Cooper-Brad convinced her to.

He goes on, "But neither of our offers will last for long. So get down here and bring back her goddamned laptop."

The screen goes dark. Huh, that does have a nefarious vibe.

I immediately start texting Blaire about the steak but stop just short of hitting Send. It's not right to involve her. And if I wind up in jail, she's the one I'd call.

I duck inside the ballroom to nab a server, place the order for the steak (nut-free) and the wine, and pass her a hundred bucks from Hartley's wallet (and, yes, I've got a mental tab going). As I do, Hartley's license falls to the floor. Except it's not a license like I'd thought. It's a membership ID for a New England romance writers' association. I hold it up to the light and squint at the small type underneath her photo. Redheaded Hartley is not a Hartley at all. She's a Genevieve. Genevieve Lily.

"You've got to be kidding me."

Genevieve Lily.

Author of the glassblower-and-dreamy-sand-guy story.

Of course, she is.

So much for being a master plotter, Sofie.

"Uh, ma'am?" The server is still standing before me. "Is it the cost? Because I'm sure the conference would comp—"

"It's fine," I say, the shock still reverberating in my chest. I ask the young woman to deliver the meal to me in one of the small conference rooms at the end of the hall.

There, I prop my foot up on a chair, nostalgic for a younger body able to bounce back from stubbing a toe, and pull Hartley's laptop from my tote.

Except it's not Hartley's laptop, it's Genevieve's.

She may be a liar, but perhaps she's not also a thief.

Though the room is empty, I still check to make sure I'm alone. Goose bumps light up my skin as I open Hartley-Genevieve's computer, ready to find anything and everything I can to hold over her.

I start with her browser, googling *Genevieve Lily*, who has more than a dozen self-published books including the one Anika told me about: *Transparent*. Only the bio of the first book lists her age, but the releases date back to when she would have been in her early twenties. She's younger than me by twelve years. Her hormones have yet to betray her. No perimenopausal mood swings and sheets drenched in sweat. Her joints are still kind. Her skin still elastic. Her metabolism not yet a traitor. She dyed her hair white and donned those drapey clothes to appear older, to appeal to a more mature readership, like mine.

Because not all of her self-published books do, I realize, as I scan the titles and premises. At random, I click on one, and the sample chapter fills my screen. A quick skim shows the writing is decent, like Anika said. Maybe even good. The concept may lack that extra hook that's needed to more easily grab an agent or editor, but the foundation appears solid. I click on another, and then two more, coming to the same conclusion. There's skill here. And yet, all of these "Genevieve Lily" books were written before the ushering in of AI. *Love and Lawlessness* is the only book released after AI hit the public domain.

Maybe she has a connection. Maybe she's in tech and had access before the rest of us. I hesitate, then fully invade her privacy by moving from browser to desktop. I scan her folders, open the one labeled "writing," and sweep my eyes over the interior folder and file names.

"Story ideas"
"Pitches for current books"
"Pitches for future books"
"2010 Query letters"
"2013 Query letters"
"2020 Query letters"
"Decoding self-publishing"
"Keys to Amazon ranking"
"How to craft meaningful character arcs"
"Story beats from Save the Cat"
"Story beats from Story Genius"
"Notes from Grub Street class"
"Romance tropes and how to use them"

On and on and on. The mark of a writer stamped on every folder and file name. The craft and marketing articles we read and download, forever looking for the secret to success. Which Hartley found by using AI. And me.

Her "finished projects" folder includes subfolders for each of the titles I've just seen online and more. In them are character profiles and outlines and tracked-changes drafts and files labeled "final" and then "final final" and "final, use this one."

None of what I'm seeing matches her recounting of writing *Love and Lawlessness*. All of it is true to the messy behind-the-scenes of a working writer.

I search the internet, but no other titles pop up under "Hartley West." I do see her name attached to that pilgrim-themed craft fair where she met Cooper-Brad. It lists her as selling just *Love and Lawlessness*, not a single one of her Genevieve Lily books. Backlist is where the money is, especially in self-publishing. Readers are ravenous and loyal. If they like you, they'll tear through everything you've ever written down to your grocery list. Especially romance readers.

Hartley has enough novels published to understand this. Changing her name for *Love and Lawlessness* does a disservice to the others—considerably, now that the book is doing well. Authors most often use a pen name to differentiate between categories (say, middle grade and adult) or when works will appeal to wildly varied audiences (sweet romance versus erotica). Genevieve Lily's books don't seem very S&M at first blush.

Authors also use pen names to distance themselves from the abysmal sales figures of previous books. A new name wipes the slate clean and tricks the big chain stores into thinking you're a debut. No sales history is better than a crappy one. One bomb of a book can tank an entire career. A pen name is like a reboot.

Is *Love and Lawlessness* that much better that she didn't want to be associated with her previous work? Or the opposite? That much worse? If she always intended for the truth of AI to come out, perhaps she was safeguarding herself against the backlash that could have come. She'd still have her "career" (such as it was) as Genevieve Lily. She was hedging her bets.

The publisher had strongly encouraged the same for me when they acquired the first two Jocelyn books. Blaire went to bat for me. She convinced them to let me use my own name. Something I'd forgotten until now.

I return to the folder of completed manuscripts on Hartley's computer and choose two of the titles whose first chapters I've already skimmed. Online samples are always the first chapter, which we authors revise ad nauseam, knowing that's what agents and editors and readers will use to decide if they want to see more. Flatware in Buckingham Palace shines less than an author's opening chapter. Here, I push past and skim chapters from the middle.

The writing in these pages holds up. It's reminiscent of what I've seen in *Love and Lawlessness*. Perhaps a little less stylistic. A little less "me."

Which makes sense, considering she used my writing as the prompt to create *Love and Lawlessness*. Except she claimed she was using AI not only to be able to sound like me but to be able to write, period. That she had no training, no skill. That she only understood what made a good story, not how to craft the prose to express it.

None of that describes Genevieve Lily.

Yet, Genevieve Lily became Hartley West and used AI to write a bestselling novel. AI that I have never used.

Like voluntarily swimming into the mouth of a crocodile, I sign up for an AI account. As I wait for Hartley's steak, I type *Genevieve Lily, author* in as a prompt, not sure if it will be able to identify her. But it can. It describes her as a lesser-known author of romance novels, often with a paranormal or period element, like *Heartbeat, Heartbreak, The Moons of Caramoor,* and *Magic in the Mist.* I then ask it to write a short story in the style of Genevieve Lily.

It seems to be thinking, the wait time longer than before. Still, within seconds, it spits out a response apologizing for not having enough specific information about this author and the author's work to complete the request.

My fingertips hover over the keyboard. But then I do it. I open the files and copy the opening chapters of *The Moons of Caramoor* and *Magic in the Mist* and paste them into the AI. I then ask it to write a short story in this same style. It draws on Genevieve's material in less time than it takes me to blink. It's disturbing and terrifying. It feels reckless.

Dumbfounded, I watch as paragraphs and paragraphs appear before me. I read with terror in my gut. Terror that this is truly the end, like Rosie fears. And yet, the more I read and the more I compare to Genevieve's actual work, the more I realize this isn't very good. At all. Similar themes appear to be expressed— lost love, grief, a quest to find one's true self. Some of the details are the same or reminiscent—a "charmer" in *Magic in the Mist* is an "enchantress" in this short story. But the cadence and tone, even the word choice reflect little of Genevieve's style. It's like an actor adopting the affected JFK accent, thinking that's actually how people from Boston speak. It's not real.

And the story itself is simplistic and derivative. Maybe that's accurate for Genevieve's work. I haven't read enough to assess. There's only one author I know well enough to be able to judge that.

The smell of char and meat wafts in. Before I can second-guess, I ask the AI to write a story set in the Wild West in the style of Sofie Wilde. Exactly what Hartley said she did.

A deluge of words fills the screen. I don't have to describe who I am or put in any source material. It channels me, trawling through years of my work, of my life, in a blip.

What if it's good? What if it's great? What if the abundance of my writing means it could actually mimic me well enough that I could use it to write like me? I could put out an entire new series in a month, a year, space them out like serials, and Blaire and I would simply sit back and watch the zeros in our bank accounts proliferate.

I read with a mix of hope and fear. This story's prose reads marginally better than the first. The tone a stronger match for me. But it's the same playacting. Too many flowery adjectives and metaphors tossed in a blender, nonsensically combined, like a campy version of literary fiction the writer didn't intend to be campy.

"Your steak, Ms. Wilde?" says a nervous young woman with doe eyes and a T-shirt that reads I Write Your Wrongs.

I thank her as she leaves it on a chair by the door. I root around in my tote for my copy of *Love and Lawlessness*. I flip pages. The prose flows seamlessly, the dialogue crisp and true to life, the character descriptions a tad overdone but not enough to pull you out of the story. The writing is strong, nearly as strong as mine.

I close the book and trace the outline of the chocolate-colored horse on the front. Hartley using AI to write *Love and Lawlessness* would take longer than just writing it from scratch.

She's an even better liar than me.

AUTHOR INSPIRATION

COOPER-BRAD GREETS ME AT THE DOOR, HIS FACE UNREADABLE.

"Don't worry," he says. "All's quiet on the *Western* front."

Ooh, okay, good, breezy, light, a quip, a jibe, a joke. I follow his lead. "Strong literary pull for someone who writes apocalyptic worms and killer manatees."

He frowns. "Who says my apocalyptic worms and killer manatees aren't literary?"

Oops. "Oh, of course, I shouldn't have . . . Are they?" I stumble through.

"Nope. Is that a problem?"

"Of course not."

"Okay. Cool."

He's angry, I get it. He thinks I've been too self-centered. (And yes, we need the *too*.) He doesn't know I'm prepared to release his craft-fair friend or friend-friend. (Release, subject to a not insubstantial amount of blackmailing.) He doesn't know what happened at dinner and that I'm back to being BFFs with Blaire and Rosie. (Oh, just go with it.)

"Listen, Cooper-Brad," I start. "Cooper. Coop. I realize things have gotten—"

He slips my book out from under his arm. "So, I've read enough to see that you're writing about sacrifice. Which is interesting, because aren't we supposed to write what we know?"

Is he actually psychoanalyzing me in the middle of a hostage situation?

"Figure this out, Sofie," he says. "And quickly. Or I will."

The blood drains from my face as he storms out. The door slams shut, and I regain my composure as I approach Hartley, whose brow glistens with sweat.

"More than fashionably late," she says, clutching the edges of a chair behind a table in the middle of the room. "Slaughter the cow yourself?"

"No, but from the way you're sweating, it looks like you did," I say.

"Amusing, as ever." She relaxes her grip on the chair, revealing dark circles beneath the underarms of her white tee. The Bears sweatshirt lies crumpled on the floor beside her. "Except this is what it took for me to get myself here." She taps the table and points at the tray I'm holding. "Formal invitation or what?"

I navigate through the tree nut obstacle course to set the bottle of wine on the bar before sliding the steak in front of her.

She lifts the cloche and inhales the smell. Her eyes slice to the bag of Marcona almonds to her right. "Would you mind . . ." Her voice is uncharacteristically meek.

I pocket the almonds, trying to ignore the guilt winding a knot in my stomach. As I begin to clear the nuts closest to her, her knife scrapes the plate. I quietly move about the space, gathering bags and containers and fans and piling them by the door. She'd called this a phobia. I didn't really understand. Or care. I didn't care.

I circle the speakeasy one final time, checking behind the cardboard cutouts and scanning the bar, making sure I've collected everything. I grab the scissors as I go. Four pairs, including the Barbie ones, which judge me for my betrayal of another woman. (Women, technically.) With all the nuts beside the door, as far from Hartley as I can take them without putting them in the hall, I sit across from her.

She eyes me with suspicion. "What is it? Ceiling rigged to drop nuts like confetti if I make a break for it?"

"If only we'd had the luxury of time. And your creativity, Genevieve."

She stabs a piece of meat. "I figured this was coming."

"You did?"

"Despite what you may think, I am a writer. Stolen laptop isn't the most subtle of clues. And I screwed up big-time with that stupid candle analogy. That's how you found out, right?"

"Plus, your romance writer's ID accidentally fell out of your wallet."

"Which accidentally fell out of my purse?"

"Look at you following."

We stare intently at each other, until she eventually breaks the connection to dredge her meat in the sauce.

"I endured this," she says. "But I'm done being caged inside this phobia the size of the Grand Canyon. So whatever you want—the keynote, me to leave the convention, I'll do it. Let's just keep my use of this pen name between us." She pauses, fork in midair. "It is between us? Your accomplices . . ."

"Have no idea. And Cooper-Brad?"

She cocks her head. "The traitor otherwise known as Cooper only knows me as Hartley."

I try to discern if she's telling the truth as she lifts the fork and pries the meat off with her teeth. While she chews, I fish the infinity bracelet out of my pocket. I drape it across my wrist beside my bangle and pry open the clasp to fasten it. Hartley thinks her pen name is all I've discovered, and yet she's capitulating, offering me everything I want. An outsized conceding of defeat. Which proves that I'm right about the rest of it. The bracelet slides off my wrist. I try again and again, each time lining up the clasp and each time watching the string of infinities slither away.

Finally I say, "The pen name though, that's not actually the most titillating piece of the story, is it?"

She continues chewing, but a flash of fear crosses her eyes.

"And the most titillating piece of the story negates all else." I continue to lose my battle with the bracelet clasp, reinforcing my preference for bangles (and my need for reading glasses). I let it go and look directly at Hartley. "You wrote *Love and Lawlessness*."

Hartley doesn't look at me as she says, "We've been over this. We have to expand our definition of *write* to incorporate—"

"I know, Genevieve. And the reason I know will give you the ultimate satisfaction." I swallow past my hubris. "You're too good. Or AI isn't good enough. But the combination means you actually wrote *Love and Lawlessness* the same way you wrote all the books already published under your real name. Let's skip to why you would pretend otherwise."

"I don't know what you're talking about," Hartley says.

"Yes, you do." I surrender to the prowess of the clasp.

Hartley stares at me, and for a moment I doubt myself.

Then she says, "Fuck it." She pushes her plate to the side and reaches across the table. Instinctually, I jerk back, my plotting mind expecting to see the glint of her steak knife. Instead, Hartley picks up the bracelet and gestures for my arm. I extend it slowly, and she grabs hold of my wrist. She loops the bracelet around and her young eyes allow her to fasten it with ease. "So now what?"

"Now you tell me the truth."

"About what?"

"I want to know why you lied."

"Isn't it obvious?"

"Not to me."

"Look at where I am." She scans the room. "Not literally."

"You couldn't have known it would lead to this—that readers would embrace you. An author who admits writing a book using AI is easy prey for cancel culture."

She shrugs. "I made a bet and won."

"It's not that simple."

"Damn straight." Hartley stabs the last piece of steak. "I told you earlier: I didn't do this on a whim. Any of it. Or without trying the traditional way. I walked that path. I crawled down that path. I dragged my limp, pummeled body down that path. If I printed the number of query letters I've sent to agents, it would deforest the Amazon. For every *much to like here* and *extremely talented writer* and *gripping premise*, there were hundreds of *not connecting with the voice* and *not a fit for me* and a thousand no responses."

Hartley became someone else in order to do this. Not out of shame. She wouldn't have made herself a co-panelist at Harbor Books or taken the stage here if she were ashamed. But she wanted this part of her life to be different. She wanted to be someone else. And I suddenly feel a kinship with Hartley-Genevieve that I never felt with another author before—not Rosie or Fiona or Grace, not even Lake.

I spin the bracelet around my wrist. "So the system isn't perfect."

"The system isn't a system, it's a dumpster fire. Great writers get missed because an intern wanted to start their weekend early so they trashed the slush. Mediocre writers get snapped up because high-concept trumps storytelling. How is it remotely fair that to even be considered by an agent or an editor, we have to write the whole goddamn book—two, three, four *hundred* pages—and they get to decide after reading a single page, maybe five? That opening chapter can never represent the full arc of a story—and if it did, we'd be called out for being too rushed and heavy-handed. And yet, that's all we get. Years of our life dismissed in less time than it takes to cross and uncross your legs. It's a miracle that anyone makes it in this industry."

She's not wrong. But she's not entirely right. Signing with Blaire showed me just how much agents have to juggle. Author egos and self-doubt and missed deadlines and fights over covers and sobbing over not getting put on tour or selected for a best-of list. Agents are thinly veiled therapists. Treating a breed of human arrogant enough to believe that, despite the odds, their work will rise to the top and yet crippled by a lack of confidence and constant need for validation.

Hartley has only seen one side of it. She can't see past it yet. "I was there, you know that. Still, I'm not sure what the alternative is."

"We can build a spaceship and land on Mars, but we can't find a way to make this less soul-sucking? This is all before we even get to publishers and the fight we don't know we're in for marketing dollars." She jiggles her head. "Whatever, okay, so self-publish. We do it among the hordes whose only actual talent is the ability to click Upload. We do it among the very talented who have publishing contracts and decide to *dabble* in the hybrid world *for fun*. Can I have something? Some. Thing. Please? A chance?"

I think back to my Harbor Books rant and finally understand how the wrong delivery can obscure the right message.

"I had to stand out, somehow," she says. "So I hitched myself to someone else and gambled that grabbing headlines would help me beat the house."

"So all of that about needing to be saved . . . about being lonely . . . your dead cat—"

"I never owned a cat." She thrusts her chair back and stands. Her arms hug her chest, and I don't know how to respond. So I wait. Eventually, she faces me again. She reaches for the wine bottle I left on the bar, pours two glasses to the rim, and slings one across the bar top. Drops of wine decorate the bar like polka dots. She settles herself onto a stool and takes a long sip. "I hate cats. Cats are just lying in wait for the chance to eat your eyeballs. But yeah, my tissues were on a monthly subscribe-and-save that still wasn't enough."

I park myself on a stool two down from her beside the flapper. This doesn't feel like a toast moment so I simply drink. "Life's . . ." I have no idea how to do this ". . . not always easy."

She snorts. And drinks. And snorts.

Christ, do I wish Blaire were here. She would know what to say and how to say it. Earlier, when she said we were friendly but not friends, I wanted to protest, but she's right, of course, she's right. Me thinking I loom as large in Blaire's life as she does in mine is delusional. I am one of many, an important one, but still an author, not her partner or child or sister or mother. Those are relationships built on more than contracts and hand-holding, ones I've convinced myself I don't need. Blaire's words now hit me like a slap across the face. For someone who prides herself on a deep understanding of human nature, I have been profoundly naive when turning that lens on myself. While it's entirely accurate to say I've created a life where I don't need anyone else, wanting is another thing entirely.

In the moments when I allow myself to stop caring about

not being good enough or funny enough or likable enough, when I admit that I've cut everyone off at the knees before they can do the same to me, it's there. That feeling boxed and stuffed in the far reaches of an attic, covered with dust and infested with mites, supplanted by the characters I write and the fans whose books I sign and the occasional cocktail in a pink chair above a bookstore. It has both been enough and at the same time not enough.

I fight the sting in my eyes, and then, I don't. My cheeks grow hot like a fresh sunburn and I face Hartley. "Life isn't easy. Sometimes you just need a win."

Hartley's face goes slack. She then nods, surprise at my words ebbing as the honesty behind them sinks in. "It was my mom. Is my mom. She's not dead, though some days death would be preferable for both of us."

I drink again.

"This is . . . Well, it is what it is and what it is, well, it's Parkinson's. It's been a while, it's been something we've known and seen happen over time. At first, it was just her body shutting down, but now . . ." Hartley taps her head. "She knows it too. She sees the signs, the dreadfully slow descent into losing herself. I'd give up everything to be able to fast-forward through it for her. For us both. But as it stands . . ." Hartley drinks a long pull of her wine.

I do the same.

Hartley watches me and laughs. "You are so uncomfortable."

"Me? No, I'm fine." I kick my dangling legs. "I'm used to my feet not touching the ground."

"That's not what I meant."

I fiddle with the stem of my wineglass. "I'm more used to the problems of fictional people."

"Because people people suck."

I look at her with surprise, and she shrugs.

"I mean," she says, "a lot of them do."

"Especially the ones tricking the world into calling them *the next Sofie Wilde*."

We maintain eye contact, each waiting for the other to break. She does. She grins, then pours us both more wine.

"The rest is true, then?" I ask. "You were lonely and sad about your mom, not your cat—understandably." I get credit for adding that, right? "And you turned to AI but realized it wasn't good enough, so you wrote the book yourself?"

She laughs. "I don't even have an account. I wrote the book originally as me. My mom loves Westerns. Saloons, player pianos, bandannas, all of it. It was a love letter to her. I was about to publish it when I realized I couldn't take what she loved and relegate it to the abyss—again. She deserved more. I wanted us to be able to celebrate at least one of my books being read by more than a couple hundred people before she couldn't remember I was a writer. Or her daughter. I read some article about a writer testing AI and writing the same story in the style of everyone from Ernest Hemingway to Danielle Steele to *Game of Thrones*. And that's when I thought of you."

I roll my eyes. "I'm flattered."

"You should be. I said I hitched myself to someone. I should have added *to someone I admired*."

That warmth that comes with a fan's adoration floods me. No need to fill my pockets with rocks, I sink low enough all on my own.

"I should say I've learned my lesson, shouldn't I?" Hartley says. "Because if someone I admire could be turned into a kidnapper to prove a point doesn't teach you about right and wrong, what will? The thing is, after being asked to be there for your series celebration and then receiving the call about getting a *Times* review, my mom and I shared a magnum of champagne and three pizzas."

The night I got my first review in the *New York Times*, I took a cab to the beach with a take-out box of sushi and a bottle of vintage Veuve Clicquot. It was February. Lacey made me keep her on speakerphone so she'd know if I died of frostbite.

Hartley smiles wistfully. "I've never seen my mom so drunk or bloated or happy. I'd do it again."

"But your mom isn't seeing you succeed. She's seeing Hartley West."

"She knows it's me. We came up with the pen name together." She trails her finger along the rim of her wineglass. "It was the only way this could work. If people knew I'd written books before, it undermines the entire story. Besides, debuts are the unicorns of the publishing world. We love our Cinderella stories. No one prizes years of hard work."

Entirely true. Even so, I don't understand how Hartley could relinquish credit. "But no one else knows? Doesn't that bother you?"

"Why should it?"

"You queried. You wanted to find an agent and a traditional publisher. You wanted a book deal."

"Sure, but the name on the cover doesn't matter. Think about it, Sofie, doesn't Genevieve Lily sound a little too perfect for the name of a romance author?"

It is perfect. But it didn't occur to me with all the Fionas and Lakes and Tara Karas around. "Genevieve" fits right in. "That's a pen name too?"

She tips her glass to mine. "Can't have a preschool teacher writing romance novels."

I shudder at the thought of being covered in snot and slime and whatever else it is that seems to ooze out of young children with reckless abandon. "So, seriously, that means you've never written anything as . . . What's your real name?"

"Mary. Mary Rogers."

"Okay, fine, point taken. Still, don't you want people to know it's you?"

"People, like who?"

"Everyone," I say. "I've always wanted people to read my books."

"Obviously, me too. I did all of this to get the chance to reach more readers. It's what we all want, isn't it? Our books in more readers'—"

"Hands," I say.

"Hearts, is what I was going to say."

"And all this? The crowds? Going viral?"

"Exactly what I hoped. I told you I planned this. I studied marketing campaigns and book banning and what gets a book trending online. Saying I used AI is one of a dozen strategies I considered. And when I landed on it, I gamed it out, including setting up fake accounts to petition for *the next Sofie Wilde* and Sofie Wilde to meet."

I can't help but smile. It's not just *Love and Lawlessness* that mimics me. She took a risk, the same way I did by using my own name when the publisher didn't want me to. By having Jocelyn choose herself at the end of book one. By killing off Vance. Risks, but not uncalculated ones, same as Hartley. She recognized the system was broken, gave up fighting against it, and schooled herself in how to use it to her advantage. I didn't have social media to manipulate my way to what I wanted, but if the tools she has now were available to me fifteen years ago, I probably would have done the same. Except there's no "probably." I would have.

Rosie and Cooper-Brad are right. I've been focused on what

Hartley West writing a book using AI means for me. Not other authors. Not other artists. Not the creative community as a whole or the readers and consumers of our work. Riley Moore said that for something to take hold, it requires a tipping point. Perhaps I've just reached mine.

Hartley drinks more of her wine. "I chose AI because it was flashy, but also because I was primed for this to work. Being Genevieve was good training. I've always had to shy away from author photos and websites. No one but you and my mom knows I'm also Genevieve. When I met Coop at that god-awful pilgrim craft fair, I only had books with one name on them: Hartley West. So now, yes, all this attention means I may no longer be a preschool teacher . . ." She crosses her fingers. "But I still get to be Hartley West. I love being Hartley West. But they can call me whatever they want, so long as they read my books and invite me back. I do want to come back. All the five-star reviews online will never make up for this. The passion and energy of these fans . . . you must know how lucky you are. You're here for them, and they're here for you."

A pang in my chest—the energy of my fans is my oxygen. I've absorbed it, greedily, without pausing to recognize that it comes with a responsibility. To give something back. And to *want* to give something back. At the first panel, Hartley had said something about me not interacting with fans online. I don't, because in-person is what fuels me. *Me.* But not everyone can afford to come to conventions or the bookstores I frequent only because they report their sales to the list (not all do).

This business isn't a meritocracy for any of us—authors, agents, editors, bookstore owners—and readers. Machines aren't the real threat to art. We are.

"And if it all went away tomorrow?" I say slowly. "If this

came out and you were canceled or if no one wanted your next book, what then?"

"I'd up the frequency of my subscribe-and-save. And write more books."

"To try to hit it with the next one."

"Yes, but mostly because I will always write. Even if no one reads a word."

I barely manage a nod.

"Oh, no, truly?" she says. "You'd stop writing? I don't believe that."

"What would be the point?"

"The point is you remain who you are. And you are a writer. Nowhere in the definition is the requirement of *reader.* Or seven-figure advances."

"But both are nice."

"I'll drink to that."

And she does, the rest of her glass, which she refills along with mine.

"Did you really sign with Max Donner?" I ask.

She gives a wry smile. "Not yet."

"Don't," I say firmly.

"I was hoping I wouldn't have to. I was going to use him as leverage." She drains the bottle of wine into our glasses, giving me the heavier pour. "What would you say about giving me a referral to Blaire?"

SURPRISING BUT INEVITABLE

MY HEART AWAKENS BEFORE ME, *THUMP, THUMP, THUMPING* IN my chest.

"Hands. In the air!"

I peel my cheek off the bar. The flapper smiles coyly beside me. I'm dreaming. I'm drunk. I close my eyes.

"Hands! Now!"

The barking jolts me, and I tumble off the stool, the Burberry knockoff that had been sprawled across my shoulders falling to the floor. Hartley's already on her feet, hands in the air, lips crimson from the wine. She's wearing the Read or Bleed hat, which I don't remember her putting on.

"What's going—" The beam of a flashlight blinds me.

Two police officers of the non-cardboard variety block the doorway. One inches forward, hand on the holster at his waist. "Up!" he says with force.

"Sofie!" Hartley whispers.

I drive my hands above my head, which swims in confusion. The cops move deeper into the room. Behind them is Cooper-

Brad and the convention director and a small group that must include the hotel manager and staff.

My entire adult life has been one of relying on myself. I brainstorm on my own. I write on my own. I edit on my own. I don't use beta readers. I don't collaborate. I don't toast contract signings or fat royalty checks with anyone. I sip wine in my recliner and am happy. Because the alternative is this. Being disappointed when Cooper-Brad rats you out.

"On the bar," says the first cop with the meaty build of an ex-linebacker on a diet of Cheetos and Guinness. "Both of you."

As Hartley turns toward the bar, I study her face. The steak, the wine, the story about her mom . . . was she simply stalling? Giving Cooper-Brad enough time to bring the cops here? Does she actually not care if everyone finds out she lied about using AI to write *Love and Lawlessness*?

My brain feels foggy, a step or two behind from days of unending stress, too much wine, and too little sleep.

Hartley spins toward me. "I didn't," she murmurs, and I believe her, even though I have no reason to and it goes against the entire life I've led until now.

Cheetos cop takes position behind us. "Ma'am," he says to Hartley. "My apologies, but is it all right if I pat you down real quick?"

Her head bobbles assent, and I hear the rustle of his hands over her clothes.

"You can step aside, ma'am." He takes hold of her elbow and transfers her to his partner. Then, he moves to me, asks me the same question with more force and an additional accusation of, "Do you have anything that is going to stick me or hurt me?"

I mumble yes to his first question, no to the second, and feel my face burning. The skin on his fingers is unexpectedly soft and he smells faintly of vanilla. His hands begin at my bare feet (*when did I lose my shoes?*), skim my calves, thighs, hips—and stop. He leaves one hand on my pocket, while the other travels my torso and arms. He spins me around. "What's in the pocket, ma'am?"

"I'm sorry?" This feels a little foolish, like I'm part of an acting workshop.

"Pocket. Draw it out slowly, or I will have to confiscate it myself."

"Pocket?" I can't understand what he could possibly—

His arm flies out, and he grabs my wrist, bending it behind my back like a chicken wing. His other hand disappears into my pocket, and the crinkle of plastic makes me remember the small bag of Marcona almonds.

"Are these laced?" he says.

"I'm sorry? They're nuts."

"They don't look like nuts."

"They're Marconas. From Spain?"

"Look like edibles." His thick but soft fingers press on the nuts, and the bag pops.

Hartley's face pales.

"Close them!" I leap for the bag. "She's allergi-phobic!" comes my own grammaphobic cry.

The officer lifts the almonds higher like he's teasing his little sister. "Tommy, any idea what this one's talking about?"

"The nuts!" I prop up on tiptoes, and he rams his hand out to force me back. But one benefit of being short is the ability to duck. I limbo beneath his arm and swivel my head to find my tote. It's by the door. I'll never make it in time.

"Cooper!" I say. "My bag."

He's standing stock-still, as if unable to comprehend this scene he's put into motion.

"Now, Cooper-Brad, now!"

He startles back to life, finds my bag, and races toward me. He holds it open while I fumble for Hartley's purse and the EpiPen that must be inside. I clench the thick plastic in my fist and whip to her side. "How do—"

Her hand folds over mine and guides me in flipping open the cap and sliding the injector out of the tube. She points the tip toward her thigh, and I begin to thrust downward.

"Wait." Her hand travels to her throat.

"Are you dying? Shit, she's dying."

She presses her fingers to her chest and inhales deeply. "I'm not. I'm breathing . . . normally." She inhales again. "Fine. I'm fi—"

But Cooper-Brad is already pushing me aside, hunching over Hartley. "Too far," he says with a tremble in his voice. "Too, too far."

Hartley starts to shake her head, but the terror on his face must be preventing him from thinking clearly. He wrests the injector from my hand. "On three!"

"Wait," I say, placing my hand on his. "She said to wait. I don't think she needs it."

But Cooper-Brad isn't listening and lifts the injector into the air, ready to drive it into her thigh.

"Coop!" Hartley snaps. "Enough." She swivels her body, evading Cooper but sending his plunging hand and the needle directly into Tommy's calf.

"Fuck!" Tommy cups his leg. "Goddamn, that hurts."

Cheetos police officer who smells like vanilla barks, "All of you, back it up." He approaches slowly. "You doing okay there, Tommy?"

Tommy nods, and Cheetos police officer ambles past him to line up three chairs, each about a foot apart. He commands the three of us to sit.

A distressed Cooper-Brad claims the one on the far end, Hartley the middle, and I take the last chair. Cheetos positions himself in front of me, one hand still holding the Marconas.

"I promise you those are nuts. Delicious. You should try them, but not now because . . ." I point to Hartley. "She is allergic, maybe even to fumes, we just don't know."

Cheetos eyes me skeptically but buries the nuts in his pocket. "Full story, now."

He's talking to me, but it's Cooper-Brad who answers. "Like I told Ms. Caulder." He tips his head toward the shocked convention director who hasn't left the doorway. "Sofie Wilde kidnapped Hartley West."

The flat tone to his voice sharpens the sting of his betrayal.

"And why would she do that?" Cheetos asks.

"So Ms. West wouldn't be able to participate in the convention. She was jealous."

Cheetos nods, loops his fingers on his vest, and says to me. "You. Five feet on a good day. Kidnapped her. Nearly Tommy's height. Who helped?"

I want to shout Cooper-Brad's name, but that would be akin to confessing.

"No one?" Cheetos says. "You did this alone?"

Tension tightens every muscle in my body, and I let my face transition into resting bitch face.

"Sofie," Hartley says, her voice softer than usual, the more shy tone she had when we first met at Harbor Books. "They need to know the truth."

I hear her say the words, and my heart sinks. Without even realizing it, I had hope. Hope that we had come to an understanding. That Hartley wouldn't do what Cooper-Brad has done.

"Sofie," she says again. "I know this is hard. All these plans upended. But we have no choice. We have to come clean."

Time seems to slow. I swallow, starting to stand and—wait, did she say *we*?

Hartley rises out of her chair, faces me, and claps. She brings her hands together, over and over, the *thwack, thwack, thwack* drawing confused looks from everyone in the room. "You did it. We did it." She pumps her fist. "Go us!"

I do the only thing I'm trained to do: move from resting bitch face to polite half smile.

Hartley addresses Cheetos, sidling closer. He stations his hand on his weapon. She stills, but continues. "We should apologize that we were so entirely convincing. We wrote the script, sure, but who knew we'd be able to act too?"

Since when did we become a *we*?

Cheetos looks at Tommy. "Take the extra shift, my wife said. Didn't want me underfoot on her book club night. My last extra shift had a guy shooting ghosts in Walmart and teenagers stealing llamas from the Lincoln Park Zoo. Extra shifts always come back to bite me." He grimaces at Hartley. "Now, ma'am, this gentleman came to us because he thought you were in danger. I can assure you that you are not. You have no reason to fear this woman." He juts his chin at me. "But I need a straight answer: did Sofie Wilde kidnap you?"

"Yes." Hartley bobs her head with enthusiasm. "Because I let her."

I'm sorry, what?

"See, there was this hashtag," Hartley says.

"Hashtag?" Cheetos says.

Tommy interrupts, "An online thing. For trends and—"

"I know what a hashtag is."

But the look on his face makes it clear he doesn't. He stares at me, looking for me to corroborate. Hartley does too. Her eyes are wide and pleading.

I stand, slowly, keeping track of the distance between Cheetos's hand and his holster. "WildeWestShowdown. Sofie Wilde." I curtsey (*I what?*). I gesture to Hartley. "Hartley West. The fans are clever."

"And unfortunately feed off feuds," Harley says. "We wanted to play into it, make it seem as though we were giving them exactly what they wanted—a showdown." Her lie comes as easily as breathing. "But then flip it on its head. Perhaps get them to rethink the ingrained pitting of women against one another and why they wanted it in the first place. And give them something better."

She turns, tossing me the balls she's been juggling. I can let them fall to the floor, and we can do this separately. That way there's no chance of someone disappointing me. I don't owe Rosie or Grace or Fiona or Hartley anything. Or I can swoop in and we can bring this to its surprising but inevitable conclusion together.

I look her square in the eye and prepare to catch. "We faked it," I say. "The kidnapping. I mean, nuts? Who would actually use nuts as a weapon? A bit over the top." See, she's not the only one good at this. "And that's coming from someone whose constellation-superhero Lupus used his snout to sniff out a field of deadly mushrooms."

"Diabolical that Scorpius," Hartley says. "Intent on poisoning the entire water supply of Cincinnati."

Cheetos mumbles, "No more extra shifts. Ever."

"Right, yes, well," Hartley says, "the point is: we dreamed up this whole thing. And filmed it." She points to her open laptop on the bar.

"For what?" Cheetos says.

Hartley looks at me and my plantsing brain lands on: "For a book trailer."

"What does that even mean?" Cheetos says.

"Like a movie trailer but to advertise a book," I say.

"In this case, the authors of the book," Hartley says.

"Who are adept at self-promotion."

"And who are writing about a fake kidnapping."

"Together," I say, the dialogue writing itself. "It's very meta."

Hartley comes to my side. "Sofie Wilde and the next Sofie Wilde are now coauthors." Her lips twitch into a slight frown. "Though this wasn't the way we intended to go public. We planned to pull an all-nighter editing the trailer to present at our joint keynote."

I start laughing. I can't help it. Even I can appreciate an artist at work. Even when it's of the "con" variety.

WRITE WHAT YOU KNOW

THE LAST BANDS OF PINK STREAM ACROSS THE SKY, AND COOPER-Brad's fingers entwine through mine. He tilts his head, and the puffer vest he's wearing crinkles. "Here it comes."

At the front of the parking lot, a team snaps the projection screen into place.

An uncharacteristic warmth brims in my chest and I trace the outline of the compass rose tattoo on his wrist. If I were a character in one of my books, I'd probably already have a matching one. (And be making myself nauseous.)

I look over at him. "To think. The silver screen."

Cooper-Brad nods, then cocks his head. "It was, you know. In the early nineteen hundreds, movie screens were painted with a reflective metallic silver that better displayed the—"

"Not now, Coop," says the woman beside me. She takes my other hand and squeezes. "You hate this, I know, but let me have it, for a millisecond?"

For a single heartbeat, I squeeze Hartley's hand back, and

the fading sunlight reflects off my grandmother's ring—resized to fit my middle finger.

Fans and locals continue to settle into the tiers of seating brought in days ago. With tourist dollar signs in its eyes, the town enthusiastically supported transforming the main parking lot overlooking the harbor into an outdoor movie theater. A much better use. Maybe I can convince them to keep it.

Hartley, Cooper-Brad, and I sit in the cushioned VIP chairs up front, breathing in the scent of salt and fish and listening to the clank of boats against the dock. Along the water side, individual tents house vendors selling steak sandwiches and macarons and dirty martinis. The seafood store offers lobster rolls and fried clams. Ice-cream cones and sundaes drip in the lingering heat. Roxanne sells my book amid her own curated list of "Roxy's Rocking Reads." She's trying to make it a thing. I'm helping. (Or rather, Lacey's helping me help.)

It is the height of summer. It is a year and half since Hartley and I saved ourselves from being arrested by making up that preposterous story. A year and a half since we delivered our joint keynote at the Romance US convention.

I'd like to say I embraced her as my co-speaker. That after Cheetos took our statements and our offer of free copies of our books for his wife's book club and Tommy wrapped an ice pack on the bruise forming from the EpiPen, we were all singing campfire songs and sharing s'mores.

Cooper-Brad had betrayed me.

Hartley had protected me.

Each for their own gain.

I admired them and despised them equally.

Cooper-Brad had been intent on playing me by playing the hero. He took a metaphorical page from Hartley's book and gambled that "saving" Hartley West from the clutches of Sofie

Wilde would be a boon. He figured that all the attention he'd receive for thwarting the kidnapping of an in-the-headlines author would skyrocket him to fame. Agents and publishers would be clamoring for his work.

Or, at least, that's what he let me think. Hartley did too. For a little while.

Music plays through the tall speakers flanking the screen. A group of women all blaming the other for taking too long in the porta potties or at the cocktail tent or browsing at Harbor Books shush one another as they fill their VIP seats. Rosie, Grace, Fiona, and Tara Kara with Lake and her sexual storyboarding husband on video.

I booked them all rooms at the inn in the harbor. I didn't want to find notes from Fiona in my container of jasmine rice or stuck beneath my vaginal dryness gel. Besides, the guest rooms in my house were already claimed by Hartley, Blaire, and Lacey.

Claimed being the operative word. I didn't offer. Apparently forcing themselves upon me as houseguests is some type of intervention for my lack of social graces.

All I can say is they use a lot of towels.

The opening credits begin, and the title glimmers onto the screen: ROMANTIC FRICTION. As the names of the main actors and director pop up, Lacey nudges Blaire, who leans across Hartley to wink at me, clutching her long-stranded pearls. Because of what is coming next.

"Written by Sofie Wilde and Hartley West"

"Based on the novel Romantic Friction *by Sofie Wilde and Hartley West"*

We're a Riley Read, a Read with Jenna, and a Reese selection. The trifecta of book club picks. A first. One of many firsts. The novel is the first writing collaboration for both of us. It is my first non-romance title and hers too. And it's certainly the first time any of our books have been made into a film. All done without AI but because of AI.

Hartley was right. (I hate that she was right. Except I don't. Not really.)

We wrote our story. Our actual story. Meet-cute and all. Details changed (Chicago became New York) and embellished (bruised toe became broken ankle) and invented (torrid romance with "Hunter-Jon"). My actual torrid romance with Cooper-Brad started after my tour when he and Hartley admitted that they'd planned the police raid—the whole EpiPen thing a pantsing opportunity Cooper-Brad took full advantage of. They waited to tell me, conspiring as armchair psychologists that my rage at Cooper would allow me to better bond with Hartley.

The police raid and the "filming" of the fake kidnapping was his idea. He gave me an exit strategy at the cost of me having to share the stage with Hartley. She had planned to stick with the story she started with: that the fake kidnapping was our way of tearing down the hashtag. It was me blurting out "book trailer" that sparked her to upgrade to coauthoring.

She had me on video. Still, Blaire had been sure she could come up with some contractual excuse that prevented the use of my name on anything but solo projects. Lacey too was hesitant. As interested as she'd been in having Hartley and I partner at Harbor Books, the discussions at the convention were beginning to resonate. She feared a backlash was coming.

It did. Led by Hartley West. She admitted her actions were a ploy to draw attention to the consequences of authors using AI. And the reasons why they feel they need to. This industry that could and should be better. Our keynote centered on it. We prompted a new hashtag: #WildeWestTakeAim.

We were booked for speaking engagements for months.

"Sofie," Hartley whispers and I turn to her. Her face glows

with joy (and the bronzer she borrowed from Lacey). She tucks her arm through mine and draws me close. She's going to ruin this moment. I know her. She can't help herself.

We're partners. Friends, if the definition includes sometimes thinking dancing on broken glass would be less painful than being in her company. Our cowriting came alive with the same rush I felt with Cooper-Brad as we weaved a backstory for the waiter with the bald patch. Our cowriting also came close to putting one of us in an early grave. She randomly shows up at my house now, living only an hour away. She made herself a key, and I'll find her in my recliner drinking my wine by penguin candlelight.

I really should change the locks.

She is one of my phone favorites though. Just ahead of my massage therapist. Roxanne says that's progress. It's profitable, I'll tell you that.

My fifteen-city tour that Roxanne saved ballooned to twenty, with Hartley joining for half. The dates we added included her hometown and the one where I grew up, where my parents still live.

They would have come tonight except my dad fell while lunging during pickleball and broke his wrist. Lacey set up a link for them to watch from home. They texted a photo: their house filled with friends and neighbors and probably random people they pulled off the street. Exactly who they've always been.

Thanks to the convention, tour, and previously made plans ensuring she would indeed have enough copies in circulation, Hartley hit the list for a week. I hit at number five, hanging out for a solid twenty weeks. A personal best. And Roxanne didn't have to buy a single leftover copy.

Hartley's "Genevieve Lily" books were acquired by a traditional publisher and rereleased under Hartley West. She now has a solid fandom and steady sales. News leaking (is it leaking if your own team does it?) of Riley Moore wanting to age down Jocelyn prompted the Hollywood A-list of older female actors to clamor for the part. Season one premieres next spring. The more complicated and expensive production meant it would come out after *Romantic Friction*.

I don't mind the wait. I'm writing another romantasy (spoiler: Vance is back!) *and* a contemporary novel. I'm not going anywhere. Even if that means one day writing with the help of AI. This is a game, and even if the rules change, you can't win if you don't play.

Hartley tugs harder just as the first frame of me (but not me) peeking through the shelves at Harbor Books (but not Harbor Books) flashes on the screen.

"What is it?" I hiss.

"It's just . . . I'm ravenous. Do you have anything to—"

I push aside my own long strand of pearls that still feels foreign to me. Hartley wears a matching one—a movie tie-in, sold at bookstores nationwide. I click open my small sequined clutch and shove aside the packets of stevia stolen from Starbucks, because yes I am now my grandmother, to pull out a nut-free protein bar. A year of touring with a hangry Hartley taught me a lot.

"Add it to my tab," she says.

"Your tab is two thousand seven hundred and twelve dollars." She thinks I'm joking. But I have a spreadsheet and everything.

"That's a lot of protein bars."

"Includes interest. And hazard pay."

A hand cups my shoulder. I spin around to see Rosie's smiling face.

"Adorable, truly," she says, her eyes traveling between me and Hartley. She's pushing the idea of all of us forming an imprint.

Be the agent of change. A role model for others. "But can you please shut the fuck up."

The more time we've spent together, the more her vocabulary includes the f-word. I'm pretty sure it's not a direct correlation.

Under the joint byline of Sofie Wilde and Hartley West, I found the courage to write about something other than love. Something I wasn't sure I needed. Something infinitely more devastating when it goes wrong and exponentially more rewarding when it goes right. I wrote about friendship—the kind the whole world thinks we have.

But remember: we both lie for a living.

And we're very, very good.

★ ★ ★ ★ ★

ACKNOWLEDGMENTS

ROMANTIC FRICTION IS MY SIXTH PUBLISHED NOVEL. AND THE word *published* there is key, for I've written more than six novels. Five more, in fact, with just one of those under contract and making its way into your hands soon (that is, if you liked the one you're holding now, and hey, even if you didn't, how about considering this one a fluke and trying the next—ah, see how ingrained promotion truly is?).

This novel owes its existence to those books that have come before—both published and not—because with each novel written, I learn more. That translates to better premises, stronger characters, more intriguing plot twists, and books that take what I see and hear in my mind and translate that to the page. But this novel also owes its corporeal existence (if an inanimate object can be corporeal . . . oh, let's just go with it) to those previous books because they taught me the business of publishing.

And that word there is key too: "business." Writing is art,

but done like this, it's for-profit art. It's entirely dependent on sales figures and performance, and we writers have no guarantees that we'll keep these damn cool jobs we have. Much of why that's the case is contained within the pages of this book. This novel is an open love letter to this industry that has the highest of highs and the lowest of lows (and if that's melodramatic, well, I *am* an artist!).

This year, almost to the day of the release of this book, marks ten years since the release of my first novel. With that book, I entered this wildly fulfilling, frustrating, competitive, camaraderie-filled world of publishing. The authors I've met along the way who have been willing to privately share their experiences contributed to the authenticity of the "behind-the-scenes" of publishing that you find in these pages. I owe this book's existence to their transparency. I am profoundly grateful to every writer I've met over the years, from the students in the classes I teach to the authors I've shared bookstore and festival panels with to the writers who have turned into the best of friends. Many of the latter have read and helped to shape not just this book but all of my writing, and I can't thank them enough for their brilliant minds, generous hearts, and never-ending text chains.

I also owe this book's existence to my agent, editor, and the entire team at MIRA who didn't flinch even once (at least that I know of) at pulling back the curtain. An enormous thank you to my powerhouse agent, Jill Marr, and the Sandra Dijkstra Literary Agency for grabbing me and this book and delivering us both to Meredith Clark at MIRA. To have an editor who not only gets my quirky humor but will allow me to call a character "Cooper-Brad" without question while also offering insightful and whip-smart notes is more than one can ask for. To my new team at HarperCollins, I'm honored and thrilled to be here and can't wait to see what we can do together.

This book, and all my books, wouldn't be here without one other person. I have more craft to learn to truly be able to find the words to thank Marc, my partner in all ways, for all he's done to support me. You not only listen to my every half-baked idea, but you stay with me, through nights by the fire and walks on the beach and random notes I ask you to save in your phone as I'm falling asleep, to help those ideas become characters and plot twists and books. My first reader of everything. Thank you for supporting me and for every time you say, "Ooh, I love it."

One final note, this novel is the first of my books that will publish without my father being here to see it. He and my mother made me a reader, which made me a writer. Their love and support are with me always. We miss and love you, Dad.

And that's why we are all here, doing what we're doing—because we love it. All of us in publishing want books to continue to educate, to entertain, to offer readers an escape. It's a privilege for us to get to do this thing, no matter what the future and technology holds. In the words of the inimitable TS, AI, "try and come for my job."